Evil Side of Money

By

Jeffrey Robertson

RJ Publications, LLC

Newark, New Jersey

RJ Publications
mtymn19681@wowway.com
www.rjpublications.com
Copyright © 2007 by Jeff Robertson
All Rights Reserved
ISBN-10: 0978637321
ISBN-13: 978-0978637323

Printed in the Canada
October 2007

2 3 4 5 6 7 8 9 10

ACKNOWLEDGEMENTS

I would like to first, thank God, for the gift he has given me, and the understanding of the responsibility that has been bestowed upon me to accompany this gift.

I'd like to thank Lela and Richard Robertson for their bond in 1967, which made this all possible.

L. Renee' Robertson for her love and support, you're the genuine article baby!

J'nae, Jayla, and Jazmyn, daddy's babies!

Richard Jeanty for believing in the talent, the project, and me. It's amazing what can happen when brothers help each other!

Thanks to Daveda L. Flute for your work. Keep your head up lil' sis!

Thanks to Ms. Eve, the Lab, and Forilla Records for the MySpace page loved it!

Torrian Ferguson and Ferguson Literary Group for getting me out there!

…..And thanks to all who have supported me through this project by reading and encouraging me to live out my dreams, there are too many of you to name individually. May God bless you all.

Chapter 1

Humble Beginnings

I remember meeting Nate for the first time during the summer of '76. I was outside walking around because my mom was getting high again, and I just didn't want to see the filth that usually came with her binges. I remember it being pretty hot; In fact, very hot. Maybe it was because I was wearing corduroy pants. My mom never bought me new clothes; the money usually went up her nose, or into her arm, so I wore the same clothes year round. I remember thanking God that I didn't have a brother or sister, because if I had, it would have been another person to look after, but at the same time I remember being real lonely.

This was a new neighborhood, the third in the last two years, and this one was pretty good. My mom managed to get on section 8, and we actually lived in a decent neighborhood for a change. Chicago was alive then. This was before drive-by shootings, gangster rap, crack rock, and all of the other madness the city is plagued with nowadays. People were friendlier, more approachable; the city was genuinely safe, so safe that an eight-year old kid could wander a mile or more away from his house, and his only worry would be the neighborhood bullies.

And that was always my worry. I was a skinny little kid who seemed to attract bullies like a magnet. Most kids were bigger, and I suffered for it. I usually tried to get along and befriend the bigger boys, to keep the bullies off. It had worked before, but I wasn't sure about this neighborhood. I had already been around for half the summer and none of these kids seemed interested in being seen with me.

I remember seeing Nate coming toward me on the sidewalk. He was a nice sized kid, and I had already heard that nobody messed with Nate, that he was just cool. I had heard that he played Little League, and was good, too. As he passed, he said, "Waz up man, want to play some strikeout?"

"Yeah," I said. "Where are we gonna play?"

"Right out here, up against the wall."

In those days, we would get a can of spray paint and paint a huge box with an "x" in it on a wall, and use it as a pitching target. Kids seemed to be much more creative in those days than they are today. This was before home video games and MTV. A kid had to be creative and have an imagination to have fun then. Of course, I knew I would be the pitcher for a while because he could really play, and I could never strike him out, but it was okay with me because I wanted to kill time anyway. What did I have to go home to, Mom lying on the floor, high out of her mind?

"What's your name, man?" he asked.

"Derrick I said dryly. I was almost ashamed, this guy was so cool in the neighborhood, and I was new and unknown. It was embarrassing. Just as he was about to run the score up to 8-0, a couple of older boys showed up. From the looks of them, they had to be at least 12 or 13 years old.

"Let me see your bat, man, so he can throw me a pitch," one of them said sternly.

"Naw man, it's mine," Nate said defiantly, almost with authority.

"I ain't gonna take it from you, little nigga," one of the others said. These boys were tough. One of them even had a cigarette behind his ear. I just stood there, petrified, hoping, in fact praying, that Nate would just give it to them so they wouldn't beat us up.

Nate gave him the bat, and his friend the ball, and they played for what seemed to be an hour. Nate finally said, "Okay, give it back." The guy with the cigarette behind his ear pitched the ball again and his friend knocked it clean across 71st street.

Nate was furious. "Go get my ball!"

"Nigga, shut up," the big kid said, as he gave Nate the bat.

" Fuck you, go get my ball!" Nate shouted.

Oh, God, I thought, why did he say that, now they're gonna beat us up.

"What did you say, little nigga?" the tough kid said. "Little nigga talking' shit!" his buddy said. The tough guy backhanded Nate across his face, and Nate fell to the ground.

I don't know what got into me then, but I kicked the tough guy between the legs. His buddy gave me a fist to the face, and I fell to the ground next to Nate. The guy I had kicked gave me a kick to the stomach as well. They both laughed at us and walked away.

As they walked away, I looked at Nate, who was staring angrily at them as if revenge were already on his mind. "Who were they?" I asked.

"Titus, Titus Thompson, he likes to mess with all of the younger kids," he said. "I hate his ass."

"Is he a gang member?" I asked.

"Naw, not yet, but he's one of the toughest guys in the neighborhood. He's gonna join the Disciples any day now."

The Disciples were one of the most ruthless gangs in Chicago during the 70s and 80s, but the gang members our age were mostly into petty theft, knives, truancy, small time battery, and maybe a little reefer.

That was about it. But to the straight-laced kids of the time, like us, that was a lot. It was enough to scare me, but it didn't seem to bother Nate. He always seemed to be in his own little world; nothing either intimidated or impressed him much.

"You a little G, the way you kicked him," Nate said. "You wasn't scared, man?"

"That punk? Naw, man, I was just standing' up for ours, man." In the inner city, if you weren't tough, you had better be a damn good actor; many times it was more about survival than fitting in.

"Let's go home, man, ain't nothing else to do," Nate said.

"Okay, but let's go to your house, I don't feel like going home."

"Where you live, G?"

"Over near 73rd and St. Lawrence, where you live?" I asked.

"72nd and Eberhardt, down the street. Let's go there, I'm hungry and it's lunch time," Nate said.

Lunch time? I thought. His Momma actually fixes him lunch? I got some cereal in the morning, whatever candy bars or chips I could steal during the day, dinner at night, and that was it.

"Momma we're home, can we eat?" Nate called as we walked in.

"Who is we ?" a woman answered.

"My friend G and me, we're hungry," Nate said.

"What happened to you two, have you been fighting?"

"Yeah, Momma, they took my ball."

"We have to do something about these bullies. What else happened?"

"They started picking on us and we stood our ground, just like you told me to."

"That's good, honey, but just be careful when you do."

Nate's mom was a real looker, a fair-skinned woman with a fabulous body and beautiful hair. Looking back, I can see she was a very proud woman because she kept an immaculate home. Her house always smelled good, and had the cleanest walls! Most of the walls in the houses of women with children were usually grimy with fingerprints, crayon marks and all. But not her house; Mrs. Williams's home was top notch, better than any home I had ever been in. I later found out it was because she entertained all the time, usually guys and friends of hers, she said. She had great furniture, and I remember she had a white carpet, imagine that, a white carpet! She made us take off our shoes when we came into the house.

"Would you two like grilled cheese sandwiches and French fries?" she asked.

"Yeah," we said in unison. I would have liked anything. As I said, I was used to getting nothing for lunch, so anything would be an improvement.

"Where do you live, G? G, that can't be your real name, what is your real name?"

"My name is Derrick, Derrick Jones."

"How did you get a name like G?"

"I gave it to him, Ma," Nate said, "Because he helped me fight those guys, like a gangster, that's why I called him G."

"Well, you two are not gangsters, and that's not a good thing to be, understood? Where do you live, Derrick, nearby?"

"On 73rd and St. Lawrence."

"With your mom?"

"Yeah."

"I see. I'd like to meet her one day."

Well, I can't say that I was happy to hear that. I really loved my mother, I just was ashamed of what she was into. I guess the pressure of raising a child alone in the inner city was too much for her. I never knew my father. She did the best she could. I wished at the time that she could have been more like Mrs. Williams.

I was a little ashamed at how fast I ate my food. Both Nate and his mother looked at me as if I had inhaled it. I couldn't help it, I was hungry.

"Let's go play racecars man, I bet I can beat you!" Nate said, after we were finished.

"You got a racing set?"

"Yeah, let's go."

"Be careful, and don't run in the house!" Mrs. Williams said sternly.

Nate had a real little boy's room. He had Spiderman on the wall, a carpet, and a bedroom set. He also had all the cool toys of the time, and to top it off, he had a bed shaped like a car! We must have played for hours, game after game. We enjoyed each other's company, so much that I lost track of time, and it was dark.

"Derrick, I better take you home, your mother's probably worried sick," Mrs. Williams said. I wanted to walk home by myself, but I knew she would never let me. She even had a car, a red 76' Volkswagen beetle. I remember because I always thought they were ugly cars. Ugly or not, she had one, and in those days people didn't have the nice cars they have today. My mother and I didn't, we were on the bus wherever we had to go. I remember asking Nate what his mother did for a living. He said "She's a counselor." At the time I really didn't know what that was, being nine years old and all, but whatever it was, it seemed to be doing well for her.

As we approached my street, I was a nervous wreck. Even at the age of nine, children are very self-conscious, and can be embarrassed easily. I didn't know what condition we would find my mother in, or if she would even be home. This was not a very good time for us to be showing up. I remember trying to jump out of the car, hoping they would just leave. I tried to convince Ms. Williams that I would be okay, but she wouldn't have it. "I can't let you just walk up there by yourself, Derrick, I have to walk you up. What floor do you live on?"

"Second," I responded. During the whole walk up the stairs I was so nervous I was dizzy. I remember the hallway smelled like piss, a huge contrast to the way Nate's mom's house smelled. We knocked on the door; no answer. Nate's mom knocked again, but this time harder, and I remember hearing my mom dragging herself to the door. "Is that you, boy? It better be!" she yelled.

When she opened the door she was a pitiful sight, just as I had expected. Her hair was standing up all over her head, the clothes she had on looked as it she had worn them for days, and she smelled.

"Boy, where the hell have you been?"

"I was over Nate's house, Momma."

"Who the fuck is Nate?" My mom was so high she didn't even see Nate and his mother standing there. Suddenly she noticed. "Oh, I'm sorry, I'm so sorry, I didn't see you standing..."

"It's O.K., I just brought him home. He was over at my house playing with my son Nate. I am Nate's mother, Mrs. Williams. How are you doing?"

"I'm O.K. now. I was so worried about Derrick, he never does this."

"It wasn't his fault. Actually, I should have gotten him here sooner. I am the one who lost track of time."

"I would invite you in for a drink or something, but it's late and shit, so..."

"It's okay, but maybe we can get together another time."

"Yeah, okay maybe sometime." I was so glad they didn't come in. I didn't want them to see how my house looked and smelled. It was horrible!

"What's your name, little man?" my mom asked.

"Nate," he said.

"So you're the one keeping' my son out so late. Little niggas trying to hang out late already," my mom slurred. She thought she was being polite and amusing; it was so embarrassing!

"Well you have a nice night," Mrs. Williams said. "I didn't get your name."

"I didn't give it," my mom said, slurring and laughing. "But it's Betty, my name is Betty, and I hope to see you again, and thanks for bringin' my boy home."

"No problem," Mrs. Williams said.

After my mother closed the door, she told me to get undressed and go to bed. Before I could get my pants off, she had shot some heroin and fallen asleep. Thinking back on that night, and many others, I remember how much I really loved my mom. She had given me many embarrassing moments, but I still loved her. You see, my mom was a victim, a victim of the inner city social order. My mom fell in love and got pregnant with me when she was very young, fifteen to be exact. When my grandparents found out about it, they kicked her out, and she went to live with her cousin on the West Side, somewhere near W. Jackson Street. My father, whoever

11

he was, couldn't stand the heat and didn't want the responsibility, so he split. I remember hearing that he had been pretty young, too.

My mom had lived with her cousin, who was 22. I heard that my cousin was the worst example my mom could have had. She turned my mom on to men and drinking. From what I heard, they used to party every other night. I don't know all of the details, but when I was older, I heard from family members that my mom and her cousin had met some West Side niggas, and they had turned the women on to drugs and orgies.

I think what hurt my mom the most was not how my dad had left her, but how her parents had rejected her. She had no guidance and no love, so like most inner-city women in her position, she looked to other things for comfort: booze, drugs, and sorry-ass niggas. Before long, my mom was hooked on coke, along with her cousin. I never got decent care, and my grandparents threatened to call DCFS, drop a dime on my mom and get custody of me, so my mother took me and ran off. We have been living like nomads ever since. When she heard that her cousin had overdosed and died, she sank deeper into depression.

I have always blamed my grandparents for my mother's demise. If they had just given her love and forgiveness, maybe she would not have had to go through what she did. Some people are so concerned with their little reputations that they try to protect them by destroying loved ones. Her parents helped make my mother a victim. It is such a common story in the inner city, and it is a shame. So many women are looking for love and acceptance, and other people (mostly men) take advantage of them. As I lay in my bed listening to my mother snore, I thought that maybe Nate wouldn't want to be my friend anymore, that he would tell all of the kids in the neighborhood about my mom and how we lived. I cried myself to sleep.

I was wrong about Nate. When I saw him the next day, he acted as if nothing happened. When I tried to explain the scene by saying my mom was sick, he just went along, and I appreciated that.

Nate was a great baseball player; he could field, hit, catch, and run with the best of them. Therefore, when his Little League coach heard that he was quitting the team, he was pissed. Nate said he just didn't like it anymore, he said it was boring. I later found out that he had gotten bad grades, and his mom made him quit. Nate made bad grades the whole school year. He hated school. It's not that he wasn't smart; it's just that Nate got bored with things fast; he always had a short attention span.

His mom told Nate that he would never play ball again unless he got his grades up, so I volunteered to help him when school started. I read all of the time... that's how I would entertain myself while my mom was high. I read magazines, newspapers, books, periodicals, everything. I didn't have much going for me, but I was a good student. Mrs. Williams asked me to try and help Nate that school year, so he could play ball the next summer.

Nate worked hard on his reading and math the whole school year. During that time, we became good friends. We did things together, and what we had grew from a friendship into a brotherhood, into a kinship. He always had my back, and I always had his. People began to associate us with each other; we were always together, never with outsiders. We trusted one another, and we experienced true brotherhood.

When I turned 13, Mrs. Williams decided to give me a birthday party. I was excited, because my mom had cleaned herself up and said she would be there. We invited a few friends, and had food, cake, and ice cream. It was the first birthday party I ever had. I truly loved Mrs. Williams for thinking of me in that way. I have never forgotten that day; it was a real turning point in my life.

Everyone was there except Mom. People came and gave me cards with money in them; lots of money, too. Most of the cards came from Ms. Williams' guy friends. I remember feeling bad that my mom wasn't there yet, but with the kids and grownups making so much fuss over me, I felt better. We played games, sang "Happy Birthday," played more games, danced, and enjoyed ourselves.

At last, it was nearly eight o'clock, and my mother still had not shown up. I was starting to get a little scared; I had a feeling something was wrong. Mrs. Williams kept everyone distracted, but I could tell she was concerned also. After everyone left, we counted my birthday money; it was $100 dollars in all! I felt like the luckiest kid in the world, but I was still worried about Momma.

"Let's go home and see what happened, Derrick, she probably fell asleep and just forgot," Ms. Williams said. She was a sweetheart; she knew something was up, but she didn't want to alarm me. During the whole ride over to our house, I felt a knot in my stomach.

Somehow I could always tell when something bad was about to happen. I always could sense impending doom. As we walked up the stairs, I remember having my birthday hat on and my gifts in a bag. We wanted my mom to see how much people had given, and how much they cared. Mrs. Williams and my mom had grown close; my mom had shared her story with her, and confessed that she was a user. Mrs.

Williams never judged her. I suspected she just wanted to be an ear for my mom. When she found out my mom was a user, she looked after me even more. Many days I spent more time at Nate's house than at home.

We knocked on the door. There was no answer. I knocked real hard and the door just swung open. We looked in her bedroom and she was not there, but we found her in the living room. My mom was laying on the couch, with a needle on the floor beside her, lines of coke on the table, and a half bottle of gin sitting on the floor. My mom had overdosed. The three of us knew she was dead; she looked pale and lifeless, and was stiff and cold to the touch.

After picking things up a little, Mrs. Williams just stood over her with tears running down her face. I noticed a letter balled up by my mother's body. It was from DCFS. With the help of my grandparents, they had tracked us down. The letter said that they were going to take me away from her and give me to my grandparents. It also said that the agency was considering pressing charges against her for child endangerment and neglect. I guess the pressure of it all made my mom get high.

By this time, tears were rolling down all of our faces. I was in complete and total despair. How can a person have the happiest day of his life and the saddest one at the same time?

Mrs. Williams put a blanket over my mom and said quietly through her tears, "Rest girl, it's all over. I'll take care of him, you just rest." I went over to my mother's body and kissed her on the lips. "Bye bye, Momma, I love you."

Nate was crying too, and asked his mother if we were going to call the police. She told him we would, from home. We all took one last look at my mother's body, and quietly walked out the door. My mother was 29 years old.

My mother's funeral brought out people in my family that I had not seen in a long time. I saw uncles, distant cousins, friends of the family, all coming to pay their respects. I could not help but wonder where they had been when my mom was alive and needed them the most. We black people have always been "after the fact," taking care of things after it's too late.

It was nauseating, looking at all those strangers and listening to them tell me how smart and cute I was. *People are such hypocrites,* I thought. It was easy to be so glib and encouraging now, when my mom was no longer here to ask for anything. Despite all their fine words, I noticed that none of them mentioned taking me in. Some of them even offered me money, but no one wanted the full-time responsibility of raising a child.

Mrs. Williams was great; she paid a lot of the expenses of the funeral. My mom didn't have life insurance, so the state had to bury her. Mrs. Williams paid for the flowers, the programs, even the plot and headstone. Once again, I found myself wondering what exactly it was that she did for a living. Maybe she could have gotten my mom a job where she worked. Mrs. Williams even bought me my first suit. We went to Zayre, Sears, JCPenny's, Venture's, everywhere looking for a nice suit for me. I remember her saying, "I can't have my little man looking shabby when he says goodbye to his mom." That meant a lot to me.

Nate never said too much about the events of my birthday; it seemed he just tried to keep me playing and happy. He shared everything he had with me as if we were brothers. This was the family I had never had, the family I had always wished for.

I didn't cry at my mom's funeral. I remember feeling a lot of hate for everything and everybody. Hate for my so-called family and grandparents for abandoning my mom, hate for the state for sending my mom off like some homeless bum, even hate for the preacher, for preaching such a long eulogy, as if he had really known my mom. He went on and on about being saved, whatever that is. He went on and on about Jesus and blood and crosses, while I just wished he would stop.

At the repast, everyone again wanted to be encouraging. My grandfather walked up to me, along with my grandma. I had heard that after the funeral was over, he was going to try to get custody of me, but I had decided I wouldn't stay with him. I would rather have stayed in a homeless shelter; to me, he was a piece of shit! As he bent down to talk to me, something came over me and I spat right in his face. I told him, "That's for my momma, and how you treated her. I know you trying' to get me to stay with you, but I ain't gonna, I hate you!"

Mrs. Williams screamed at me, "Derrick, don't you act like that at your momma's funeral, those are her parents!"

"Mrs. Williams, if they're her parents, why did she spend our entire time running' from them? They're monsters, and I still hate them!" Then I ran off to Nate's room. I remember hearing her tell them as I ran off that it was gonna take time; yeah right, like a lifetime! Adults need to remember that children have remarkable memories, and when you hurt someone that they love, you can forget about ever getting their trust. I didn't know what was going to happen to me and I guess the pressure of so much uncertainty pushed me over the edge.

Nate came in the room and asked me if I wanted to play G.I. Joe or racecars.

"Nah, I don't feel good."

"C'mon man, don't cry, my momma's gonna make it all right for you, you'll see."

"How do you know, Nate?"

"My mom loves you, just like you are her own son, and she told me she was gonna try and keep you herself. She said she would do it for your momma."

That just about made my day. I really wanted to stay with them, but I didn't know if it was possible. It was then that I started to understand that it had meant for me to meet Nate and his mother.

My mom's parents didn't put up much of a fight to keep me. I guess the episode at the repast let them know I really didn't want to stay with them. They were also pretty old, and maybe didn't want to put up much of a fight. They also liked Mrs. Williams, and felt that I would be in good hands.

Life at Nate's house was interesting; it was much different than what I was used to. Their house was much more structured. Mrs. Williams ran a tight ship, but she also entertained a lot. There were always friends of hers in the house. Many of them were very cool, but I remember finding the situation very strange. Nate didn't like it much either, I remember him saying that he sometimes wanted to have just us around, and not so many "outsiders."

At school, Nate was always the most popular kid, because he always had the best clothes, and was always outgoing and charismatic. Now I was along for the ride. I would no longer have to be the loner, the peculiar, smart, goofy nerd. I had status when I was with Nate. I continued to help him with his grades, and we were a good team.

The new school year was going to be different. We were entering high school now, and it was a bigger stage. Mrs. Williams was torn between Robeson High School, and Mendel, the all-boys Catholic school. Nate and I were definitely not interested in any all-boys school, but Mrs. Williams insisted that it was a better school than Robeson. Unfortunately, Mendel was also much more expensive. I remember her not wanting to pay such a high price for education, and her friends telling her that we would excel in whatever school we attended.

During that time, Catholic schools were the "in" thing in the Black community. Catholic schools signified status back then, and status has <u>always</u> been an important vital aspect of the Black community. Not everyone shared that view, however. One of Mrs. Williams "special friends" told her that the Catholics were just robbing the Black community, that their schools didn't teach any better than the public schools, and that she could pay a bill with all the money she would be sending to the Vatican.

After endless debates and tug-of-war sessions with Nate and me over the summer, she made her decision. She would send us to Robeson for one year to see how things went, and if we got into trouble, off to Mendel we would go. We were fine with that, since Robeson was where we really wanted to go in the first place.

Robeson was a tough school, located in Englewood. It was a school where many inner city kids were hungry. They were hungry for money, status, and attention. Many kids came from families that were...well, dysfunctional. Many of the kids there were angry, jealous, and envious, and if you had anything going for yourself, you had to watch out. Kids came to school with their new clothes, handbags, popular gym shoes, and other nice things, just to have them stolen.

Many of the problem kids were underprivileged, and came from bad backgrounds. Many of these kids' parents were alcoholics, drug addicts, or other losers. The kids had to find other sources of love and attention, and many of them found what they needed in the street gangs. High schools gangs were taking form, and terrorizing kids all over Chicago.

We straight-laced kids were nothing but food for the gangs. We were not used to being tough and fighting. We didn't share the raw nature of these kids, and they knew it. Many of us were bullied and robbed everyday. We had no choice but to give in to this element. Parents complained, and some kids were hassled by the police, but it didn't help. On top of all the other things that kids have to go through, we also had to worry about being bullied.

Well, now it was Nate's turn, and mine. We were among the straight-laced kids about to attend one of the toughest high schools in the city. Nate was optimistic, but I was terrified.

"Maybe Mrs. Williams was right, Nate, maybe we should go to Mendel. I don't know if I want to go to Robeson," I said.

"Why not?"

"'Cause it's tough over there at Robeson. I don't want to fight every day at the end of school."

"We won't have to," Nate said. "It's not as bad as everyone says it is, you just have to know how to survive, we will make it, you'll see."

I wasn't as optimistic. I stayed up all night the night before school started, wondering, thinking, and worrying about the next four years.

The next day we ate breakfast, and put on our new school clothes. Mrs. Williams bought us all of the latest fashions for kids. New Levis jeans and the new Izod shirts, and the latest new leather gym shoes on the market, called Nikes. We looked crisp, clean, and new. We looked privileged, and we didn't fit in. Not that there weren't other crisp, clean kids there; there were, but the two of us were on our own. Nate was known and liked in the neighborhood, but Robeson had an enrollment between two and three thousand kids, and none of them knew us. I just felt like a sitting duck. It did feel nice to be clean, though, in nice new clothes. I looked the best that I had ever looked.

As we got into the car to go to school, Mrs. Williams gave us all of the rules; be nice, be attentive, don't fight, come straight home after school, and above all, don't look for trouble. However, as soon as she let us out of the car and drove off, we didn't have to look for trouble, it found us.

"Hey man, look at these little niggas, where the fuck y'all think y'all going? All these new shoes and shit, these motherfuckers think they on Happy Days or something. Look at them!"

Of all the people we could have run into, we had to run into Titus Thompson and his boys. By now, Titus was in the Gangster Disciples, and he was worse than ever. Nate called him a punk under his breath and Titus heard it.

"What, nigga? You better shut up or I'll take that shit from your ass, you and your goofy ass friend!"

"Yeah, Potsy and Ritchie looking' niggas!" his friend said.

21

"How you know about the names? You must watch the show, fool," Nate said. I started to get a sick feeling in my stomach.

At that moment, a police car drove by and the tough guys walked away, but not without bumping us as they went by. "I'll see your ass after school, little nigga."

Titus had joined the Disciples and had an earring in his right ear as a sign of his devotion. He had what was then called, "buttas" on his head, a permed hairstyle with huge waves going toward the back of the head, and a blue streak on the right side. He also sported black slacks and Foti shoes. He thought he was big time now. He had also developed a real hatred for Nate.

We had heard that the Disciples had given Titus a block to sell some reefer, and that he was making good money. In any event, we thought it was good money—two to three hundred a week. Titus was in his third year at Robeson, and had a notorious reputation. Many of the teachers were afraid of him, and they were passing him in the hope that he would graduate and leave. By this time, he already had several arrests. He made most of his money by selling dope to school kids, their parents, and to others in the community.

There was a killer tension between Nate and Titus; one that I could never understand. I have always heard of people who just didn't care for one another, but this was something different.

"Why does he hate us so much?" I asked Nate.

"It ain't you, G, it's me, he don't like me."

"But why?"

"I don't know, my Momma just said he is jealous, and he's a bully."

"Oh," I said, but I still didn't understand.

The classes at school were standard. I didn't know what classes to take. There were a lot of things I liked, but I didn't have the slightest idea what I wanted to do. Nate was interested in accounting, but I didn't...I didn't like numbers. One of the biggest tragedies of the Chicago Public School system at that time was that many counselors and teachers just didn't know how to inspire students, or guide them toward what to do with their future. I considered myself a pretty smart guy, but I was disappointed with high school. I thought that it would cultivate my mind and satisfy my thirst for knowledge, but as it turned out, high school did just the opposite. I got through the classes, but I wasn't inspired. I just wanted high school to end.

Nate was different; he loved high school. The girls, activities, sports, social life, everything...he was just there for it. He did pretty well in the classes, and the teachers seemed to like him. The only bad thing was the criminal element seemed to keep calling us. No matter how hard we tried, the culture of crime was always there.

One time early in our sophomore year, we were going to the bathroom and found a couple of guys shooting craps against the wall. A quick glance showed us there was at least a couple of hundred bucks on the floor. Nate turned and asked me "Can you shoot dice, G?"

"Nah, never have, what about you?"

"Once or twice, let's try."

"I don't have any money," I said.

"You don't need any. Watch this. Hey y'all, can I get in?"

"It'll cost you five dollars, you got it?" one of the kids on the floor asked.

"Yeah, in my locker. Let me in and I'll give it to you after fifth period. I've never played before and it looks like fun."

The two players looked at each other as if they had caught a fish, and one of them said "Cool, c'mon in, but you gotta pay us the five bucks, plus whatever you lose, cool?"

"O.K., let's play."

Of course I just watched and held his winnings, but Nate played great. He got into a craps game with no money that day, and left the bathroom with seventy dollars! As we left, he whispered to me, "See, G, it's not about having money to get in, it's about having money when you leave!" He gave me half his winnings and told no one about it.

Soon the bathroom craps game went from four guys to about fifteen guys a week. Nate and I cleared about 400 dollars over a couple of weeks, and it was going pretty well until the disciplinarian and the principal found out. Nate was pretty angry about it and said that somebody had told, maybe someone who was angry about losing. The good thing was Nate had saved a good portion of his money. The bad thing was, we were immediately suspended for a week, and Mrs. Williams exploded.

"What are you two doing, shooting dice at school? Nathan, I am talking to you, you better answer me!"

"Nothing Ma, we were just playing. We won't do it anymore."

"I know you won't, because you two will be at Mendel next year, and that is a promise! I told you two I would snatch your asses out of that damn school if you got into trouble. Well you blew it, and now you're going to Mendel."

Well I was glad, to say the least. I'd never liked Robeson anyway, but Nate was livid. He said all-boys schools were for faggots and squares. Mrs. Williams did not seem to be as mad at me as she was with Nathan. I guess she was always trying to be tender with me because of my mother, but I did not want sympathy, I wanted to get yelled at, too. I know it sounds crazy, but I did.

Yet her harangue raged on. "And I'll tell you two another thing, your asses are gonna get jobs, no more sitting around here watching television, and talking to those pissy tailed girls all day!"

Pissy tailed girls? I thought. They never smelled like pee to me!

"Now, Nathan, get your ass in here and take this garbage out!"

"Ma, why you never yell at Derrick, you always yell at me, he was rolling dice too!"

"Boy, don't you back talk me. I'll beat your ass. Just take that garbage out!"

Mrs. Williams would never have hit either of us, really. Her bark was far worse than her bite, but she had a helluva bark!

"Mrs. Williams, Nathan was right," I said. "I was shooting too, and I don't want you to make a difference between us."

"Boy, I know what I am doing, both of you are being punished, but Nathan knows how I feel about things, and yet he does them anyway. That boy is just rebellious, and I don't like it."

"I know Mrs. Williams, but..."

"Derrick, call me Momma Williams. I'm your momma now, you don't have to call me Mrs. Williams. Now get your narrow ass in there and help your brother!" As she said that, she shot me a smile that warmed my heart. I loved Momma Williams. She was a strong woman, and I really admired her for that. I only wished my own mom could have been that strong.

From the time my mom died, I had trouble sleeping. I would wake up, and it would take a long time before I could go back to sleep. Most times I would just pull out a book, or sneak out and watch a little television. Sometimes I would have bad dreams about my mom, or nightmares about seeing her in that coffin, or hearing her calling me; whatever the nightmare, it would wake me up and keep me up. Usually, it would take me a couple of hours to drift back to sleep.

One night I had another of my nightmares, and sat up in bed. I looked over at Nate and he was in deep dreamland. Then I heard a strange noise coming from down the hall. I got up and walked toward it. It was coming from Momma Williams's room, and as I got closer, I knew those noises were sex noises. It gave me a real weird feeling in my stomach. I was embarrassed and ashamed. I heard a man's voice, but I couldn't remember ever meeting the guy. I ran back to our room to see if Nate was still sleeping, and then I ran back to Momma Williams's door to listen.

"Are you staying the night tonight, or running home to your wife?"

"Gloria, don't start, O.K., you know what this is all about."

"Oh yeah, I know you're supposed to be my john."

"That's not fair; you know I don't feel that way."

"I can't tell. You only want to come over here and see me at night, that's usually what johns do. I call it like I see it."

"Well maybe if you stop hooking, maybe I can stop feeling like a john! You've been telling me for almost ten years that you were gonna stop, and you haven't!"

"Yeah, just like you've been telling me you were gonna get a divorce for ten years, but you haven't."

"It's more complicated than just leaving; I *have* been married for twenty years!"

"That's bullshit and you know it, that's why you haven't introduced me to any of your co-workers down at the precinct, you don't want them to know that you have a thing for a black hooker on the South Side, do you?"

"You know I love you. I have told you that for years, and I have shown it for years."

"You have said it and you have shown it, now I just want you to prove it. This shit has gone on too damn long now, and I just don't want to hear anymore lies and stall tactics from you. You don't have any intention on getting a divorce, I see that now and it's time for you to face it, too. I must have been crazy all these years listening to your bullshit, about how you're so tired, and you need a change. All of my friends have been telling me about your ass, in the end you ain't no better than the old slave master hopping the fence at night to be with the wenches, you ain't shit!"

Boy, Momma Williams was giving him the business. She really had a lot of bark. I have come to realize in my older age that men are no match for women and their mouths. It's a fight we just cannot win, and I guess the guy on the receiving end was just tired of trying, because I heard what sounded like a slap. Damn, he hit her, I thought.

"Damn it, woman, I love you, you know it, and you talk to me this way."

"I want you to show it and stop saying it." It sounded as if she were saying it through gritted teeth.

"I have gotten you this apartment, furniture, helped you take care of Nathan. I have shown it, for ten years!" he said.

"Things...that's all you give me is things, and that is supposed to pacify me? I'm tired of being your little dirty secret that you drop by and see and screw after midnight. If you can't get a divorce and keep the promises you have been giving, I want you to leave here tonight, and never come back!"

There was about a five second silence and then he said, "You mean that?"

"With all of my being, I want you all in, or all out of my life, starting tonight."

"I need to clear my head and think, I..."

"You've been thinking for ten years, it's me that ain't been thinking, now get out!"

"Gloria, let's talk about this, we've been together too long to just end it like this, I just want to talk to you."

"Harry, it ain't about you, it's about me. I want to change my life. Nathan is getting older, and he's asking questions that I don't really know how to answer. I can't keep lying to him. And now I got Derrick too, and it's just wrong. I don't want to keep living like this."

"I understand." And with that, I heard him start toward the door. I had to run to our room and hide there with the door cracked open to hear and see the rest.

"Goodbye Gloria, I'll call you tomorrow..."

"Didn't you hear what I said? Don't!"

After he walked out of the door, Momma Williams stood in the middle of the hallway with her head in her hands, sobbing. She composed herself, walked back into her room, and put Christopher Cross's song "Sailing" on her record player. I remember that whenever she was sad she would always play that song. I could smell her light a cigarette, and I imagined her in her recliner with her feet on the ottoman, crying and smoking. I realized at that moment that my mother wasn't the only victim in the world; Momma Williams was too, in her own way. Over the next week or so, Momma Williams just wasn't herself. She always seemed to be sad or distant. Nate said she was just moody, but I knew what it was, she missed that guy.

That guy was detective Harry Trent, soon to be Inspector Trent. He was a big time cop with the Chicago Police Department. He was a tall white guy with a slightly olive complexion. He was married with three kids, two girls and a boy, and his wife was from a prominent family. They had been married for years, but Det.Trent was always known to like the "darker women."

He had met Momma Williams at a party in the late sixties, when he was a patrolman. He came from a long line of Chicago cops that dated back to his great-grandfather, so he had a lot of clout in the system. He and his father even played golf with old Mayor Daley on several occasions. It was always believed that his mom and dad had pressured him to marry his wife, because her father was a well-known doctor in the Bridgeport area, known throughout the city as Daley Town.

People used to say that if Trent had never married his wife, he surely would have married Momma Williams, but I doubt it. This guy's family was too big on reputation and appearances for him to totally go against the grain and marry a black woman. They would have disowned him, so he took the easy and safe way out.

He and Momma Williams had more in common; they liked the same music, movies, and topics of conversation. The great thing about their relationship was that he didn't have to "act black," and she didn't have to "act white;" they were free to be who they were. One of the worst things to see is a Black person acting like a "sambo" so he or she can fit into the white culture, or a white person trying to be "down" with the brothers and sisters in order to fit in. It is a truly repulsive scene.

Trent and his wife were married in name only; I heard they even slept in separate beds. It was a marriage strictly of convenience, his wife's convenience. After they met at the party, Trent was told that Momma Williams would occasionally sell a little "love" to make ends meet. Momma Williams didn't think of it as prostitution, she thought of it as survival.

Urban legend has it that he fell for her not too long after they met. It started out as a casual thing, but when you fall for someone, you start hanging around a little longer after orgasm, just to talk. After a few weeks, they were said to be "getting to know each other." A few weeks turned into several months, and now they are "friends." Then he hit her with it..."Gloria, I want to take care of you and Nathan."

"What do you mean, take care of us?"

"You know.....I want you to be with me exclusively. Let these other guys go and be only with me, I know why you are doing this, and I think you have much more to offer. Let me help you."

Momma Williams dug him, but she was no fool. If she was gonna take up with this guy exclusively, she had to make it worth her while. Something like this could end at anytime, and she and Nathan would be left out in the cold. At that time, Momma Williams and Nathan were staying in The Gardens, a shitty housing project full of crime and scum, a real ghetto.

"Look baby, I'm doing well on the force, and I'm gonna do even better," Trent said. "I've been looking for someone like you all my life and I am scared of what will happen if I lose you. Let me make you happy. Tell me what makes you happy, and it will make me happy to do it."

"Is that right?"

"Yeah, at least think about it."

"What about your wife?"

"We're talking about our happiness, not hers; besides, she's already happy. Let me get you outta this place and put you somewhere nice, you deserve that, you and your baby."

Momma Williams had to think, so like most women would do, she put him on ice. "Let's take a week or so and think about it."

"I don't need a week."

"Yeah, but I do!" she said.

"Ok, I'll call you in a week…"

"I'll call you."

"O.K., if that's what it takes. Call me at the station."

The next day, he sent her four dozen red roses, and a card that said "Thinking of you, dreaming of you." Two days later, Momma Williams went to the office to pay her rent and the lady told her some cop had paid it up for two months, and left a card that said, "Thinking of you, dreaming of you." Momma Williams, like any woman, was impressed at this point, but he hadn't gotten to her yet. Two days later the mailman delivered a 200 dollar coupon good for baby clothes at the Marshal Fields department store, a gift for Nathan. This time the card read, "Thinking of him, dreaming of you!"

Gloria Williams also noticed that the guys who were usually shooting dice on the sidewalk in front of her house had been gone for days. When she looked out of the window, she saw a patrolman looking at her from his car, and he tipped his hat at her. She walked over to him and asked him what he was doing out there. He told her he was instructed to keep an eye on this apartment at night. Well, that did it, but she couldn't let Trent know

31

right away. But when she did, it was needless to say, pleasing. From that point on they were an item, so to speak, but they were an item that also was not an item, and that was what bugged the hell out of Momma Williams. She hated being treated the way she was being treated, and on the night I heard her fight with Trent, I guess she had finally decided to take a stand.

During the summer of '83 there was a lot going on in Chicago. Black people were uniting behind a brother named Harold Washington, who had decided he wanted to be mayor. There was a new music craze going on among the teenagers in all of the local high schools, something called "house music." This was something different, a seemingly endless variety of high volume, old school music from the '70s, cut and mixed with fresh new tracks. This music brought on a complete revolution among the young people that even influenced our dress code. Many people were now considering themselves "preppy," a style marked by Argyle socks, beautiful sweaters, and designer jeans by Calvin Klein, Guess, and Girbaud. Girls were carrying Gucci and Coach Leather handbags, and brothers were carrying Louis Vuitton attachés. Parents all over the city were buying expensive clothing and accessories for their kids to take to school, and the gang bangers were trying to steal every bit of it. There were always stories of kids getting their lockers broken into, purses stolen, and gold chains snatched right off kids' necks. Some kids even got beaten up and stabbed for their designer clothing at that time. But Nate and I weren't. We didn't have the money to be preppies.

Momma Williams had just stopped seeing Mr. Trent, and that meant the money had also stopped. This was good, because it forced a career decision. She decided to enroll at Kennedy King College and enter their nursing program. Momma Williams was serious about taking control of her life. I was very proud of her, but money was tight. She couldn't afford to give us all of the expensive clothes the other kids were wearing, and wouldn't have even if she could have. "All of these parents buying these kids expensive clothes to wear to school like they are movie stars and most of them can't afford it!" she said.

"Aw, Momma, we want some Reeboks, we're tired of Nikes, all the kids are wearing different shoes, they don't wear the same type shoe all the time, they change up," Nate and I protested.

"Shit, not my kids, if I am paying for it, you will wear what I can afford! But I will tell you what I will do. If you two get jobs, I will pay for half of whatever you want to wear, and you can pay the other half."

We didn't like it, but it was fair, plus we felt it was a way we could help Momma Williams out with some of the bills. So we got a job at McDonald's, on 87th Street in Oak Lawn. It was pretty cool, except that we were the only black guys there. It was a bit awkward at first, but we adjusted. All of the kids that worked there were trying to be nice, and feel us out, just like we were trying to feel them out. It is a shame blacks and whites are so uncomfortable with each other. It took about 6 months before we were all comfortable together. I guess they wanted to make sure we weren't hoodlums, and we wanted to make sure they weren't rednecks.

I took to the job pretty well, but Nate hated it. He hated all of the hard work we had to do for minimum wage. Mopping, frying hamburgers and fries, washing dishes, and cleaning grease vats and windows just weren't Nate's things. "All of this bullshit just so we can have some gym shoes and clothes. I don't like it!" Nate argued. I always thought about what I heard some guys say on television one night, that there was dignity in all work. I believed it then, and I believe it now. On that point, Nate and I couldn't have disagreed more.

I will always remember when we received our first payroll checks. Momma Williams was so proud she took a picture of us holding our checks before we cashed them. It was so funny to see me holding mine with a wide grin, and Nate holding his with a grim scowl! Our first checks were for $110.56, Nate was furious. "Look, they worked the shit out of us for two weeks, and this is all we get?"

"Be cool man, at least it's ours, and we can buy what we want. To me, it feels good to have a hundred dollars in my pocket!"

"That's you. I feel like I've been raped!"

Nate wanted to quit so bad, but he didn't want to disappoint his mom. It got so bad that he would complain from the time we got on the bus to go to work, until we got on the bus to go back home at night. By law we could only work until 8 or 9 o'clock at night, because we were minors. We only worked four to five hours a day, but it was four or five hours of hell as far as Nate was concerned. He really started getting on my nerves with all of his complaining. Sometimes I wished that he would quit, so I could have some peace.

The only time when Nate was not complaining about our new jobs was on the weekends, when we would party. Now partying for kids in Chicago in those days was different. "House music" had taken over the city, and house parties were the happening thing. There were many places to party during those days; Mendel, The Playground, The Bismarck, and others. Most kids decided where to go based on who the DJ was, and Chicago had the best. There was Kenny "Jammin" Jason,

Farley "Funkin" Keith, Frankie Knuckles, Scott "Smokin" Silz: they were considered the "Hotmix" five. Other people liked Li'l Louis, but our group loved Ron Hardy. This man did it for us; we would follow Ron Hardy to anywhere he was spinning. The way he mixed the old school cuts with the hot new tracks was great.

Ron was the usual DJ at The Music Box, so we kept going there. The parties would usually start at about 10:30 P.M. or so, and we would party until about 4 A.M.. How would a bunch of kids get out of the house that late and party until 4 A.M.? Don't ask. There were about five of us in our clique back then, and it took a combined effort to pull it off.

Our friend Pete was the oldest, so he had the ride, his grandmother's car. Pete's parents had been killed in a car accident, so his grandmother had raised him and his brother Mike, affectionately known as "Big Mike." We called him that because he was huge; six feet tall and 210 pounds and this by the time he was 16. Then we had Donnell, a guy who had come up from Florida with his family, and had kind of taken to us. We had known Donnell for about 4years, and that is an eternity for kids.

Finally, there was "Fingers." Fingers' real name was Cordell, but we called him Fingers because of his penchant for stealing. Cordell could steal anything, and he liked doing it. I think he really got a rush out of it. Fingers didn't know his parents. He was adopted by this affluent couple from "Pill Hill," on the South Side of suburban Chicago. They only had Cordell for about 6 months, and he was already robbing them blind. He would take anything; food, watches, even money right out of their wallets and purses. I think they knew he was stealing from them, they had to; but I also think they wanted a kid real bad, and Cordell could be very charismatic when he wanted to be.

At any rate, a usual night out would begin like this. Pete and Big Mike would have their grandmother in bed by about 9 P.M., and she was about 65, they knew she wouldn't be awake too long. Pete and Big Mike would raise the garage door, put their grandmother's car in neutral, and ease it out of the garage. I will never forget that car; it was a 1978 Buick Electra 225, affectionately known in Chicago as a "deuce and a quarter." That car was so big and so long, it could have been a boat. Pete would steer, and Mike would push the car down the street about half a block, so when Pete started the car up, grandma wouldn't hear the roar of the engine.

Nate and I would wait until about 10 P.M., because Momma Williams would go to sleep early after studying. We lived on the first floor, so we would quietly raise the window and jump down, and we were out. Some nights we would play hell trying to get back in, because Nate had let the window close too far. Once we were out, we would wait for Pete and Mike at the rib shack, or by the tavern on 71st Street. Nate used to like to look into the tavern and talk about all of the big booty ladies dancing to Johnny Taylor, or B.B King, and laugh. By 11 P.M. the other guys would drive up, and we would head toward Lake Shore Drive to the party.

When we were a block away, we could already hear the music. "Aww shit, time to party," Donnell said.

"How many numbers you gonna get tonight, Nate?" Donnell asked.

"I don't know, man, my mind been on other shit lately."

"Something other than females? I can't think of anything else more important," Mike said. "What about you, G, what you gonna do?"

"G don't get numbers, he scared of females!"

"Shut your ass up, I ain't afraid, a lot of times I'm just picky."

"Picky my ass, nigga, you scared," Mike said. I wasn't gonna argue, not with Big Mike.

Partying in those days was safe; there weren't any kids shooting guns, or anything like that. Most of the time, they were just exchanging phone numbers, and getting high off the music. But the music wasn't the only thing they were getting high from. Reefer was a main staple at these parties. Sometimes kids would do a little acid, but "bud," as it was called, was the drug of choice. Kids would get high off what we called the "wicked stick," and dance out of their minds.

The Music Box was just that, a box. It was so tight and hot and sweaty in there, I sometimes thought I would pass out. But the atmosphere was just cool; all of the women, the music, and the drugs sprung a feeling of euphoria that couldn't be beat.

During that time, I think, many kids used the party as a means of escape. Many kids had problems at home, at school, or in their social lives, and the party served as a sort of release from the pressures of those problems. At the party you could be who you wanted to be, say what you wanted to say, and belong to something in a weird sort of way. The trouble was; many kids were caught by the dangers of the party. Kids became hooked on drugs, many girls fell in love and got pregnant, and still others simply lost their desire to do anything else. The party had that kind of affect on some of us. All of a sudden attending college, or starting a career, just wasn't important anymore. Many of those who did go to college took that same party mentality along with them, and partied themselves right out of college. There was a mass of kids that got lost during those times, and were never found.

As for our group, well, we just had a good time. We never sampled the drugs, we were always afraid to. I believe that's what saved us. We would lie to others and tell them we were high, or we would drink a little, but we never did "bud." Nate and I were never big on dancing. We would simply enjoy the music, grope some girls, and try to get their numbers. This was enough fun for us. We felt we were too cool to dance and get all sweaty. We met and dated plenty of girls during that time, and had a lot of fun.

On that night, however, the party was cut short by an incident that changed the course of our lives. We didn't realize it at the time, but this particular night set off a chain of events that many of us are still feeling the effects of, to this day. Even today, I go over this night in my head, and ask myself what would have happened if we'd stayed home that night, or if we had gone straight home after the party instead of stopping. I thought at that time it was all just bad luck, but it wasn't. That night was meant to happen, I know that now.

It was Saturday night, our usual party night, and everything had gone as it had always gone. We sneaked out, met on 71st Street, drove to the party, had a good time, and left. This time we collectively decided that instead of going straight home, we would make a quick stop for some food. Everyone seemed to be strangely hungry that night. Since it was close to 3:30 A.M. and everything else was closed, we decided to go to the White Castle on 79th Street, which was open 24 hrs.

"Man, I don't want any sliders. I won't ever be able to get to sleep tonight. I can't eat that shit this late at night!" Donnel said.

"Man, you sound like an old-ass man, just get some onion rings or something," I said.

"Okay, who's going in?" Pete asked.

"Why don't we all go in, since all of us are eating something?" Nate reasoned.

After we went in, placed our orders, and sat down, in walked Titus with a few of his guys from the block. "Oh, shit, here we go," I said in disgust.

"Just be cool, dude, ain't shit gonna happen, we just gonna get our food, and be up an' outta here," Pete said sharply.

"Nah, this nigga don't ever let us get by without starting some shit, but I'm ready for his ass tonight!" Nate said with confidence.

By this time, Titus was a true gangster. We had heard he had been "upped" in the GDs and given a chunk of the West Side to sell dope for the gang. He had purchased a car, some new clothes, and was also sporting some gold teeth.

"What are you gonna do, Nate?" Pete asked.

"Just follow my lead, you all, this motherfucker's gonna get his tonight!"

My heart sank into my shoes. As soon as I saw Titus, I knew it was gonna be a bad night.

"Look at all these little house motherfuckers, sitting' in here trying' to be growed up," Titus said. "It's past y'all's bedtime, ain't it?"

Nobody said anything; we all just sat there.

"Hey, man, look at that big fat motherfucker, sitting over there looking like they daddy!" The whole restaurant started laughing as Titus lit into Big Mike. "Let me put my order in before this big motherfucker do, 'cause there ain't gonna be no food left."

By this time half the place was doubled over in laughter. Big Mike looked at Nate, and Nate shook his head, as if to say don't say anything yet.

"Hey ya'll, get some veggie burgers back there for his big ass, 'cause he need another cheeseburger like a hole in the head!" Titus said. Still more laughter.

Our order was finally ready, and we stood up. Nate said, "Remember, follow my lead, and Mike, the first motherfucker you put your hands on, you try to kill him. I'll take care of Titus."

"What? No, you don't. Mike, Nate, don't do this shit," I said. "You don't want to fuck with these guys. Let's just get our food and go!"

"Fuck that, G, we been kissing' this motherfucker's ass for six years. No more, no more kiss ass, we gotta teach him tonight!" That was always Nate's personality, short on patience and with an even shorter fuse.

This was a sticky situation, because the side door of the restaurant was locked after midnight, Titus's group was standing by the main entrance, and we had to go through them to get out. I just wanted to run and go home, I've never been one for much confrontation.

Titus said, "Oh shit y'all move out of the way for his big ass, you know he coming' up here to get some food, we all liable to get ran over!" Nate nodded for Mike to go ahead, and it was on.

"Fuck you, Titus, you ain't shit!"

"What you trying to raise up, you fat fuck? I'll split your motherfucking head in this bitch. Y'all better talk to this big ass before…." Just as Titus came to the end of his rant, Nate clocked him square on the jaw, almost knocking him out. Mike grabbed one of Titus' guys and choked him with one hand while sticking a thumb into his left eye with the other.

"Pete, get the fucking car!"

I pushed over a table and a couple of displays to roadblock the other two guys, and we all ran out. As Pete ran to get the car, I heard the restaurant manager tell someone to call the police. I looked at Mike, and his thumb and part of his hand were covered with blood. In the background, the guy he had assaulted was screaming in pain. It seems that Big Mike had pushed the punk's eyeball all the way into the back of his head. Titus was trying to shake off Nate's punch, and looked stunned; I guess he couldn't believe we had the guts to make a move like that. He quickly recovered though, and pulled out a .45 pistol from the small of his back. "Little motherfuckers! Look out, man," he shouted at his partner.

When I saw that gun, I started running like a four legged animal. It seemed like my feet were running so fast, the rest of my body couldn't catch up! The faster we ran toward the car, the further away it seemed. The first shot broke all of the glass in the window of the restaurant. Just as we were reaching the car, a second shot tore into Donnel's back, thrusting him forward. Big Mike scooped him up and kept running, almost without breaking stride.

By then police sirens were howling. Titus and his crew picked up their one-eyed buddy, and screeched off in their car. Nate and Titus had started out as a neighborhood rivalry, but now they were full scale arch enemies. And I was smack dab in the middle.

As I looked at Donnel's face and saw the life leaving him, I asked God why, why hadn't we just gone home tonight? "Pete," I shouted, "Take Donnel to Jackson Park Hospital, down Stony Island, make a U-turn here, and hurry up!" Big Mike cradled Donnel's head in his lap and cried, trying to talk to him, trying to keep him alive. "Hold on man, don't die, we almost there, just hold on!"

We were all terrified. I kept thinking about everything that happened, and suddenly something in me just snapped and calm came over me. I opened my mouth, and even I couldn't believe what was coming out. "We can't rat Titus out, don't anybody say anything. If we finger Titus as the shooter, the GD's will kill us all."

"What, that's bullshit, G he gonna go to jail for what he did to Donnel!" Mike said.

"No, Mike, he ain't going to jail, he's gonna die for what he did, but not now," Nate said. "G is right, if we rat him out now, the GDs will hunt us down and kill us. We can't finger him."

"Man, this shit ain't right; you mean if he dies, he just gonna die for nothing?" Pete asked.

"No, we'll get him back, but it ain't the right time. Just trust me and don't say nothing y'all, I promise you we will get revenge," Nate assured us.

I looked down at Donnel and his lips were quivering as we pulled up to the emergency doors of the hospital. "Get a fucking doctor out here, our friend's been shot!" Mike screamed. By now there was blood all over his clothes. The doctors took Donnel's seemingly lifeless body from us and began to work. As we sat in the waiting area, we went over our stories, from back to front.

Twenty minutes later everybody started pouring in, all of our parents, the police, the press, everyone. You see, up to 1984 there had been no shootings of kids by kids in Chicago, so this was news. I knew I would be able to hold up under the pressure, but I wondered about my friends, especially Pete, who was a consummate worrywart. He held up, barely. The police bombarded us with question after question. We denied everything.

Donnel's mother begged us to try to remember what the shooter looked like, but we just kept saying we didn't see anything.

Some of the people from White Castle gave a general description of Titus and his guys, but nothing concrete. Then our parents lit into us, after they saw that we were O.K. Everyone rallied behind Donnel's parents and family, helping them dig for information.

Then this lady cop came in. She looked hard, but cute. She had her hair back in a ponytail, and I remember that she had hard hands. She said she was Officer Jackson, Diane Jackson. She approached me first, for some reason, and started with some small talk. I knew the snow job, and I knew where it was going.

"I want you to know, Derrick, that I want to help you, but you have to help me," she said. "Donnel is very sick, and we all want to help him, do you understand?"

"Yeah."

"Now just tell me what happened tonight, very slowly." So I went over it again just as we all rehearsed it. I said it was an attempted carjacking, and she looked at me with such calm and motherly look, I could tell she knew I was lying through my teeth.

"There's only one thing I cannot understand, though, Derrick, how could it have been a carjacking from inside the store?"

"Some of us stayed in the car, and some went in to get food, and they approached the car and tried to jack us."

"O.K., so tell me, how did they shoot Donnel in the back?"

"I don't know, I was keeping my head down, I didn't see anything, I just heard the shot."

"Your friend Peter said there were several shots, how did he hear more?"

"Look, Ma'am, I don't know anything about several, I was just trying to keep from getting shot."

Momma Williams chimed in, "That's enough. These kids have been traumatized enough for one night. I don't know about the other parents, but I'm taking mine home."

"I have some more questions, Ms. Williams."

"Not tonight, you don't. Call me in the morning. As far as I am concerned, we're done for the night."

After about a month of the TV reports, newspaper interviews, and police questioning, people started to leave us alone. Somehow, I felt that some of the parents knew we were lying, but they couldn't figure out why. Some, like Momma Williams, felt we were afraid, so they didn't push the issue.

Donnel had three operations in the month after the shooting, and wasn't faring well; they said that if he lived, and that was a big if, he would be paralyzed from the waist down. Five weeks after he was shot, Donnel slipped into a coma and died. It broke all of us up real bad. We thought Donnel would pull through, but it just wasn't meant to be, I guess. I missed him. It all seemed so unreal, so unfair, and so final.

The funeral was a circus. Everyone was there; the press, the police, thrill seekers, people from the community, everyone. There were hundreds of people, most of whom didn't even know Donnel or his family. Even some of the kids from the Music Box came to the funeral. All of the kids took it so hard. Many of them came up to give short eulogies about Donnel, but were so broken up they couldn't finish. All of the DJs turned out, to my surprise. Some of them left gifts and money for the family. Everyone came up for one last look at Donnel, and the tears and crying were just overwhelming. To this day, it was the saddest funeral I have ever attended. When I walked past the coffin, the boy in it didn't look like Donnel to me; he looked like all dead people look, like my mamma had looked, waxy and dead.

Something changed in all of us. We weren't the same; we lied to the police, deceived the press and our parents, and watched our friend almost die in our arms. We couldn't have been the same. Looking back, we all could have used some therapy. Nate said we shouldn't talk about Donnel anymore, except among ourselves. We were holding a terrible secret, and had vowed revenge. That summer we came of age, our innocence was gone. We had crossed a line too wide for fifteen and sixteen year olds to have to cross. We were coming of age; we were becoming men.

Chapter 2

Descent

Times were changing. Times were changing nationally for poor minorities at the hands of what was called "Reaganomics," a socioeconomic ideology that allowed the rich to get richer, and the poor to become destitute. Steel mills and factories were closing or relocating, leaving countless Black men without jobs. While many upper middle-class and rich whites enjoyed an era of prosperity and excess, members of poor minorities wondered where their next meals were coming from.

Momma Williams said it was because many Blacks were not educated, and weren't equipped for the changing of the times. "The days of working on an assembly line making twelve or thirteen dollars an hour are over. In the future, education and career training are gonna be the keys, and black people had better get them."

Too bad that many people didn't heed the warning. We watched as whole cities shut down because of steel mill closings, mega mergers, and company relocations. Cities like Gary, Indiana, a city that heavily depended upon factories for its economic and employment stability, were now becoming ghost towns.

There was a bright spot, locally. Black people all over town rallied behind Harold Washington, the city's first black mayor. I remember there were voting drives everywhere. People who didn't vote in years were now registered voters. Nate and I were too young to vote, but we were certainly in touch with what was happening. I can still close my eyes and remember Harold, as he was affectionately called by blacks, standing at that hotel podium telling the crowd, "You wanted Harold, you want Harold, well... you *got* Harold!" Harold Washington had won the election by an overwhelming margin, and Momma Williams said she was proud of her people that night. It wasn't just a victory for Washington; it was a victory for minorities in Chicago, who were tired of machine politics and business as usual. Now we had a voice; we had someone in City Hall that represented us.

Things were changing for our group, too. We didn't want to party anymore; it just didn't seem the same without Donnel. Donnel's parents decided to move back to Florida with his little sister. I guess with all that happened they felt better just going back to familiar surroundings. Cordell kept talking about how he wished he had been with us that night; his parents had put him on punishment for what else...stealing. He kept going over how he should have been there, as if he would have made a difference.

Momma Williams put the hammer down on us, too. Now she didn't want us to go anywhere but school, home, and work. We couldn't date or anything. Nate hated it because he would have to stay at McDonald's, with nothing else to do after work. The death of Donnel had an impact on all of our lives. We just were not the same anymore. We didn't want to attend any school football games, pep rallies, school dances, or anything. It all seemed juvenile to us. Somehow, we had outgrown all of that.

We all kept talking about how one day we were gonna get even with Titus for Donnel's death. From time to time the police would stop us and ask us questions, especially Detective Trent. I think he really wanted to get back with Momma Williams, and wanted to use the case as an excuse. One day when we were home, he rang the doorbell, asked Momma Williams could he come in, and assured her it was concerning the case.

"I don't know what you could possibly want to ask, we have answered all of the questions anyone could ask," she said.

"I just want to run a couple of names their way and see what they say."

"Derrick....Nathan.....come out here!"

"I am so proud of you, Gloria, for the way you have taken control of your life, " Trent said.

"Thank you," she replied.

"Don't you miss me at all? I miss the hell out of you," he said pitifully.

"You're still married?" she asked.

"Yeah."

"Oh well, you haven't missed me *that* much," she said sarcastically.

As we walked in, I immediately began to study Detective Trent. It had been a few years since I had seen him, and he seemed to have aged some, but he was still intimidating. "Sit down, boys. I want to ask you some questions," he said.

"Is it about Donnel? Cause I ain't answering no more questions about it!" Nate said emphatically.

"Oh yes, you will, Nathan, or I will ground your ass so long you'll have a gray head before you see the outside of this house again, and you will be respectful!" Momma Williams said.

"Does the name Titus Thompson mean anything to you two?" Trent asked.

I didn't answer. I thought I should let Nate answer first. "Don't know him," Nate said, looking out of the window.

"What about you, Derrick, are you familiar with him?"

"He doesn't know him either." Nate said sternly.

"Let him answer for himself. Well, do you, Derrick?"

"Like he said, we don't know him."

"Nathan, don't make me knock the shit…" Momma Williams was getting real angry at Nathan, and she was starting toward him when Detective Trent stopped her.

"Mrs. Williams, can I speak to the boys for a minute alone?"

"Five minutes," she said.

After she left the room, Detective Trent put his pad down, and looked Nate squarely in the eye. "You want to hit me, Nate, go ahead. We may as well get all of this out into the open. I know all you little punks don't like the cops. If you think you are a man, go ahead, hit me."

"Don't come to me with that cop shit, this ain't got nothing to do with you being a cop. I know you used to see my momma, playing her like some slave woman. You're right, I can't stand your ass, but it don't have nothing to do with you being a cop!"

That was the first time I had ever seen a cop at a loss for words. Trent didn't know that Nate knew about him, and he looked back stupidly. I looked at Trent with sort of a half grin on my face, waiting to see what his response would be.

"I see. I am sorry, Nathan. I am sorry things worked out the way they did, between me and your mother. But let me assure you, I have all the respect in the world for your mother, and I love her too, Nate."

"Yeah, her and your wife. All of you pasty ass honkies are the same. You don't give a damn about black people. You just use us for your own greed and self interest. Go to hell!"

"Hey, who the hell do you think you are talking to? I have helped you and your mother for years because I cared for you both, and I still do."

"I didn't ask for your help. I didn't want it. I wanted my mamma to have a black man."

By this time they were both standing, eye to eye, like men. I respected Nate for his stance, but I must say I disagreed with him.

"Oh, a black man. She had one, and he left her with you!"

Tears welled in Nate's eyes, along with raw rage. This was the first time I had seen it. I think if he had a gun in his hand, he would have shot Trent right there. I stood between them.

"Look, you two, Momma Williams is coming back. Let's just cool it!" Nate's fists were balled up. I could tell he wanted to hit Trent so bad he could taste it. Trent picked up all of his things and stormed out the door, slamming it behind him. He was so pissed he forgot to finish asking us about Titus.

"Hey, what about the questions Harry, what happened in there?" Momma Williams was just coming back into the room.

"I'll call you later, Gloria, I have to go!"

"Harry, wait, wait a minute!" Trent got into his Crown Victoria, and screeched off down the avenue.

Nate told Momma Williams he knew about her and Detective Trent. Momma Williams was surprised, but not shocked. She knew Nate had to know more than he had let on through the years. The painful part for her was Nate's knowledge of her on again, off again years of prostitution. I imagine no mother wants her son to know about her sexual encounters, but this was far worse. To my surprise, Nate knew all about it, and he had harbored feelings of shame. There was a lot of hurt inside Nate, feelings that were never addressed. Momma Williams thought that if she didn't mention it, it would never come up, and maybe Nate just didn't know about it at all.

One of the biggest mistakes parents make is underestimating their children. Children know far more than they are credited for, sometimes. They may not know all of the details of a given situation, but their understanding is usually in the ballpark. I guess talking to Nate about something so graphic and shocking would have been too much for her to handle, so she pretended it didn't happen. By this time, Momma Williams had gone to school, gotten her Associate's Degree and moved on, so why go back and re-open old wounds? The years of teasing by the other children, and the shame of it had taken its toll on Nate. Maybe that's why we had taken to each other so well. We both had had some of the same issues with mothers.

For a long time, Nate couldn't really look Momma Williams in the eye. It never occurred to him that Momma Williams had done it so they could survive. Looking back on it, I can see he dealt with it the way most young men would have.

Momma Williams insisted that we keep our jobs at McDonald's, much to the dismay of Nate, who was desperately trying to find a way to quit. I, on the other hand, wanted to try to get a schedule that did not coincide with Nate's, because of his complaining. Momma Williams wouldn't have it, though; she said that with all of the publicity of Donnel's death, and the fact that gang members may be involved, she wanted us to work together.

The police dragged Titus in for questioning, but with no witnesses, no murder weapon, and no real evidence, they had to let him go. Titus was going around town bragging to people inside the Gangster Disciples that he had gotten away with murder. It really made us mad, but we had promised to take care of him ourselves.

The Gangster Disciples were so impressed with Titus that they gave his crew three-quarters of the West Side to sell drugs in, along with enforcement for the entire West Side. The fact that Titus had been selling drugs for close to ten years, and now had killed a guy without ever being collared, gave him colossal street cred. Titus was growing in the crime world while we flipped burgers and fried fries, but that was about to change.

Most of the white people at work were really starting to warm up to us, especially the girls. The white guys seemed to be a bit afraid of us, especially after all the talk in the press about us being involved with a gang killing. Most of the girls seemed strangely intrigued, though, always asking questions and wanting to take their breaks with us and socialize.

One particular girl named Heather was especially interested in Nate. Heather was a brash young blond dishwater girl who partied a lot. She was always late for work, and she smoked cigarettes like a chimney. She had two or three girlfriends who followed her around the restaurant all the time. Nate was apprehensive; he felt they were up to something.

"I don't trust those white bitches G, they up to something, always smiling in our faces and wanting to eat lunch with us and shit."

"Maybe they are up to something, but so are we, you know what I mean?"

"We ain't up to shit, that's you. I like the sistas!"

I think Nate had a problem with white girls because of his feelings about Detective Trent and his mom. It really didn't bother me, though. People were people, the girls were cute, and I wanted them. Whenever we were eating or talking with them, Nate would often just sit there, not really saying anything and somehow that seemed to interest them even more.

"You don't talk much, Nathan, what's wrong?" they would ask.

"Nothing."

"Nate isn't feeling well today," I said, covering for him.

"Oh well, we're having a party this weekend at my house, would you two like to come?" Heather asked.

"Sure, what time?"

"It starts at nine thirty. Do you guys have a ride?"

"Nah, we'll just catch the bus over there. Is it near 87th Street?"

"You don't have to catch the bus; we will come over and pick you up."

Wow I thought, that would be real cool, having some white girls come to our neighborhood and pick up a couple of black guys. That would be saying something! The only problem was Momma Williams. She didn't want us going anywhere, and there was not going to be any sneaking out like the old days, so I had to think of something quick.

"Don't we have something to do that day?" Nate asked.

"No, Nate," I said. "We'll be there. Maybe we will just meet you on 87th Street near Halsted. That way you won't have to drive all the way east," I assured them.

"O.K., we will meet you both on Halsted at eight fifteen, is that cool?"

"Yeah, are your parents gonna be there?"

All three of the girls looked at each other and started laughing, as if it were an inside joke. "No, silly, why do you think we are having a party? They'll be out of town."

Jackpot, I thought. It was obvious these girls were hot for us, and if everything went right, it was gonna be a good night. The only problem was Nate; he was being a real stick-in-the-mud.

"Man, I don't know why you made a date with them white broads," Nate said later. "I don't want to spend the night listening to their stupid conversation, and they're boring!"

"Nate, you never know, it might be fun, it's not like we are doing anything else!"

"O.K, Mr. Know-It-All, how do you plan to get us to 87th Street at 8 o'clock at night, and what are you gonna tell Momma?"

"I haven't figured that out yet, but I will. Whatever I say, just go along with it."

It didn't take me long to come up with the perfect plan. I was going to ask Heather to call Momma Williams and pretend to be the store manager at McDonald's. She was going to ask if we could do some work at her house after hours for double the pay. She was going to praise our work, and talk about the future work she may have for us. I told her to tell Momma Williams that we would be out until at least 1 A.M.

"Ingenious, G, that's a good plan. It might even work, too."

"It will work. She doesn't know Heather from a can of paint, and she won't expect a thing. It'll work."

It did work, like a charm. Momma Williams was proud that we seemed to be getting preferential treatment over the other kids at McDonald's. She told us to just make sure we weren't over there playing butler and maid, shining for the white folks. Since Heather was supposed to be the store manager, she could come all the way over to the apartment to get us. Heather played it up real good, too. She drove her father's Mercedes, and even came in to get us. She wore a lot of makeup, dressed older, and it worked perfectly. I kept thinking, these girls must want us to come to their party real bad, to go to all this trouble.

Soon, we were in the car headed toward Oak Lawn. "Try some of this," Heather said, "It's real cool." She handed me a joint. We had tried weed before, and it wasn't our favorite thing, but I had to be cool. I didn't want to seem square, especially in front of some white girls.

"Don't smoke that shit, G, you don't know what it is."

"It's grass, Nate," Heather said. "It's not going to hurt him, it's cool."

I took a pull from it, and I had to admit that it was good weed, real good. It was better than the stuff we had tried before. It was smooth, and had a good aroma.

"Hey, this is good shit," I said. "Try it, Nate. For real, it's good shit!"

Nate took a pull, and he agreed that it was good reefer. Not that we were experts on marijuana, but we knew this stuff was different.

"Where did you get this stuff from?" I asked.

"A friend, he sells to us all of the time. We don't buy from anyone else," Heather said.

After Nate got a little buzz, he started acting much better. He loosened up so much that he started to actually enjoy himself. Once we got to the party, we saw that our hostesses had purchased about a pound of marijuana, which was the most reefer I had ever seen in my life. There were about eight girls there, plus Nate, this other guy named Jon, and myself.

The house was beautiful. Heather's father was a dentist, so he had plenty of money. I wondered what he would have thought if he knew his daughter was spending it on drugs. The music was loud, and everyone was smoking joint after joint. We were literally going through it like candy. Jon went to the store to buy some beer. While he was gone, Heather made her play for Nate.

"Come upstairs, Nate, I've got something to show you."

Nate was so high, he just followed without asking any questions, and Heather's other friend Jessica started flirting with me. Jessica had the most beautiful cobalt blue eyes I had ever seen. They were hypnotizing.

"Do you like white girls?" she asked.

"I like girls, it doesn't matter to me if they are white or not, do you like black guys?"

"Definitely, if it ain't black, take it back."

"Oh yeah? What is it about black men that you like so much?"

"They are confident, confident in themselves, and they have such an alluring swagger. They are beautiful."

Of course, that was all B.S. She was just jungle curious. While saying that, she started rubbing my chest and kissing my neck. Since I had never had sex before, I was nervous that I wouldn't be good enough. I asked her if she was sure she wanted to do this.

"Yeah, does it seem like I am having second thoughts?"

She pulled my pants off and started to perform oral sex on me, right there in front of the other girls! Jon walked in from the store, saw what was going on, grabbed one of the other girls, and they started doing their own thing. Jon and I had sex with all of those girls, right out in the open. Drugs and alcohol will make people do some crazy things. There's no way I would've been so irresponsible if I had been in my right mind.

I didn't see Nate for the next hour or two. I knew what they were doing, but I had to check things out for myself. After we were "finished," I walked upstairs and opened the door slightly. They evidently had sex already, and were asleep in the bed. When I came back downstairs, one of the girls grabbed some pillows and blankets, and crashed on the floor with Jon. I grabbed one of Jon's pillows and a blanket and did the same. There we were, nine people lying on the floor with about a half pound of reefer spread out on the table, and beer cans all over the place. It was wild!

Nate was excited the next day, and had a whole different perspective on white people. He told me all about Heather, and what she had done to him, and what he had done to her, the whole thing in graphic detail, like brothers do. He also told me that Heather got the reefer from a mutual friend of Jon's, some Mexican guy named Hector. He said that Heather told him they did that at least twice a month. Nate said he really didn't like reefer, but that stuff was so smooth you wouldn't know you were smoking it if not for the smell. "Man," Nate said, "we should get some of that for ourselves, while we are still in good with Heather and her friends."

"What do you mean, still in good? They're cool people. I thought you liked them."

"I do, G, but you know this shit ain't gonna last forever. As soon as the novelty of it wears off, they're gonna break it off."

Nate underestimated Heather and her friends, as our "partying" went on for about nine more months. Sometimes we would drive downtown and get high near Buckingham Fountain. We were having the time of our lives. Once, we skipped school to get high, and drove down to Brookfield Zoo. Jon did impressions of the lions and monkeys, and had us dying with laughter. On the drive back, Nate asked Jon about the reefer.

"So Jon, how much do you guys pay for all of this reefer?"

"Why? We haven't asked you for any money." Jon was like that, real quick witted.

"I know, man, I'm just asking. I might want to get some for myself."

"About sixty or seventy bucks a pound, but I don't reveal my contacts man, so don't ask."

"I know, but what if I wanted to buy some, could I buy from you?"

"I ain't no drug dealer, man." Jon kept driving and bobbing his head to the music of War. He loved that group. As a matter of fact, that's all I ever remember him listening to. Still, it was strange to see a white boy listening to War.

"I know, Jon, but I want to buy some, and I know some other people who do, too." I looked at Nate strange. We didn't know anyone who was looking for reefer!

"How much they looking to buy?"

"I don't know, about two pounds."

"Are you sure? Who the fuck wants to buy that much reefer if they ain't selling it?"

"Look Jon, will you help us or not?"

"What's in it for me, do I get a cut?"

"Yeah, I'll cut your throat," Nate said jokingly.

"Let me see what I can do, and I will get back to you," Jon said, laughing.

After Jon dropped us off on the sidewalk, I asked Nate about his exchange. "Why did you ask him about two pounds of reefer, weren't we only looking for a little for ourselves?"

"I had to make it look big, so we can get the contact. He won't give it to us for two joints, G."

"Say he gives it to you, what will you do then?"

"I don't know. I will think of something."

Just then Big Mike and Pete walked up. Until now we hadn't told them about Heather and her friends, as we wanted to keep this to ourselves. Nate always said when you start telling a whole lot of stuff to niggas you're asking for trouble. It's not that we didn't trust Big Mike and Pete, but you just never know.

"Man, where have you two been, we been looking all over for y'all," Pete said.

"Just hanging out, what have you all been up to?" Nate asked.

"Nothing, we heard Titus is the new king on the West Side, he got the whole area locked down now," Pete said.

"I know, I heard it too," Nate said.

"Man, you sure we shouldn't drop a dime on his ass?"

"Nah, his time will come, just be patient," Nate said.

"I'd like to break his fucking neck, that's what I would like to do," Mike said.

"You and I both, Mike, but something is just telling me we should wait," Nate lamented.

While we were standing on the corner, Jon suddenly drove up in his Camero, seeming to come out of nowhere. "Hop in guys, got somewhere to take you."

"Nate, who the fuck is this guy?" Mike asked.

"Don't worry about it, he's cool, I'll be right back, man."

"Cool, call me later," Pete said.

"Hey, where is Fingers?" Nate asked. "That's what I have to talk to you about. Come see me later," Pete told us.

As we were riding around, Jon ran down all of the details. "O.K., I'm gonna introduce you to the contact, but you need to have the money on you, 'cause he ain't taking no shit."

"How much do we need to have?"

"Two hundred."

"Two hundred dollars? We're buying reefer, not cocaine!" I shouted.

"You wanted two pounds, right? That's the price, take it or leave it."

"C'mon Jon, you know that's too high, you said you pay sixty or so for a pound, how come we have to pay two hundred?"

"Hey, man, that's what he told me you had to pay. He knows whoever buys it is gonna be selling it, so I think he upped the price. And I suggest you don't try to bring him down. All of his prices are non-negotiable, especially with people he don't know."

Now we were in a mess, Nate and I together had about twenty bucks between us. We hadn't expected it to go down like this, and we were screwed big time. Nate looked at me with a get-me-out-of-this-look on his face. So I thought fast, and said,"Well, we don't have the money on us. Can you take us back to the house to get it?"

Now we were really reaching. We only had about twenty more dollars at the house. "I figured you wouldn't have it. I'll loan it to you until you get it back from whoever needs the stuff, but I need it back this week!" Jon insisted. He reached into his pocket, pulled out two one hundred dollar bills and handed them to Nate. "Now don't fuck with this guy. He's cool, but he's a hot head.

If he thinks you're fucking with him, he will cut your throats, and then cut mine for bringing you to him, so don't screw up!"

It seemed as if we drove for hours. During the whole ride I was trying to think of a way to get us out of this. Best case scenario: We would be sitting in our room tonight with two pounds of reefer and no clue about what to do next.   Worst case scenario: Momma Williams would be making our funeral arrangements later this week. I had to think fast.

"Hey Jon, can you turn that shit down? I can't hear myself think!" I shouted.

"You don't like War? I thought all of the brothers liked War."

"I like it, but damn, it's too loud!" Jon turned the music down a little, and I got back to thinking. I needed to know more about this guy.

"What's his name, Jon?" I asked.

"Hector, but I will formally introduce you three when we get there."

"How long he been in the game?" Nate asked.

"A few years, he's got the Hispanic community locked down. I go to him 'cause his shit is good, he gets it straight from Mexico. He wants to expand, though."

"Is he with the Mexican gangs?"

"Hell no, he hates gangs!" That was a relief; nobody hated gang bangers more than we did. "Is that who you are buying for, 'cause if you are......"

"No, hell no, we hate those fuckers too!" Nate insisted.

As he drove, I kept trying to think of a plan to just get the reefer and get the hell out alive. "Who turned you on to him?" I asked.

"I met him through a mutual friend when I was at University of Illinois at Chicago a couple of years ago.

Since then I have turned him on to customers here and there, and have earned some respect from him, something I hope you two won't fuck up tonight!"

He was hoping, I was praying! This guy sounded big time, and Nate and I were a couple of school kids looking for kicks. We had never even sold candy bars before, much less drugs. This guy was gonna sniff us out immediately, and then kill us. I had to think. Jon had put his reputation and maybe his life on the line for us with this guy. We had started out looking for a couple of joints, and now we were probably gonna get killed!

We were on First Avenue in the Hispanic community, and my heart was in my throat. My heart was beating so fast, I was sure Nate and Jon could hear it. We pulled up in front of this house, real quaint and inconspicuous, but I noticed there were guys, big guys, sitting on the porch, along with some Mexican girls.

"O.K., this is it. You two got anything you want tell me before we get out of this car?"

"Nope," Nate and I said in unison.

"Are you sure?"

"Yeah, we're sure motherfucker, let's just go!" Nate said.

"You better be!"

Chapter 3

Hello's and Goodbyes

As I got out of the car, I took a good look around to get my bearings, in case we had to run. As we approached the house, the big guys came down to the bottom of the steps to meet us. These were the biggest Mexicans I had ever seen. One had a long mustache, a ponytail, and the word "outlaw" tattooed on his arm. "Who are you hear to see?" he said with a thick Spanish accent. "You're cool, we know you, but we gotta check the others."

"They are with me," Jon acknowledged.

"I don't care, man," one of the other guys said. As they frisked us, I couldn't help but think what they would do if they found a gun.

"They're clean," the big one said. "Hey Jon, what's up Homes, how have you been, man?" I noticed that they did not open up until they knew we were clean.

"Cool, I'm just bringing in more business," Jon said.

"Hey, that's what we like to hear, Homes, come on up." As they invited Jon into the house, we naturally followed.

"Not you two, homes, we don't know you, you two gotta wait here."

"C'mon Julio, they're clean, and they are with me, it's cool," Jon said. The guy Julio stared at us for what seemed like an hour, looking us up and down, "O.K., follow me."

I could smell someone cooking in the kitchen, and it smelled pretty good, too. There were kids in the room playing, but the Julio guy quickly closed the door so I couldn't see. There were two guys walking about a foot behind us, talking Spanish, and three guys in front, including Julio. I had never felt so vulnerable before in my life. I remember looking for exits, windows, any route out of the house, but there were none. Everything in that house was sealed or secured, and we were sitting ducks.

A large woman emerged from one of the bedrooms with a plate of what looked like nachos and dip. "Hey, Rosa, what do you have there?" Jon asked. He was trying to make us feel relaxed by showing his familiarity with everyone.

"Food, boy. Look at you…you need to eat. Here." Jon took one of the chips and ate it. Rosa looked at us strangely, giving us that I-don't-know-you look. Jon may have been relaxed, but we weren't relaxed with them, and it seemed that they were not relaxed with us. Jon turned to me and whispered, "That's Rosa. She can cook her ass off. Whatever you like, she can make it, and she's great!" To hell with Rosa and her food, I thought, I just want to get out of here.

Soon, we approached a long stairway leading up to a room. "O.K., you know the rules, Homes, let's go," Julio said.

"What rules?" Nate asked.

"Keep your hands out of your pockets and speak only when spoken to," Jon answered. As we walked up the stairs I noticed the Spanish conversation behind us had abruptly stopped. The stairway was dimly lit and steep. I also noticed the sudden change in temperature; the higher we went the hotter it got, which did nothing for my nerves. Julio gave two signaling knocks, listened for a response, and swung open the door.

There he was, Hector Gomez, the drug kingpin of the Hispanic community, sitting at a large desk eating nachos and reading a newspaper. There were two large men with assault rifles behind him, and about five other men with handguns around the room. I also noticed two exotic looking women sitting on the couch counting money. To me, it looked like thousands of dollars.

"Ah, Hola` amigo, I see you have brought your friends you spoke of, no?" Hector's accent was the thickest of all. He sounded like he just arrived in the states about an hour ago

"Yeah, Hector, they're cool, we're ready to make our purchase."

"Hey we will talk business later, I haven't seen you, cabrone`, introduce me to your compadres." We all exchanged greetings and then Jon asked about the reefer.

"Who is buying, and why?" Gomez asked.

"We are," I asserted.

"Oh. Señor Jon, can you excuse me and your compadres, and let us talk business."

"Hey, Hector, it's cool, man, they are on the up and up."

"I know, but let me talk to them first, you know, let us get to know each other." Hector smiled at Jon, and Jon gave a nervous smile in return as he was escorted to the door. "Don't worry, my friend, they will be fine," Hector assured him.

After Jon left the room Hector's smiling face quickly turned to stone. "So how long have you been in the business?"

"Oh, a few years, doing a little bit here and there," I said, trying to sound convincing.

"Can we just get the stuff and go?" Nate said impatiently.

"In due time my friend. What's wrong, you don't like my company?" Hector asked.

"No, it's not like that, man. I just have somewhere to be soon."

"Patience my friend, you will get there. So are you two with the local gangs, or no?"

"Naw man, we don't fuck with gangs, we work alone," Nate said strongly. "Hey, man fuck all of this talking shit, are you gonna sell us this shit or what?"

Hector got up from his chair. Nate had struck a nerve. Hector walked over to us and got about two inches from our faces. His breath smelled of hot salsa. "Mind your fucking tone with me, son, or I will cut your fucking throat!" He walked around us, looking us up and down. "You know what, if you two are dealers, I am the President of the United States. Kill them!"

"Hey, wait a minute Hector, what the hell is this? We heard in the 'hood that you were a stand up guy, what's up with this shit?" I asked.

He motioned for his hired guns to wait a minute. "What is up is I don't know you, or who you represent, and I have never been to your 'hood,' as you call it."

"Jon said that you were cool, and the guys in my neighborhood that get high on your stuff said you were cool."

"Fuck Jon, he is dead, and what neighborhood are you talking about?"

"South Side, my area," Nate said.

One of Hector's people whispered something in his ear in Spanish. He gave the guy a strange look, and then a nod of approval.

"I apologize for acting so strongly, it is business, you understand?" he said to us. "Now, let me make you a, how do you say, a proposition."

"Like what?" Nate asked.

66

"Let's say you come in and work for me, let's say we make a deal of twenty pounds a quarter, at a 70/30 split. Now surely if you are dealers, you can move that," he reasoned.

"You don't know us and you are gonna trust us with twenty pounds of stuff?" I asked.

"Fuck no, we will start with the two pounds you came here to buy, you move that and bring me back five hundred dollars, and we have a deal," he said, as he lit a cigar.

"Wait a minute, if we do that we don't get anything!" Nate said.

"Oh yes, you do, you get to leave here with your lives," he said.

"But seventy-thirty? What 'bout the gangs? You want us to sell drugs in their territory, and only get a seventy-thirty split?" I asked incredulously.

"That is your problem, not mine. You said you are dealers, then deal. What's wrong? I am taking a chance on you, compadre, but you do not want to take a chance for me?"

"Naw, not with our lives!" Nate said.

"But what is stopping me from killing you now, and keeping your money, all for free?" He had a point. We were doomed the minute we walked in there pretending to be something that we weren't. A seasoned dealer like him sniffed us out the minute we walked in the room. We screwed ourselves.

"Do we have a deal, or do we have a funeral?" Hector Gomez asked.

"No deal until we see our friend alive," Nate demanded. A door was opened and Jon was sitting there in the next room, duct taped to a chair, with a gag in his mouth.

"Do we have a deal?" Hector shouted.

What were we gonna say? If we refused, we were all gonna be killed, 'cause these guys were not playing with us. We had walked into something we definitely couldn't handle. We agreed to the deal, if that's what you'd call it. Jon was released, and Hector kind of half apologized for his aggressive behavior, but now we had a real problem on our hands after leaving Hector's place.

"What the hell are we gonna do now?" Nate asked.

"I don't know, but you guys should have told me about what was going on before we got in there, we almost got killed!" Jon said. I really expected Jon to be angrier than he was, but he always had an easygoing personality. I, personally, would have been livid.

"We are going to have to deal drugs, what else?" Jon said.

"But we don't know anything about drug dealing. Shit, I don't even know what to charge!" Nate pointed out.

"That's easy. Find out what the going rate is and go a little cheaper. Hector's shit is good, and I am confident that it will basically sell itself," Jon insisted. "I will show you how to clean it, bag it, and weigh it. You will have to figure out the rest."

Jon showed us how to get all of the sticks and seeds out, and package the product. Since Hector had given it to us in brick form, we had a little work to do before we could hit the streets. We spent about two hours cleaning the stuff, and another two hours weighing it and bagging it. We agreed to sell nickel bags for seven bucks and dime bags for twelve. We hid the stuff in a ragged suitcase that Jon gave us, and we left his house to go home.

When we arrived home, Momma Williams was in bed with the flu, so she never got to see what was going on. We left the suitcase in the hallway until the coast was clear. Once Momma Williams was asleep, we sneaked it in and hid it in the back of the closet behind all of our clothes and shoes. Nate and I sat on the bed and looked at each other. We were in a world of trouble, and we had to agree on how we were going to get out of it. "Maybe we should tell the police and Momma Williams," I suggested.

"Are you crazy? Those guys will kill us, and besides we are just as bad as they are. You forget, we just bought two pounds of reefer!"

I was fully aware of the lunacy of my suggestion. I just wanted to check out Nate's mindset on the situation, and his commitment level.

We started out selling at Robeson. Since we always knew people who wanted to buy reefer, it wasn't hard to get started. Heather also took some reefer to sell at her school in Oak Lawn. We made a rule to never sell to people we were not familiar with. Most people bought "nickels" and "ounces;" the "dimes" didn't sell that well. I could never figure that out. Most times people would buy a "nickel," smoke it in a couple of days, and then come calling for another "nickel." That seemed so crazy to me; it made better sense just to buy the "dime" in the first place.

To be perfectly honest, Heather sold better than we did; the white kids went crazy over that reefer! Of the two pounds we got from Hector, Nate and I only sold about a quarter of a pound, and Heather sold the rest. I liked it that way, though, since most of the reefer was sold outside our community, the gangs couldn't catch on. The prospect worried me a lot. The Vice Lords, Black P. Stones and the Gangster Disciples had certain areas that they sold in, but who was gonna get wise to reefer being sold in Oak Lawn?

Big Mike caught up to us and told us he heard that we were selling "bud."

"Who told you that?" Nate asked.

"A little bird, but don't worry, it's all on the hush. I want to know why you didn't let us in on the whole thing, I thought we were friends," Mike said.

"We are, dude, I just didn't want a lot of people involved. We are dealing with Hector Gomez, and I just didn't want to take any chances," Nate confided. I could tell Mike was a bit hurt, but didn't show it. "But now that you know, we want you to work with us. This needs to be a collective effort."

"Where is Fingers, what's happened to him?" I asked.

"That's what I wanted to tell you all. His people sent him back to the boys' home, man. Fingers was robbing them blind. He would steal their shit and fence it with this guy over on Wentworth Avenue."

"Damn, he had a good deal with them. What's wrong with him, couldn't he just chill out?" Nate asked.

"I guess not. He's up north, and we don't know how to get in touch with him."

"What's the name of the boys' home?"

"I don't know. Maryville or something, I don't know," Mike conceded.

"We've got to go up there, but for now we need your help with this deal. Come on, let me fill you in," Nate said. Nate told Mike about the whole situation, and how it had come about. Nate wanted Mike's help with security if we decided to take Hector's offer to deal for him. Nate wanted Mike to tell Pete about it, too. Nate wanted a meeting with everyone eventually, but he had to talk it over with me first to see if it was a wise move.

Everything hinged on how well we did with the first two pounds. And we did well. Hector gave us one month to get rid of it. We sold it in two weeks, making seven hundred dollars instead of the five hundred he asked for. Jon was right, the stuff really sold itself. If a person were into "weed," all he had to do is try it and he would be hooked, so to speak. I remember sitting down with Nate after school to discuss it. Momma Williams had gone to the doctor for her flu, so we didn't have to worry about her hearing us.

"Well what are we gonna do?" I asked.

"I don't know, we could give him his money back and just quit and walk away," Nate said.

"Do you think he would let us do that?"

"Who's to say? We could deal for him and when it starts to get old, get out. It's not like we are selling coke," Nate reasoned.

"I don't know. This has been the easiest money we have ever made, especially since Heather did the bulk of the work."

"Yeah, no shit. But it's all his, G. We keep two hundred, but the other five are his. All of the risk for a fraction of the cash, I don't like it!" Nate confessed.

"True, but we don't have a choice. We are not in a position to make demands. We either do this, or we don't."

"With the people we have right now, can we do twenty pounds a quarter?" Nate asked.

"Hell yeah, if we can sell two pounds in two weeks," I said.

"What about the gangs? We can't deal twenty pounds of reefer out here without dealing with them. Heather did good, but she won't be able to move twenty pounds of stuff in Oak Lawn. We would have to sell on the block," I said.

"Let's see," Nate said. "Neither of the gangs has established the South Side as real territory for

71

themselves. The white boys have the North Side, and the gangs have the West Side, but the South and the Southeast sides are open for freelancers. Why can't we establish it for ourselves?"

"'Cause we have no muscle. Let's face it, Nate, in this game you have to have muscle, it's the only way people will respect and fear you. It's a vital part of the game!" I said.

"I know. I've been talking to Mike about that. I think I am gonna let Mike handle the muscle part, but I want to meet with all of you tomorrow about our plans for the future. Hey, G, what do you think about us just putting a group of people together, and doing all of this ourselves, after we finish with Hector?"

"It's a thought, but we have to be organized, Nate, no wild freelance mess. We have to have it together even while we make this deal with Hector."

"Hmmm, can I sleep on that?" Nate said.

I couldn't sleep at all that night. I knew that we were about to turn a corner in our lives, and I was nervous about it. I looked across the room and Nate was sleeping like a baby. I tossed and turned for about twenty minutes, then got up to get a glass of water.

I thought I heard something in the bathroom, so I walked closer to the door. It was Momma Williams throwing up. I knocked on the door and asked if she was all right. "Go get me a towel, baby," she said. I went to the dining room table where the clean, fresh folded towels from the laundry were stacked. When I returned I cracked the bathroom door open, and saw blood in the toilet.

"Nate!" I screamed. Nate came in running, half asleep. "Quick, call the ambulance, Momma is sick!" I remember Momma Williams was burning up, and she seemed to be delirious. I flushed the toilet, and cradled Momma Williams in my lap on the bathroom floor. Nate put on a pair of pants and was outside looking out for the ambulance.

"Momma really sick, baby, I might have to go into the hospital for a while," she said.

"Don't worry, Momma, me and Nate will be fine." I was afraid. I had already lost my real mamma; I didn't want to lose Momma Williams also. Soon, the ambulance arrived. The paramedics put in an IV, and placed her on a cart. They asked Nate and me all kinds of medical questions about her allergies and so on. We answered as best we could, but we didn't know anything about stuff like that. The police let us ride in the back of the ambulance with Momma Williams and we were off. In route, the EMT asked me if she had medical insurance. I told them I didn't know. Momma Williams managed to gasp out that she didn't. She had just started her nursing job at Michael Reese Hospital, and her medical insurance didn't kick in yet. So they took us to Cook County Hospital.

When the ambulance arrived, Detective Trent was already there, half-dressed and looking worried. He even had on his house slippers. At first, I wondered how he even knew she was en route to the hospital, but I remembered him telling her he always kept his radio on.

"What the fuck is he doing here?" Nate asked.

"Not now Nate, let's just worry about Ma."

"I know. He just gets on my nerves!"

As Trent walked over to us I looked into his eyes, and saw genuine grief. "Hello, boys, I just wanted you to know that I am getting your momma out of here to a better hospital as soon as they stabilize her. The transfer orders are already in, she will be leaving soon." Then he grabbed us both and hugged us. "I have missed you boys. She is gonna be fine."

"What did they say was wrong?" Nate asked.

"They are not sure, some kind of virus I guess, but we are getting her out of here real soon."

He was right. We were out of there in less than half an hour, and on our way to Northwestern Memorial downtown. That was the longest night. Nate paced and Detective Trent paced; they were both driving me crazy, walking back and forth. "Why don't you two sit down, all of this walking is making me nervous."

"Sorry," Nate said. Then to Trent he said, "Uh, I want to thank you for getting my mom out of the County, I appreciate that." I remember looking at Nate and feeling real proud that he was big enough to thank Detective Trent. Detective Trent looked surprised, since he knew Nate didn't care for him, especially since Nate didn't say anything to him most of the night.

"It's O.K., Nathan. I told you I love your mother, and I would do anything for her."

Nate looked up at the sky and walked toward the waiting room window. Another officer came into the room with Momma Williams's doctor. "Is this all of the family?" the doctor asked.

"Almost. Momma has an aunt, and a half brother that's coming. What's wrong with my mom?"

The doctor looked at Detective Trent, and he acknowledged that he was a friend of the family. We all sat down at a table. I remember it was round, and huge. "Boys, your mom has a very bad virus," the doctor said. "The human body has a defense system called the immune system, and it fights off diseases. Well, this virus your mom has is attacking her immune system."

Detective Trent dropped his head and got up to walk to the window. He knew what was going on.

"Well, don't you have anything that can get the virus out?" Nate asked.

"I'm afraid not. What your mother has is a virus that causes what is called Acquired Immune Deficiency Syndrome, or…"

"AIDS," I interrupted.

"What the hell is that, what is everybody looking so down about?" Nathan asked.

"Nathan, there is no cure for this disease," the doctor said.

"So what are you trying to say, my momma is gonna die?"

"I am very sorry." The doctor placed his hand on Nate's shoulder. Nate had a far away look in his eyes, for about a moment, then he suddenly snapped back.

"Man, fuck you, my momma ain't gonna die, nigga, fuck you!" Nate stood up and flipped the table about three feet into the air, hitting the doctor on the chin with it. I screamed Nate's name and grabbed him. Detective Trent jumped in to help me restrain Nate, while the doctor grabbed his chin and fell to the floor. Nate started screaming, "Momma, Momma, don't leave me Momma, let me go, I want to see my Momma, Momma!" Detective Trent grabbed him and Nate screamed at him. "Let me go, motherfucker, I hate you, you gave it to my Momma, you killed my Momma!" Trent let go of Nate and I grabbed him. He looked me in my eyes, and there were tears running down his face and mucous out of his nose. "She gonna leave us, G, Momma gonna die!" He sobbed in my arms, and I sobbed along with him. My emotions had come over me like a wave. I just couldn't picture never seeing her again. My heart hadn't been that heavy since my own mother died five years before.

I guess Nate didn't yell at me because he felt that I was all he had left. Also, he knew that I had been where he was, and that I could relate. After we got ourselves together, the doctor let us go to the window of the ICU to look in on her. I remember there were tubes everywhere, and everyone in the room was wearing some kind of suit. They had Momma Williams in some type of plastic bubble-like enclosure. There was a lot we didn't know about AIDS in 1985, and the nurses and doctors weren't taking any chances.

They wouldn't allow us to go in the room just yet, so Nate and I went for a walk down Michigan Avenue. We walked for a long time and didn't say anything to each other. We stopped under the Marshall Fields clock and just looked up at the sky. "Except for you, G, I ain't got nothing left. If my Momma dies, we will be all alone in this world."

"No. We won't be. Momma will look out for us from heaven."

"Yeah," Nate agreed. "Do you think there's such a thing as heaven, G?"

"Yeah. I don't know much about it, but that's all I heard my aunt talk about, she was in the church and stuff," I answered.

"I wonder," Nate said, looking up at the sky. That was the first time Nate and I had ever talked about God or heaven, or anything spiritual. It was strange, but I could feel a presence right then, like someone else was there with us, so I turned around and looked.

"Yeah, you felt that too?" Nate asked.

"Yeah, you think it was Momma Williams?" I asked.

"Maybe. Let's go back to the hospital, G."

When we got back to the hospital, the doctor said we could go in and see Momma Williams, but we had to put on those plastic suits before we could go in. We agreed, and went into the room. I remember looking at the clock. It was 4:30 A.M., but strangely enough, I wasn't sleepy. I don't think Nate was, either. The room was big and Momma Williams was in the bubble tent, but we could hear her. Detective Trent sat there in a chair next to her bed with tears rolling down his cheeks.

"Momma, can you hear me?" Nate said softly.

"Yes, baby, you look tired, both of you do," she said. Nate started crying again.

"Don't cry, baby, mama's gonna be alright."

"Momma, they saying you gonna die," Nate sobbed.

"Yes, but I will see you again," she said. She waved to let everyone know she wanted to be with Nate alone. We all left the room.

As I was coming out, there was a guy standing there with a Bible in his hand, wearing a medical suit. He wore a temporary ID badge that said, "Clergy." His name was Reverend Fisher. He nodded at me, and I nodded back. I remember wondering what he was doing there.

Nate was in the room talking to Momma Williams for about thirty minutes. When he came out, his eyes were swollen from crying. "She wants you, G," he sobbed.

When I went into the room I sat close to Momma Williams so I could hear her. "I am so proud of you, son," she said weakly. "You have grown to be such a strong, handsome man, and wise beyond your years. I have loved you just like a son; you know that, don't you?"

"I know, Ma," I said between sobs.

"Don't cry. I want you to hear me good. I want you to take care of my Nathan; don't let anything happen to him. You are the strongest and wisest. I want you to guide him and help him. God sent you into our lives because he knew this would happen. I love you, Derrick, promise you will take care of yourself and watch out for Nathan."

"I promise," I said, now awash with tears. She looked up at the ceiling and back at me.

"Are you going to heaven to see my mother?" I asked.

"Yes."

"How do you know?" I asked curiously.

"The minister told me. I received Jesus in my heart and now I am going to be with him and your mom in heaven," she said, still sounding weak.

"Who is Jesus, ain't he God or something?"

"Yes, the minister will explain it to you if you like. Yes, why don't you and Nathan talk to Reverend Fisher for me? You and Nathan stay out of trouble, and always do what is right, O.K.?"

"Yes Momma," I said, still crying. I kissed her hand through the plastic and she told me to send Detective Trent in. "Come and see me tomorrow, O.K.?"

"We will. Bye, Momma."

When I came out Nate was in the visiting area with the Reverend Fisher guy, eating a sandwich. Detective Trent went into Momma's room, and I saw him sit down in the seat I had been in. I joined Nate and the reverend.

"Hello, you must be Derrick, I am Reverend Fisher, how are you? Would you like a sandwich too?"

"Yeah, I guess I could use one. I am hungry."

"No problem," he said.

He seemed to be a nice enough guy; he bought us both sandwiches and drinks. "Momma Williams told me about you," I said. "She said you told her she was going to heaven. Is that true?"

"Yes, it is, Derrick. Would you like to go also?"

"Not right now, I'm too young," I said.

He laughed. "I don't mean now, I mean when you die. You can go too, everyone can." I looked at Nate, and he looked up at the ceiling sarcastically. The preacher continued, "Did you know that Jesus died for your sins, and he loves you and wants you to receive him in your heart?"

Nate stood up abruptly and interrupted him, "Yeah, Rev, we thank you for the sandwich, my brother and I, but we ain't really interested in no Jesus right now, we're worried about our Momma!"

"That is my point, Nathan. You don't have to worry about her. She is in God's hands now. She received God's son Jesus into her heart and..."

"Yeah, whatever. We gotta go, Rev."

"Nate, be cool," I said, "He's good people, plus Momma Williams told us to talk to him."

"We did, and now we gotta go!"

I was so embarrassed, and I felt so bad for Reverend Fisher, but he took it all in stride. "Here is my number. Call me whenever you are ready, it doesn't matter when."

"Thanks, we will, and thanks again for the sandwich and pop," Nathan said.

"Don't worry about it. I will be praying for you boys."

"Do that, we need it," I said.

After he left, I let Nate have it. "What is wrong with you man? That was a minister. You shouldn't talk to him like that!"

"Man, I don't want to hear that shit right now, my Momma is dying in there, and he's trying to bury me next to her!" Nate said angrily.

"Nate, man, that was ignorant," I said. "You should never be rude to people, man, we might need that man one day."

"Yeah, to bury us when we're old!"

I shook my head in disgust. I looked at the card and saw that he was from Joliet. What was he doing all the way up here, I thought. I folded the card and put it in my wallet.

Detective Trent asked us if we wanted to go back home, and we both agreed that we did. He asked us if we knew any adults that would stay with us until our relatives arrived from out of town. We couldn't think of anyone, so we gave him Jon's name. Jon was 22, so he was an adult; not a very responsible one, but an adult just the same.

We called Jon, and he was shocked to hear about Momma Williams, though he had never met her. "Man, I'm sorry to hear about your mom, guys, is there anything I or the girls can do?"

"Thanks man, you are doing enough right now. Maybe call the girls and tell them about it."

The next morning we called Big Mike and Pete to come over and talk. "Man, it's hard to believe about Mrs. Williams, man. What time are you guys going to the hospital today?" Big Mike asked.

"We're leaving in about an hour. You guys wanna come?" Nate asked.

"Sure, you want me to drive?" Pete offered.

"Yeah, man, I don't feel like fooling with CTA," Nate conceded.

"Where is she at?" Mike asked.

"Northwestern Hospital. You know, off Michigan," I said.

"Oh," Pete said. He leaned in close to talk to me so no one else would hear. "You think y'all could give me some help on the gas? I'm kinda short."

What a knucklehead, I thought. "Yeah, Pete, we'll help you out."

The girls rang the doorbell, and Nate let them in. Heather brought three of her friends, and they cooked breakfast for us. They weren't really bad cooks, either. It wasn't like Momma Williams's cooking, but it served its purpose.

"Man, where the hell did y'all find the white girls at?" Mike asked.

"They're friends of ours, I'll tell you about them later. You guys hear anything on Fingers?"

"Yeah, he's at Maryville. It's like a home for troubled kids up north. I talked to him last night, he said he's gotta get out of there quick."

"I don't know how, the state put him there, if he's gonna get out, he's gotta be adopted all over again," I said.

"You know, it's a shame Fingers fucked that up, but I don't think we can do anything about it," Nate said.

"He will be eighteen soon, and he will be able to leave under his own will. They won't be able to hold him," I reasoned.

"I just hope he stays out of trouble after he turns eighteen or he will be going to the County Jail!" Nate said.

"What's up with this Hector thing anyway?" Mike asked.

"I will tell you all about it tonight; meet me here at about eleven o'clock."

"All of us?" Heather asked.

"Yeah! All of you," Nate said. Heather was surprised she was acknowledged as part of the team.

The doorbell rang. Nate looked out of the side window and saw it was a FTD man. "What the fuck is this?" Nate said under his breath.

"Package for a Nate and a G?"

"Yeah, what is it?" Mike asked. Mike stepped in front of Nate and pushed Nate behind him to shield him, for what reason I don't know. "Yeah, I'll sign," Mike said.

It was two dozen red roses from Hector, with his deepest sympathy. The card said, "Hope your mother gets better soon."

"That's so sweet; he actually sent flowers," Heather and her friends said.

"Sweet my ass, he's trying to tell us that he knows where we live!" Nate said emphatically. At the bottom of the card it said that we could take our time giving an answer concerning the deal. "No, we are not gonna take our time, we're gonna give him an answer tomorrow. You all just be here tonight," Nate said.

When we arrived at the hospital, the nurse met us as we got off the elevator. "Are you Gloria Williams's sons?" she asked.

"Yeah, we are, why?"

"I need to talk to you." The nurse took us to a side room away from the rest of the floor. When she opened the door, we could see that Detective Trent and Reverend Fisher were already there, along with the doctor. I noticed the doctor had a bandage on his chin where the table had hit him the night before.

"Hello, boys, may I talk to you?" the doctor asked. "There is no easy way to say this, but your mother may not make it through the day. Our staff has done all that they can do, and we are trying hard to make her comfortable. She has asked for you both. Detective Trent and Rev. Fisher have already been in with her. Now, we have crisis counselors and clergy here at the hospital if you need them."

"Naw, man, I just wanna see my Momma," Nate said.

"How about you, son, are you O.K.?" the doctor asked me.

"Yeah, we just want to see her, if that's O.K.," I said.

"Sure," The doctor replied.

When we went in to see her, she had fallen asleep, and the nurses suggested that we did not wake her. We just sat there holding her hands through the plastic, and sobbing. Detective Trent peeked in and motioned us to the door. "There are a few of your friends down the hall. They have been instructed that they cannot come in here. What do you want me to tell them?" he whispered. I got a chance to get a close up look at his face; he looked beat.

"I'll go talk to them. Stay here with her, G," Nate instructed.

"Okay, how long have you been here?" I asked Detective Trent.

"All morning. I just can't believe we are losing her."

Another man in a suit motioned to Detective Trent through the window. He looked like a cop also. "Excuse me, Derrick."

As he went out, Nate came back in. "That was Jon and the girls. I told them to wait down the hall with Mike and Pete. I don't want anybody to see her like this," Nate confessed.

"I agree. I gotta go use the bathroom. I'll be back," I said.

As I approached the bathroom I could hear men talking, and recognized Detective Trent's voice. I stood near the door listening to the conversation, hoping some idiot would not come to get in.

"Harry, what are you going to do, stay here and keep vigil all week?" the other man asked.

"If that's what it takes," Trent said.

"Look, Harry, I understand what you are going through, but people are starting to ask questions down at the precinct. I'm trying to cover for you, but it's getting hard."

"I just need you to buy me some more time. I appreciate what you are doing for me, just help me out here."

"Can I ask you a question?" the other cop asked. "Have you been tested, Harry? Hey, I love Gloria too, but she was hookin' for a while and..."

"Hey, fuck you, Joe for saying that, that's a good woman in there!"

"So is your wife, Harry. Look, this is what it is, O.K.? I know how you feel, but you can't just abandon your family. Harry, look at what you are doing here! You haven't been home in two days, for God's sake!"

"I know, I know, I just... I just can't leave her here like this. Joe, she means more to me than that. I just need you to buy me a little more time, please."

"O.K., I'll do what I can. I'm still asking you, Harry, have you been tested?"

"I've been tested. Damn it, Joe I'm negative, okay, are you satisfied?"

I couldn't take it anymore, I had to walk in. As soon as I did I could see they were composing themselves, and acting as if everything was O.K.

"Hi, how are you, Derrick. Derrick is your name, isn't it? I am Detective Simmons, nice to meet you."

I shook his hand. I didn't want to let on that I had heard the conversation. "You know my mom?" I asked.

"Yeah, I am a mutual friend of your mom and Detective Trent. She is a great woman, and a fine citizen."

Yeah, right, I thought, people are so phony. He thought so much of Momma Williams that he hadn't even gone in to see her.

"Well, Harry, I'll keep in touch. It was nice meeting you, Derrick." I just watched him walk out of the bathroom. I didn't even reply.

"Any new developments?" Trent asked.

"No, nothing yet. Do you think she is gonna die, Detective?"

"I hope not. Have you guys eaten anything today?" I could tell he didn't want to discuss the notion of her dying. He had changed the subject so quickly.

"Well, yeah, we had some friends over this morning, we ate breakfast."

"What about lunch, are you guys hungry?" I knew Nate wouldn't want to eat lunch with Detective Trent, especially considering the circumstances. I politely refused, and joined Nate at Momma Williams's bedside.

The nurse informed us that Momma Williams would be resting for the rest of the night, and that if we wanted to stay, we could. Nate refused, and told me that we should go home and return the next day. He knew that we all had to talk, and felt that Momma Williams would be fine. I think Nate was in denial about the seriousness of her condition. I think that after a while he had started to believe she would recover. Dealing with her death was something he just couldn't do.

"Yeah, G, mamma is gonna be fine. This is a setback, but I think she is gonna come out of it."

"But there is no cure for AIDS, Nate, how can she recover?"

"I just believe she will. Just trust me, it's gonna be all right." I knew it wouldn't be, though. I began to expect the worst. I prepared myself for her departure from us, just as I had done with my own momma.

Later that night, Nate assembled all of us and told us his plans. "We are gonna take Hector up on his offer, but we will only do it for one year."

"How are we gonna do it for only a year? You know he wants us in it for the long haul, he ain't never gonna agree to that," Mike asserted.

"He won't know, and we don't have to tell him. We're gonna do our own thing."

"How will we be able to break from him and do that?" Heather asked.

"Let's just be honest. Hector needs us because he wants the black community, and we will sell here until we get strong, then we will make our break. Don't worry about how just yet; let's just spend the night getting organized. I have the how all figured out," Nate told us.

Nate told us that night that he didn't want us to be set up like the gangs; he wanted us to be an organized entity. He said he wanted us to have an intelligence department, because he wanted to know what was going on in the street, with the gangs, and with the police. He wanted to know what was going to happen before it happened. He went on to say that spies and plants were necessary to get this kind of information. "Our survival depends on the information we get, and what we do with it. Intelligence will also have input on whether we make certain moves or not. G, I want you to be the head of this area. As we grow, so will our intelligence, but for now we will focus on just the South Side."

All eyes were on me. I felt very uncomfortable being in this kind of position. To tell the truth, I felt uncomfortable about the whole idea. I didn't think it would work. "Why me?" I asked.

"Why not you? You're the smartest of all of us, and you have a way of knowing a little about everything, and most of all you're my brother and I trust you. Is that enough good reason?"

"Yeah. Look Nate, do you think this will actually work? I mean, we are so inexperienced at this stuff, we don't have any contacts, and we're really green," I reasoned.

"I hear you G, but we have desire, and desire is enough. Plus, if we are organized and live by our rules we will be fine. I'll talk to you more about it later, so let me finish. Finance will be handled by Jon. We want to get into this shit and then get out. Jon will make that possible by doing the right thing with our money. Look, everybody, no buying a lot of expensive stuff, cars, clothes, and all of that shit. We want to roll low key, we don't want to give the appearance of being drug dealers, so live pretty much like you are living now. Jon studied economics at University of Illinois at Chicago, so he will show us how to stretch our money out and keep it hidden."

I knew Heather and her girls wouldn't have a problem there, but I knew the rest of the brothers would. Black people are flamboyant by nature. Allowing them to make one thousand dollars a week, and then forcing them to live as if they were only making fifty, that was gonna be a feat!

Jon was a good pick for Finance because he knew money, how to turn it over, launder it through legitimate businesses, and most of all, how to hide it from law enforcement. Jon's father was an investment banker from

Barrington who made his first million by the time he was 40. And he had lost it all by the time he was fifty, through bad investments and gambling. Nate knew this, so he set up a system of checks and balances by partnering himself with Jon, to watch him. Jon's job was to keep all of our money out of banks, and to hide it in phony businesses and phantom companies. It would be pretty easy, since we were just starting out and didn't have a whole lot to hide.

"And last but not least, we need muscle. No one will respect us without it, and we have to have the most powerful forces on the street. Big Mike, that's your area. But I want you to take it seriously. I want you enrolled in a Karate class, and take gun and target classes. I don't want innocent people killed if we have to knock someone off. I will talk with you and G later about my vision of that, in private. Well that's it, what do you all think?"

We all sat there just amazed, in a daze. We couldn't believe what we had just heard. "Dude, all of that to sell a little reefer?" Pete asked.

"Well, actually I have a move I want to make later, but yes, that's it, Pete. I am a planner. I don't believe in doing things half-ass. I plan on doing this and not going to jail, and the only way to do it is to organize. We can be like the fucking gang bangers and be in jail by Tuesday, but if we do it this way, we may be able to get away with it."

"You left us out, what do you want us to do?" Heather asked.

"Just stick close to me baby, and do what you have been doing, we'll take care of the rest." Nate told me later that he did not want to involve Heather and the girls too directly, that he didn't expect them to be in it too long, and if we did get caught we would get life if we had some nice white girls selling dope for us. Never mind the fact that they were better at it than we were! We were all afraid, but since we were kind of railroaded into this situation in the first place, we had to make the best of it. We all voted that we would go along with Nate's plan, and make him the leader of our little "family." The next move was to go see Hector, and put the plan into motion.

Momma Williams's condition was beginning to worsen. We were called to the hospital because the doctors didn't believe she would make it through the night. Nate was getting very nervous, and feeling desperate about the situation. He advised me to call Hector's people and postpone the meeting because of her condition.

When we arrived at the hospital, we noticed that Detective Trent and a few of his people were already there. Everyone had a look of despair on his or her face, and there was a feeling of impending doom in the air. I worried most about Nate, because he looked like his mind was going in a thousand different directions.

"Hello, Nathan, how are you?" Trent said.

"I'm O.K., how's my mamma?"

"Not good I'm afraid. We are all praying for the best, though."

"We want to see her, can we?"

"I guess so. I have already been in. Let me talk to the doctor." The doctor gave us the O.K., and Nate and I went in.

"Hello, Momma, me and G are here, can you hear me?" Nate asked.

"She cannot hear you. She has gone into a coma. We have given her pain meds, and made her as comfortable as possible," the nurse confessed.

As we were sitting there, Reverend Fisher came in, and stood behind Nate. "She is at peace now, and soon she will be with the Lord, boys."

Nate looked at him with a scowl. "What do you want? Maybe that's why she is doing badly, you've been trying to get her into the ground ever since she got sick!" Nate spewed.

"Nate, be cool man, it's O.K."

"Naw, it ain't, G, ever since she got here he's been sniffin' around and bringing bad omens, I want you out of here, now!"

"I am sorry that you feel that way Nathan. I truly love your mother, and God does, too. I'm sorry, I will leave." With that, the minister turned and walked out of the door. I looked at Nate with what must have been a strange look because he looked back at me strangely.

"G, I don't want to hear it. I just don't like that guy."

I didn't say a word. I just looked at Momma Williams. At that moment the monitor started to "flatline." Nurses came in and pushed Nate and me out of the way and began to work on her. Nate backed away with his hands covering half of his face and tears running out of his eyes. Deep down he knew this would be it, and so did I.

As they announced the "Code Blue" over the PA system, Jon and the rest of our friends came down the hall in a panic. "Is that your mom?" Jon asked.

Nate nodded his head yes, weakly. "G, I wanna go home." I told him I understood, and instructed Mike to take him home with Heather and the girls, and to watch him. "You know what to do, G," Nate said, "I just want to go home and rest and reflect on my momma." I didn't understand. I guess everyone grieves differently, but I just thought Nate would want to be there to make the necessary arrangements.

"Are you sure, Nate?" I asked.

"Yeah, you know what to do; she was your momma, too. I just can't handle it right now. I only ask that you not let that Reverend Fisher or his church do anything, I don't want him to have anything to do with her funeral, understand?"

"Yeah, but....."

"Nothing, G. Nothing at all!" Nate had made Reverend Fisher a scapegoat, and now Momma Williams's departure was going to be his fault. I guess Nate needed someone to blame. As he walked to the exit with Mike and the girls, I could not help but look at him and remember the promise I had made to Momma Williams, to look after him. It was going to be a monumental task.

I walked back to the waiting room to think about what I would do if Momma Williams did in fact die. I didn't know any pastors or churches that I could call to arrange a funeral. I didn't know how to plan a funeral. Momma Williams had planned my mother's, and I didn't know where to start. I was only seventeen, and hadn't experienced too much in the way of these things.

I sat in the waiting room alone thinking, and in came the doctor, Detective Trent, Reverend Fisher, and a crisis counselor. "Where is Nathan?" Trent asked.

"At home. What has happened, is she gone?"

"Yes, Derrick, she is," Trent said. He had bloodshot eyes. I let out a deep sigh, and shed a tear. I looked around the room, and Reverend Fisher looked at me with a tentative look. I motioned him toward me. "Can you help me?" I asked. "I don't know where to begin with all of this."

"Absolutely, I will do all I can to help. I hope I didn't offend your brother. You know, God put us all down here to help each other," he said calmly.

"I know, sir. I just think he is very emotional right now. Please forgive him."

"I understand."

I went in to get one last look at Momma Williams. They had taken down all the equipment around her, and pulled the sheet over her head. The nurse pulled the sheet back and I looked at her. She looked terrible. I wondered if the funeral home would be able to make her look better. Reverend Fisher connected me with some people from the Taylor Funeral home and got them to give me a break on their fees.

I will always be indebted to Momma Williams for what she did for me. She helped me at a very delicate time in my life, taking me in and giving me a home, being my mother, and teaching me so much about life. I will miss her and her strong spirit forever.

"I would love for you and your brother to join us at morning service one Sunday," Reverend Fisher said.

"Maybe one Sunday. Where is your church?" I asked.

"In Joliet. We have a small congregation, but we love the Lord, and we are really dedicated to Christian growth. I think you would like it."

"Interesting. I will visit one day," I said. Minister Fisher had been so helpful that I felt I owed him something, even if it was only a vague promise to visit his church.

"Derrick, may I speak with you for a moment?" Detective Trent asked. "Do you boys need any help with Gloria's services? I would be happy to help"

"No sir, I have everything in order, thanks."

I tried to walk away, but he grabbed my arm. "Derrick, you boys need some direction. Your mom is gone now. Let me help you get good jobs and get into college. She would have wanted that." He just didn't know that we had already chosen our new career, and good jobs and college were just not in the plan. Plus, Nate had a real disdain for this guy, and I knew he wouldn't take any help from him. "I am afraid of what might happen to you two out there in the streets. Do you know what I mean?"

"Absolutely. Momma Williams raised us well. We will definitely stay out of trouble. We will be graduating soon, and we are thinking of attending one of the junior colleges in the area."

"Great, I am happy to hear that. Maybe I can get you two some intern jobs at headquarters."

"We will think about it. I will pass it on to Nate."

I was told that Momma Williams's body would be going to Taylor Funeral Home in the morning, and I let it be known I wanted the services to be held that Saturday. When I got back to the apartment, Jon and the gang were eating dinner. I asked where Nate was, and they told me he was in the bedroom, and had been in there for about two hours. I went in to see him.

"What's wrong, man, you O.K.?"

"No, I'm not. I'm gonna miss her, G. I don't know what I am gonna do without her." Nate was lying on the bed in the fetal position looking like a lost child. In a sense, he was. When a son loses a parent, no matter how old he is, he loses a sense of himself. The security blanket that had always been there was gone. Nate never knew his father, and now that his mother was gone, he was really lost.

"How do you do it, G, how do you maintain?"

"Well, I had you and Momma Williams, and you guys became my family. You two were a great support group for me. It helped me tremendously."

"Yeah, but who do I have? I got no father, and I'm not close to any of my other family."

"You got me. You have been a brother to me, and we have to really stick close to each other now," I said.

"You're right, G. I just miss her so much!" With that Nate began to cry. I just hugged him and told him it would be O.K. I missed Momma Williams too, but I think I was taking it a little better than Nate was. I figured I would change the subject a little.

"I took care of everything. The funeral will be Saturday at ten in the morning at New Love Baptist Church on 75th Street. What do you think?"

"It's cool. I am so glad I have you. G, I just can't handle all of that right now. I trust that you will do everything decently. I think I am gonna let the girls go to the mall and pick out a nice dress for Momma to wear. Do you think that's a good idea?"

"Yeah, but you better give them an idea of what you want, don't just send them. You never know what they might come back with," I said.

"Yeah," Nate said. "Look, I want to talk to you about the meeting with Hector. I have set it for later tonight. I have already briefed the rest of them. The girls are gonna stay here, and you, me, Jon, Mike, and Pete are gonna go to the meeting."

"Have you talked to Hector's people already?" I asked.

"Yeah, they're expecting us at nine thirty. I told the girls to stay here and call us after we've been there thirty minutes, so we'll have an excuse to leave. Look, we go in, make the deal, and get the fuck out, no staying around to socialize and shit; in and out O.K.?"

"Cool by me."

"I got Pete and Mike going for security. Hector seems cool, but I don't trust him."

"Pete and Mike, they got guns?" I asked.

"Hell, no, if we walk in there with guns they will probably kill our asses right on the spot! But I will let Hector know that in every meeting thereafter we will be packing."

Nate called the girls in, and briefed them once again on when to call, and what to say. He talked to all the guys and told us that if anything went wrong, to be sure we didn't leave there without killing Hector first. "Make that your chief concern. I know we are not packing, but if anything goes wrong, even in the future, make sure to kill Hector first. Always get the leader even if you get no one else."

"You think something will go wrong tonight, Nate?" Jon asked.

"Not really. I think things will go O.K.," Nate admitted.

"Then, why all of the planning?" Pete asked.

"It's always better to be over-prepared than under-prepared," Nate said. "Since we have no heat, strategically place yourselves near possible weapons; heavy objects, anything you might use to deflect or injure, and walk in looking for a way out. We are going in to make this deal; no chatting or socializing. We walk in make the deal, and then get the fuck out. Let G and I do all of the talking and negotiating. You guys are there to protect us. Jon, do whatever you can to keep his bodyguards preoccupied with talk. Everything should go O.K., but remember, our window is thirty minutes."

As we got into Jon's car, he immediately turned on his War music.

"Hey, Jon, can you turn that shit down? I can't hear myself think back here!" Nate said.

"Be cool, man, I'm nervous and War makes me calm."

"Well I'm calm, and that shit makes me nervous, so turn it down!" Nate shouted.

I, too, could tell Nate was nervous. His mind was going a million miles a minute, and he also was dealing with the loss of his mom. I was really worried about him. We stopped at a traffic light and Nate went over everything again, to make sure we were all on accord and up to speed.

As we approached the house, the same big Mexicans were on the porch, but this time they welcomed us with smiles. When we got into the house we were all frisked, and led into Hector's office.

"Ola, my friends, it's good to see you again. You have brought guests this time, no?" Hector said in his thick Spanish accent.

"Pete, Mike, this is Hector Gomez. Hector, this is Pete and Mike, they are here for security," I announced. Hector looked at one of his associates, and the guy shook his head no, confirming that we were not carrying guns.

"Security without weapons, Nate? You must teach me about this kind of security," he chuckled. "Would you like a drink, or maybe a beer for your security?" he added sarcastically.

"We are all fine, thanks," Nate said.

"First, let me give you our deepest sympathy," Hector said. "We have heard about the illness of your mother, and we pray for her speedy recovery."

Nate shot me a look. He doesn't know about Momma yet. Don't tell him.

"Thanks," Nate said.

"Now let's get down to business. Our proposal is the same. Twenty pounds a quarter, at a 70/30 split. Any objections?"

"Hell, yeah, we have objections, but we don't have a choice. But I do have a question," I said.

"Ask away, my friend," Hector said cordially.

"How long before you turn us over to the Latin Kings? Are they aware of your little expansion efforts?" I asked.

Hector looked slightly irritated. "I assure you, amigo, I am the only Latin King in this fucking community. What I say goes. You will work for me and me only. I have a mutual agreement with and respect from the Latin King gang, and that relationship will not interfere with ours. Understood?" He almost made it sound convincing.

"Not necessarily trusted, but understood," Nate said. I noticed that Jon started a quiet side conversation with a couple of Hector's men, as instructed. Everything was going according to plan so far. "Will we leave with stuff tonight?" Nate asked.

"Absolutely not. There will be a drop area for you near here. You will report to me and only me. And if anything goes wrong, or you go to the police, I assure you I will slit all of your fucking throats."

"No need for threats, Hector, we understand all of that," Nate said. At that moment, a real hot number walked in through the door, flipped Hector what appeared to be a set of car keys, and went into a side room. She was a real looker, with long black hair and a seductive walk. Hector never introduced her, and tried to divert our attention away from her, but that was impossible.

Hector spent another ten minutes instructing us on where we could and could not sell when the phone rang. Hector's guy answered it, looked at Nate, and pointed the phone at him. Hector looked at Nate strangely and then motioned for his guy to give Nate the phone. Nate said hello, and gave a series of one word answers. Looking at Hector, Nate told the caller that everything was fine, that we would see them soon, and then hung up the phone.

"Who knows that you are here, and who did you give this number to?" Hector asked.

"Security," Nate said flatly. Then it dawned on Hector; it was not the security he could see, but the security he could not see that mattered most.

"Well, our business is done here, amigo. My associate Angel will show you to the door and give you the address to your drop area. I look forward to a long and prosperous business relationship with you all."

"Yeah, prosperous for you, but not for us," Nate said.

"If all goes well, amigo, I will be more than happy to renegotiate the terms of our agreement in the future."

"How far into the future are you looking?" I asked.

"Let's give it one year, and we will see where we are at," Hector said.

"Cool," Nate said.

When we got into the car, Nate told us how happy he was with our self-control and how we handled the situation.

"Who was that broad that came in? That bitch was fine as hell!" Pete said.

"I don't know, but if G can find out about that broad, and get us some info on her and Hector's relationship, we might be able to use it later," Nate said. "I think Hector is gonna try to throw some shit into the game down the line, and we're gonna need all the ammo we can against him."

"Are you gonna let the girls keep selling in Oak Lawn?" Mike asked.

"I don't know yet. They sell good, but I'm afraid of them getting busted, so I am leaning against it. I think I want them to just work with Jon, and stay out of direct sales. What do you think G?" Nate asked.

"I think if the girls get caught our asses are burnt up, especially since they are white girls. Maybe we should just make them turn over their contacts to us and cut them out totally, Nate," I confided.

"What's wrong with them working with Jon?" Pete asked.

"It's too much of a risk, and it's too much for us to lose. I think we should totally cut them loose, Nate."

Nate looked out of the car window, thinking. "Maybe G has a point," he said. "If they get caught, you know the cops can get them to turn state's evidence on us, and then they'll fry our asses for making their 'good white girls' sell reefer. They'll give our black asses life in jail."

"Hey, what are you guys saying? Heather is not like that, and you guys know it. That's bullshit!" Jon said, irritated.

"Be cool, Jon, we know you're right. I love Heather and the girls, and we know our friendship isn't about race, but this society is. We get caught selling on our own, we get two to five at the most, but with the girls involved our time triples, and you know that," I said.

"I just think it's bullshit, that's all. They're gonna feel jilted, I know it," Jon said sadly.

"Let me and Nate talk to them, Jon. I know they will understand. We will all remain friends, that won't change," I assured him.

"No, once we start selling, they gotta go and never return," Nate said sternly. "We gotta cut them off, maybe keep in touch through Jon or something, but they have got to go."

"Who are we gonna replace them with? How are we gonna set up our sales and stuff?" Pete asked.

"G will let you all in on that. He knows what to do. He will talk about it when we get to the house, and after that, we won't discuss it anymore until after our mom's funeral, ok?"

"Sure, Nate," Pete acknowledged.

When we got home, we found the girls had cleaned up the whole house. They gave Nate a message that Detective Trent had called. "What the fuck does he want?" Nate asked in disgust, and said he would talk to Trent later.

"Girls, we have to talk to you," Nate said. "First, everything went well and according to plan. Thanks for the phone call, it worked like a charm. Second, I wanted to let you know if you could come to my mom's funeral on Saturday, it would be so important to G and me."

"Of course, we will, crazy, you know you can count on us," Heather said.

Then Nate put his head down, and I started talking. "We made the deal with Hector, and we start selling next week. Without you all."

"Why? Did that asshole tell you not to use us, or what?" Heather asked.

"No, it was our decision. We think it's too risky to have you all directly involved," I said dryly.

"Why? We've been involved all the way to this point. Suddenly you don't trust us or something?" one of the girls asked.

"Don't worry about it, it's cool. I understand it's the white girl thing isn't it?" Heather asked sarcastically.

Nate nodded his head in agreement.

"What about Jon, is he out too?" they asked.

"No, but Jon isn't a white woman. It makes a difference," Nate said.

"Well maybe we can do something else, help out in another area," one of the girls said.

"You're out, ladies, it's just too risky," I said.

"I understand. You guys can fuck us, but it's too much of a risk for us to make some money with you!" one of the girls said angrily.

"Look, Hector is only giving us a 70/30 split in his favor. There isn't any money to be made," I insisted.

"Yeah, how do we know that?" one of them asked.

"Hey, they're right. It's too risky for them. We understand, G, just call us if you ever need us," Heather said understandingly. "Come on, girls, let's start dinner."

"Fuck them! Let them cook their own food," the others said. They picked up their clothes and walked out.

Heather knew where we were coming from, and she understood. The other girls were just in it for the adventure of being with black men, and the potential of making money, but Heather was true blue to the end. "Can we trust them?" Nate asked Heather.

"Yeah, they're pissed right now. I'll talk to them and it'll be cool," she said convincingly.

"Are you sure?" I asked.

"Sure I am," she said.

"Heather, we love you and would never hurt you. You know that, don't you?" Nate said.

"Don't worry about it, baby, let's just start getting you two ready for this funeral Saturday."

Heather was hurt, but she understood. It was a chance we just could not take. Later that night, Nate called the McDonald's where we worked and told the boss he quit, and encouraged me to do the same. I kind of hated to leave that job. I liked the people and the idea of earning a buck or two. So many kids look down on fast food jobs, but they teach people life lessons about the work force and prepare them for hard work and sacrifice. Maybe if more children started out in fast food jobs, we wouldn't have a generation of kids with an attitude of entitlement.

The next day, Nate, Heather and I went to the mall to pick out something for Momma Williams. Heather picked out a lovely cream-colored dress, with accessories, and Nate had Momma Williams' hairstylist go to the funeral home to do her hair. After we had took care of all of the arrangements I asked Nate about the casket.

"Did you pick out a casket yet?" I asked.

"Yeah, but I'm not gonna describe it, it's gonna be a surprise."

"Well, I'm sure you did well," I said. I could see Nate was starting to fight back tears again. Heather looked at me, and we both consoled and encouraged him until he was better. Nate would have many episodes like that leading up to the funeral. The only time he would be O.K. was when he was talking about our situation with Hector. The rest of us had gone into the situation looking for the right opportunity to get out, but for Nate this was definitely going to be full time.

The morning of the funeral Nate was a complete mess. The funeral started at ten in the morning, but Nate didn't get up until eight thirty, and was a total shambles.

"C'mon Nate, you gotta take a shower and get dressed so we can be ready when the limo arrives."

"Fuck the limo. I'll just catch the bus. Why do we have to ride in a limo, anyway, G?"

"Nate, I already paid for it. It's O.K., let's just go."

He was sleeping in Momma Williams's bedroom, and when I went in I saw his suit was carefully pressed and laid out on the bed.

"Where are your shoes, Nate? Which pair of shoes are you gonna wear?" Heather asked.

"The black pair in our room, they're under his bed," I said. I literally had to get Nate dressed.

"I can't do this, G, I just can't," Nate said, as he plopped down on the bed. He started going through one of his crying spells, and once again, Heather and I had to console him. After much crying and hugging, we were all in the car and headed toward the church.

It started to drizzle. Many cars had already arrived at the church. I had no idea Momma Williams had so many friends and family, all of whom Nate had barred from riding in the limo with us. He said he didn't want any of the so-called family riding in the limo, pretending to be so concerned, when many of them didn't even call or come to see her while she was in the hospital. Nate said he only wanted Heather, Pete, Mike, and me in the car.

When the limo pulled up to the steps of the church, all eyes turned to it. When we all got out, everyone gave us the "who-is-the-white-girl" look. Heather handled it pretty well, though; she kept her head high and looked as if they were the problem, not her. I remember the church smelled good, and the stained glass windows were imposing. It was a beautiful church. Nate had demanded a beautiful church. He said he didn't want Momma Williams's funeral to be held at some dank storefront.

We took our places on the front row. I remember everyone coming by to give us their condolences, along with sympathy cards and letters. I purposely didn't look up at the casket until I made sure that Nate was O.K., but then I gave it a glance. It was the most beautiful casket I had ever seen, cream colored with gold handles and trim. It matched Momma Williams' dress. Nate had asked the casket makers put a glass cover over the body for protection. The floral arrangements were also beautiful. I noticed an exquisite arrangement from Hector and his people. I remember thinking to myself, how and from whom did he find out about her passing?

"Ready to go up and see her, Nate?" I asked.

"No, let's not, G, I just want to remember her as she was. Can you just sit here with me? Let Mike and the rest go up."

Jon came to sit down, and motioned for me to scoot over. "Everything looks great. You know we arranged it all, and Heather paid for the casket," Jon confided.

"You're kidding. Why? Mamma Williams had insurance," Nate said.

"That was Heather's gift to you guys. She really loves you, Nate, and she is taking our decision pretty hard."

"Stop it, Jon. This isn't the time or the place," I said emphatically.

"Cool," he replied. Jon and the rest of our friends had been so good to us during this whole ordeal. Nate and I were really grateful. Out of the corner of my eye, I saw Detective Trent sitting in one of the adjacent rows of seats, looking right at me with bloodshot eyes. He looked emotionally spent. He had some of his cop friends with him, then he mouthed the phrase "I want to talk to you" at me.   I shrugged my shoulders, pretending not to understand him.

"Nate, Trent wants to talk to me," I whispered.

"How do you know?"

"He just mouthed it to me from across the pew," I said.

"I don't want to be bothered with him right now. You can talk to him, but I won't," Nate said.

Nate held up pretty well during the service, and so did I. Many people came up to give short talks about what a wonderful person Momma Williams was. It made me and Nate feel good to see people speak so highly of Momma Williams. Many of the people finished their talks by telling me and Nate to stay strong and to make Gloria proud. If only they knew what we were planning to do, I thought.

The preacher gave a wonderful eulogy entitled "Divine Appointment" that made me really think about death and the hereafter. There was much I didn't understand in the sermon, but it sounded good. Nate seemed to be in outer space. He just sat there looking at the casket. My guess is he just couldn't believe his mother was gone. I know the feeling. At the end of the sermon, the preacher "Opened the door to Christ," and a woman sang a song called "There's not a Friend like the Lowly Jesus." The song made me cry, since there had definitely been times in my life when I felt like I didn't have a friend. There was not a dry eye in the house.

Spiritual emotion swept over the church, and a couple of people gave their life to Christ. It was a wonderful experience. For that moment, that one instant, there were no other problems in the world, no other concerns. It seemed everyone was focused on that sermon and that hymn. I think many people were giving their lives serious thought at that moment; I know that I was.

After the service was over, we laid Momma Williams to rest at Burr Oak Cemetery. It was a beautiful autumn day; October 18th, 1985.

At the repast, Detective Trent came over to talk to me about our future. He looked a mess. "You boys were the apple of Gloria's eye," he said. "She loved you both immensely. Do you need anything? Are any of your relatives going to come and live with you for a while?"

"For what?" Nate retorted. "We ain't kids, man. We will be eighteen next year, and out of high school. We don't need no babysitters!"

"Not babysitters, Nathan, but someone to look after you and Derrick for awhile, make sure you don't get into trouble, that's all," Trent reasoned.

"We don't need that shit man," Nate snapped.

I said, "We have a friend of the family named Jon that will look after us. He's pretty cool."

"Oh, did Gloria know him?" Trent asked.

"Why, man, why do you want to know?" Nate asked angrily. "It ain't none of your business. I wish all of you would just get the fuck out of my house, right now!" Mike and Pete put their soda pops down, as if to help Nate escort everyone out.

"What is the matter with you, boy?" Trent said. "Your mother would be appalled by your actions. These are her friends, her family!"

"I don't know half of these people. They're just here to be nosey. Let's go, Mike, get these people out of here!"

"What are you doing, Nate? This isn't right. Don't do this!" I pleaded.

"I want to be alone, G, and I am tired of entertaining!"

Nate was like that. He would do rude, unorthodox things out of the blue. He could be very emotional, unpredictable, and temperamental at times. I could tell the guests were appalled, and very offended by Nate's actions. It all was quite embarrassing, to say the least.

"You little arrogant asshole, you do your mother's memory a terrible disservice, and on the day of her funeral. How could you?" Trent demanded.

"Good night, Detective Trent. There is no need for you to sniff around here anymore. Momma's gone," Nate said.

Detective Trent looked at Nate long and hard, as if he were trying to find some semblance of humanity in him. "I am gonna keep my eye on you, young man," he said. "I owe it to your mother."

"Keep your eye on the streets, they are far more dangerous than I am," Nate said sarcastically.

Detective Trent slammed the door behind him, and Nate slammed himself down onto the couch, in relief.

"Hey, man, with him being a detective and all, maybe we shouldn't have done him like that," Pete reasoned. Nate just looked at him.

"Are you O.K., Baby?" Heather asked.

"Yeah, I just need some rest, that's all. I need to clear my head. G, can you get me a glass of water, please?" When I returned with the water, I asked him if we should start cleaning up some of the food from the repast. "Nah, leave it. We'll get it in the morning," he said. "Maybe we should all turn in early tonight, or maybe I should. We have to get that package pretty early in the morning."

Chapter 4

Drug lord

Nate was trying to ease the pain of losing his mother by acting out, and focusing on the Hector business. Heather ran him some bath water, and got him into the tub. Jon rang the doorbell, and came in with information about tomorrow's drop-off. "It's going to be in a garbage receptacle at Evergreen Plaza, somewhere in the back of the mall. Anyone know their way around the mall?" Jon asked.

"Yeah, I know it like the back of my hand," Pete said. "There must be a thousand receptacles back there. Is that all the information they gave you?"

"Well, he said there would be a person there, and we would know him when we see him," Jon said. "Probably one of Hector's guys that I know. Who's gonna go with me?"

"You're not going, we are," Nate said, coming out of the bathroom with a robe on.

"Why? Hector and his people are more comfortable with me at this point," Jon said.

"Exactly why you can't go. I'm not trying to make shit comfortable for him. Mike, G, and I will go in. You guys wait outside near a pay phone. We have to do this strategically. Heather and I are going to bed. Meet us here at six to go over our plan for this pickup. Six sharp!"

Soon everyone went home. I stayed and cleaned up the kitchen. I could hear Nate in the bedroom, crying and sobbing for hours. Heather came out to get some tissue, towels, and water.

"Is he gonna be all right?" I asked.

"Yeah, it's a lot harder on him than he lets on. Just kind of stick around in case it gets worse," she said.

"Maybe I should go in and talk to him. What do you think?" I asked.

"Yeah, go ahead."

As I walked in, I could see him curled up in the same fetal position as before.

"What's wrong, G?" he asked.

"I came in to see what was wrong with you," I replied.

"I just miss her so much, G," he said between sobs. "She is never gonna see her grandchildren, she won't see me get married, shit, she won't even see us graduate this June!" he said.

"I know, I thought about that today. Look, I know how you feel, but you gotta be strong. Remember what the preacher said today. We will see her again someday, both her and my mother."

"Yeah, but he also said you gotta be saved, and shit, the way we been living, we all going to hell," he said emphatically.

"Don't say that. Things are gonna be all right. You will see, it will get easier as the days go on," I said, trying to comfort him. "You just have to find a hobby or something, to help you take your mind off it."

"You think so? You think that will help?"

"Yeah, that's what I did. I started reading everything I could get my hands on, to help take my mind off the pain, and it worked," I explained.

"Yeah, maybe."

Then Heather walked in. I hugged Nate and slowly walked out. She gave him a cup of some soup she had made. "Thanks, G, I think he will be O.K.," Heather said confidently. Nate was definitely a tough dude, but losing one's mother can make the toughest person weak, and give him feelings of vulnerability.

The next morning I woke up smelling breakfast. I looked at the clock; it was five-thirty, and I was definitely tired. As I lumbered out of the bed, I could hear Nate and Heather talking about the pickup.

"Nah, I just want Jon to stay here with you, because he has to take you home after we get back. You and Jon will be here, G and I will make the pick up, Pete will be a lookout in the mall, and Mike will be a lookout outside the mall. Everyone will be stationed by phones in case something goes wrong," Nate lectured.

"I think it's a great plan, Baby," Heather said. "I just wish things could be different with us. I want to stick around to help out. I really think I could be of help somewhere."

"You're out, Heather. We love you, but we can't take the risk," Nate said flatly.

I heard Heather slam a pot down, leave the room, and close the door. I thought this would be a good time for me to come out. "Morning, how are you today, Boss?" I said sarcastically.

"Cool out, G. I'm cool, but I don't know about the white girl," he said jokingly.

"She wants in, Nate, and most of all she wants you," I said.

"I'm flattered, but you know the world we live in, G, the shit would not last. I got nothing but love for Heather, for real she has been there for me, and for all of us, but I just don't know."

Pete and Mike rang the doorbell. They were right on time, and Nate liked that. "Heather, could you get the door for me, please?" Nate called out, looking at me and smiling. We could hear Heather greeting the guys at the door, and then going back into the bedroom.

"What's up with her? What did you do, man?" Mike asked with a smile.

"We'll talk about that later," Nate said.

"Where's Jon?" I asked.

"He's not supposed to get here until eight. Let's go over this shit. G, make a fresh pot of coffee for these guys, and grab some pens and paper."

Nate went over everything we were supposed to do. He was micromanaging before the world knew what micromanaging was; he was very detail-oriented when it came to our business.

Everything went fine. The "product" and the guy were both there just as Hector had explained. When we got home, we cleaned the stuff, weighed it, bagged it, and began selling it. The only problem was Jon; he kept talking about the situation with Heather.

"Jon, we have already talked about this situation, and my answer is going to stay the same... no!" Nate said.

"It's cool. I just thought that maybe we could use her somewhere, that's all. We need all the help we can get. Hey, things went pretty cool today, huh?" Jon said, changing the subject.

"Yeah, but you have to always be prepared, you know?" Nate replied. "This sure is a lot of shit; how we are gonna sell it in three months, I don't know."

But sell it we did. Nate and I sold a great deal at Robeson, and at some of the other area high schools. But the bulk of it was sold at the parties. I mean, the kids went wild over the stuff. I've got to give it to Hector and his supplier; they sure had some good stuff.

Nate didn't want us selling on the street, so he sold the stuff out of a rented house. Jon rented the house out over on 78th and Indiana. It was a small bungalow owned by a woman who was never home. She stayed out of town most of the time, and didn't have any relatives. Nate clinched the sublet by making Jon cut his hair into one of those "conservative white boy" styles, and put on a suit. He figured Jon would get the woman's approval in a minute, being white and all. Sure enough, it worked.

After we moved in, we decided to produce the stuff in the basement, and give it to runners who would take the orders to drop-offs or to parties where it would be sold. Nate did not want people hanging out on the street and selling; it reminded him too the police busted much of the gangs who did it that way and always. Nate's thing was, "You gotta be smart, and you gotta think things through."

However, sales sharply increased. In the first quarter, we brought in thirty thousand dollars, and some people made standing monthly orders of an ounce or more. After the first eight months, we brought in eighty thousand dollars! Life was great and Hector loved us, and why not? We were bringing in serious cash from the black community, and he never had to as much as walk down our streets. And that's what made Nate so angry. Even though we brought in nearly one hundred thousand dollars, we had to give Hector nearly seventy thousand of it.

"Man, this is some bullshit, Nate, we are taking all of this risk for this motherfucker, and giving him almost all of the money. We need to get out of this deal!" Mike said.

"Mike, I know, just give me a little time to think of how we can get out of it. We have two more months, and we will have been in this for a year. I will approach Hector, but I need some leverage, something I can hold over him," Nate explained. "G, let's throw a party and invite some of our guys over. It's been awhile since we have partied."

Nate was right, because all he had done was organize us and lift weights with Mike. It was a little hobby he picked up since Momma Williams'death. He said it relieved stress. But I felt a party was ill-timed. I didn't want to attract unnecessary attention to any of us. Also, Hector's annual party was coming up, and I didn't see the need for two parties in less than two months.

"Nah, man, let's just be cool. Plus, we can go to Hector's party next month. I heard his parties are pretty cool," I said.

"Man, the way I feel, I don't want to see that motherfucker right now, much less party with him," Nate confided.

"I know, but we have been pretty incognito so far, and a party of our own might bring us a little unwanted attention." Surprisingly, Nate listened to me this time, and agreed.

During the weeks leading up to Hector's party, we heard that Heather was attacked near McDonald's by some of our former co-workers, all white people. She was badly beaten, her jaw and nose broken. It was going around town that she was hanging around with us, and people in Oak Lawn were calling her a nigger lover and other obscene names. Her father prosecuted the guys, and they received three years probation. Nate wanted to kill them.

"Fuck that, G," Nate said, "I can talk to Mike and have him handle them cracker motherfuckers. Three years probation? You know, if that had been us, we would have gotten three years or more."

"Nate, stay out of it. What's done is done, and if the courts and her family are satisfied, just let it go," I reasoned.

After a serious back and forth session between us, and a visit to the hospital to see Heather, Nate let it go, partially because Heather begged him to. Heather recovered nicely, we heard, but she never came around again. I guess being in the hospital gave her time to reflect on things. Maybe she thought about what we were into, maybe she thought about the pressure of being in an interracial relationship, or maybe she thought that Nate didn't really love her. Whatever it was, we lost contact with her.

Nate understood. Nate didn't want to see Heather subjected to such treatment, and he knew then that being with us would cause her more harm and hurt. All of us loved her, and none of us wanted her to be hurt. Deep down, we knew that Heather couldn't handle it all, especially the pressure from her family. However, there was no doubt that Nate could handle himself. He and Big Mike spent a lot of time together, plotting and scheming about how they were going to get us out of the deal with Hector.

They got their answer at Hector's annual party. Usually, at Hector's parties, there were a plethora of local drug dealers, wannabes, and loose women. This party was no different.

"This is a nice little party he put together, huh, G?" Nate said.

"I told you, I knew about his parties. This way, we can enjoy ourselves on Hector instead of taking the risk ourselves," I replied.

"Yeah, there are some fine-ass bitches here too, G. What do you think, Mike?" Nate asked.

"Hell yeah, I'm trying to find a way to get one of them home with me tonight," Mike said.

"Hey, G, you see that shit? I know that broad, don't you?" Nate asked.

"Yeah, that's Felix Hernandez's sister; you know, *the* Felix, the head of the area Latin Kings," I said.

"Yeah, I know who Felix is, G, but what is his sister doing here, and what is she doing with Hector, all hugged up like that?"

"You know they are fucking, Nate. Everyone knows that," Mike replied.

"No, I didn't know that! Now see, that's some shit we can use, G, we can use that shit to our advantage," Nate said, growing excited.

"Whoa, wait a minute Nate, don't go fucking around in that shit, it's too dangerous," I explained.

"Yeah, dangerous for Hector's ass if he don't let us out of that deal," Nate said.

After some mingling, dancing, and drinking, we were on our way out, but Hector spotted us and invited us over for a drink. "Sit down my compadres. Everyone, these are my newest business associates, Nate, Mike, and Derrick, also known as G. Have you enjoyed the party, gentlemen?" Hector asked in his usual thick accent.

"Yeah, it's real cool, Hector, but look, I want to talk to you about something, in private," Nate said.

"No problem, lets talk in my office," Hector replied.

When Nate and Hector got up to leave, I took a long hard look at Felix's sister and Hector's woman, Evangelina Hernandez. She was a real cute, hippy woman with long pretty hair, who liked to hang around gangsters. Her reputation in the drug circles was one of the gold digger hooker types. She had already been through some of the local guys, and it was apparent that she now had her sights set on Hector. Hector's reputation with women preceded him. Evangelina had a mouth on her, so it was only a matter of time before Hector laid an ass whupping on her, I thought. Which would be a real problem, because Felix Hernandez, her brother, hated Hector and his drug group.

115

Felix felt that Hector was keeping the Latin Kings from making real money in the drug game. Hector's position was too strong for them, so they had to put up with it, but they certainly didn't like it. In addition, there had been some heated disagreements between the two factions over the past couple of years that left a couple of Hector's people in the hospital and some of the Latin Kings dead. To say that there was bad blood between the two groups was an understatement. Hector's involvement with Evangelina was seen on the street as a ploy by Hector to get next to Felix and his people, and that's exactly the way Felix himself was seeing it. My only worry was how in the hell Nate was planning to make the situation work to our advantage.

I was very curious about the conversation Nate and Hector were having in the other room. I later found out it went something like this.

"Thanks for inviting us to the party man, I appreciate that," Nate said.

"No problem, forget it. We are business partners and friends. I would like to do anything I can to enhance that relationship," Hector said.

"Well, I'm glad you feel that way, 'cause I got something to ask you. Don't you think it's time we re-negotiate the terms of our deal? I mean, it has been a year now, and you're really shitting on us with those terms. Friends don't shit on each other, they work together and are fair with each other," Nate reasoned.

Hector looked at Nate hard, and took a strong pull from his trademark cigar. "In the spirit of Don Corleone, my friend, that I cannot do," Hector said flatly. "Nate, I have partners, people I have to answer to, and..."

"Don't give me that shit, Hector," Nate responded. "You said we were friends, you invite us over, drink champagne with us, introduce us as business

116

partners and shit, and treat us like this. You don't answer to anyone in this community, and you know it. How are you gonna play us?"

"In all fairness, Nate, you and your partners have made more money in this deal than you have ever seen in your lives. I made that possible. I took the risk for you. Is this how you show your gratitude?"

"Gratitude? Hector, are you serious?" Nate snapped. "In the last year we have made over one hundred thousand dollars, out of which we only took home a little over twenty thousand. If the Gangster Disciples and the P Stones knew we were dealing in some of their areas, we would probably be dead, so we are also risking our lives, and if you want us to kiss your ass for that, then fuck you, Hector, that ain't gonna happen, not with me."

"You ingrate motherfucker, how dare you come into my home and talk that nigger shit to me!" Hector said as he drew his gun from his waist and put it to Nate's nose. "I could've blown your little nigger brains out, and you wouldn't have made the twenty thousand you made with me. Don't you know there are little niggers in line to be in your position, asshole? You little nigger fucks come a dime a dozen. I could kill you and replace you tonight. But I won't. I will take your little outburst as a mistake, for which I demand an apology right now, and if you don't give me one you will have to find new partners, because I will kill all of the ones you have downstairs tonight. Now adjust your tone and address me appropriately," Hector demanded.

I'm sure it took everything in Nate's power to apologize to Hector, but he did it to save our lives. Hector knew Nate was the brains and balls of our group. He could easily have killed us and forced Nate to keep working for him. "I apologize, I was wrong. We'll keep

117

the current arrangement. Feel free to adjust the terms when you feel like it," Nate said through gritted teeth, seething.

"Good. Ah, enough business talks, Compadre, let's go downstairs and eat, no?"

As they came into the dining area I noticed a small cut on Nate's right nostril, and a look of fury in his eyes. "Hey what the fuck happened up there?" Mike asked.

"Nothing, Mike, sit down," Nate said, still through gritted teeth.

"Everyone, let's eat. I am starved," Hector announced.

"We can't stay, we have an appointment," Nate said, full of suppressed rage.

"I insist that you stay. We would be offended if you left before dinner," Hector said, squinting at Ante with pinched lips. Everyone knew then that Hector had punked Nate up in that room. It was one of the most embarrassing situations I had ever been in. I just wanted to leave.

During the drive home after dinner, Nate made us stop at a pay phone so he could call Jon. He talked to Jon for about ten minutes, and got back into the car and slammed the door. He didn't say another word for the whole drive. But then again, he didn't have to, because we all knew what was on his mind.

When we got back to the house, he told Mike to join him in the workout room. "Mike, let's go work out," he said flatly. I got up to join them, but he stopped me. "Just me and Mike, G, we got shit to talk about. I will fill you in later."

Now what was this all about, I wondered. Nate was on fire with rage and he was still secretly grieving over Momma Williams, so I was worried about his mental and emotional state after what had happened at Hector's. The doorbell rang. It was Jon, with a real serious look on his face, so serious he didn't even speak. He asked where Nate was, then went into the workout room and closed the door. Then the music got loud. I could hear the clanging of the weights and some talking, but I couldn't make out what anyone was saying. They talked in that room for over two hours, so long that after I went to get food and came back, they were still talking.

When they emerged, Nate was so angry his eyes were bloodshot. "I'll talk to you all in the morning. Give me a call about ten, Mike, and tell Pete to be here at about noon," Nate instructed. "You got it," Mike said dutifully.

After Jon left, I started to ask Nate what was going on, then decided not to. If he really wanted me to know, he would have told me. It kind of bothered me that he didn't.

For the next three months or so, everything went pretty much as usual, except that Pete replaced me as Nate's chief pickup man. Hector had become pretty comfortable with us, and allowed us to pick up dope from his house instead of the mall. Nate told me to drive Pete on the pickups, and to let Pete go in and get the stuff.

One particular month, Pete was pretty sick with the flu, and asked me to go into the house and pick up the dope while he sat in the car. Of course, I obliged. As I walked up the stairs, I was greeted by the usual bodyguards and the door opened without my knocking.

I could see Evangelina half hiding behind the door with dark glasses on, trying to hide the black eye that Hector had presumably given her.

"What's up? Is Hector around?" I asked.

"No. The stuff is on the table. Where's the money?" she asked flatly.

"Here, want to count it?" I asked, handing her the attaché case full of loot.

"No need," she said, dabbing her eye under the shades.

One of Hector's people came down and quickly eased the tense atmosphere.

"What's up, G, how's everybody?"

"Everybody's cool, what about on your end?" I asked.

"Just trying to make it, man. Is it all here?" he asked.

"You know it is," I answered.

"Cool. Oh yeah, give Nate my best, and tell that fucking Jon to send my 'War' tape back this week he's had it long enough."

"I'll tell him," I said. I took notice of Evangelina stumbling up the stairs, looking beat up and coked out.

When I got back to the car, I told Pete what I had seen, and he flipped out. "Pull over, pull over at that pay phone, and hurry up!" he yelled through his obviously sore throat.

"O.K., motherfucker, hold your horses!" I yelled back.

Pete hopped out of the car and ran across the street, almost getting hit by a car. He made a phone call and talked for about five minutes or so, then got back into the car, smiling.

"O.K., what the hell was that all about?" I asked.

"Oh, nothing. I just had to make a phone call and I almost forgot about it, that's all," he answered slyly.

"Well, motherfucker, if I knew you had that much energy, you could have taken that damn money up to Hector's house and got the stuff," I said, glaring at him.

"Sorry," was his only reply. I knew something was going on, and I decided I wasn't going to wait too much longer before I insisted on being told what it was.

When I got home, one of Nate's new girlfriends was there and told me that Nate and Mike had gone to a meeting and would be back soon. When Nate returned, he was in the best mood he had been in weeks. Mike went straight to the side room and dumped a load of about fifteen guns, with ammo, that he had gotten on the street. Still, I was left in the dark about the newest developments.

The secrecy went on for the next month or so. There was so much slipping around, so many ambiguous statements, that I couldn't take it any longer. After my usual restaurant breakfast with Jon, I decided to see Nate and demanded to know what was going on.

After I dropped Jon off, I stopped at the local store for a newspaper. After flipping through the first couple of pages, I saw a picture of Evangelina and a headline that said "Local Mother Beaten to Death: Left under Viaduct."

I was shocked. I had just seen Evangelina a few weeks ago, and now she was dead. The thought of it made me forget my plan to talk to Nate. I had to drive around and get my head together. I knew Hector hit his women, but what could Evangelina have done to make him kill her and dump her dead body under a viaduct? I remembered a conversation I had with Hector. He said that people knew about how he slapped his women around, but he said he just did it to keep them in line and that he would never really hurt them. Plus, Hector knew the incredible heat the Latin Kings would bring down on him if he killed Evangelina. None of it made sense.

I stopped and read the article again; it was pretty light on specifics. After driving around and thinking for

121

about an hour, I came to one conclusion. Hector didn't killed Evangelina. Somebody else did, and I was gonna find out who.

As I walked into the house, I heard Nate and Mike in the workout room, so I went in. I saw Nate huffing and puffing out repetitions on the bench press. "Nate, I need to talk to you," I said.

"Cool, G, hold up," he gasped. "Let's take a break, Mike. What's on your mind, G? Oh, hold on, G... Mike, tell Jon he better call me about that money!"

"I will," Mike said.

As he sat down on the couch, Nate said, "I took your advice, G. You know Mike and I have been lifting weights to relieve stress and frustration. You realize it has been almost six months since Momma died?"

"Yeah, I thought about that at breakfast with Jon," I replied.

"I feel like going to the cemetery tomorrow. How about you?"

"Cool, just let me know what time," I replied.

Nate nodded in agreement. "What's on your mind, G?" he asked.

"Who killed Evangelina Hernandez?" I asked.

Nate looked down at some papers and replied, "We all heard about that, G, we were fucked up about that, too. I think Hector did; the stupid ass."

"Nah, I know that's what's on the streets, but who really killed her?"

Mike and Nate looked at each other with little sly grins. "Mike, give me a minute to talk with G alone...on second thought stay put, I want you to hear this, too," Nate said

"Have a seat, G." Nate said, gesturing to the couch. As I sat down my mind was racing at about 100 miles per hour, trying to figure out what he was about to say.

"G, it was we, or more precisely Mike, who killed Evangelina," Nate said softly.

"Aw, Nate, no. No, Nate, why?"

"G, you know Hector was never gonna let us out of that deal, right?" he said in a fatherly tone.

"Yeah, Nate, but killing Evangelina, how does that connect?"

Nate went on to recount exactly what Hector had said to him that night at the party, in explicit detail. "G, after he said that, I made myself a promise right there in his office to never let another motherfucker talk to me that way again and live to tell about it. So Mike and I devised a plan to wait until Hector started hitting Evangelina, and then kill her and frame him for it."

"I'm sure Hector has a great alibi and will convince the police he didn't do it, Nate," I said desperately.

"G, Hector is dead. The Latin Kings hit him at about four thirty this morning. Julio, Mantra, Angel, all of Hector's bitches, all his people got smoked, and the house was burned to the ground. We helped the Kings set it all up, and helped finance it. The Latin Kings don't have to worry about Hector anymore, and can deal freely in the Hispanic community. And we got our freedom and some guns out of the deal. I also talked to Hector's contact. Jon and I made a deal to get fifty pounds of weed and about twenty pounds of coke every quarter, free to sell as we please, and we get to keep all of our profits. That will net us about one million dollars a quarter, without Hector's bullshit. We had to do it."

Listening to it all, I felt a sick feeling in my stomach. "Why didn't you tell me about it? I thought I was your brother," I said.

"You are my brother, but you're a cautious brother. I knew you would have talked me out of it. Anyway, I am telling you now."

"Yeah, and after the fact that all sounds real good, Nate, but you forgot one thing. What about Evangelina? She was innocent in all of this, and now she is dead. And what about her daughter? Now, she doesn't have a mother. You forgot about the innocent people," I said, frustrated.

"Innocent? That bitch wasn't innocent. Do you know what innocent is? Innocent is the old man sitting with his grandson at a baseball game. Innocent is a mother getting off the bus to go home and cook dinner for her family. Innocent is a father working two jobs to support his family. That's innocent, G, and that bitch wasn't none of that. Everybody knows Evangelina has never been nothing but a drug dealer's whore. She was totally into the dope game, G, and you know it. Listen, G, none of these bitches are innocent, they hang around all of us using their asses and looks to get cash. They're along for the ride.

"Plus," Nate continued, "It was only a matter of time before the Latin Kings used her to turn state's evidence on Hector and do us all in. She was a security risk. That's what the District Attorney and the cops do, get bitches like Evangelina to turn on their drug dealer boyfriends, and send them upstate. A bitch just turned state on our man Dollar Bill up in Maywood, now he's doing a dime in Stateville and that bitch is in witness protection somewhere living it up. Naw, I ain't going out like that, G, fuck that bitch, and fuck Hector! I tried to reason with that nacho-eating motherfucker, but he wouldn't listen. Hector was just gonna use us and then kill us, and I wasn't gonna wait around for him to do it. And as far as Evangelina's little girl is concerned, my heart goes out to her, but these bitches should think about their kids when they're fucking and chasing drug boys all over the place, and that's how I feel about the whole matter!" Nate concluded angrily.

I listened to Nate's entire tirade, and then it dawned on me. Nate had decided long ago that he liked this life. Nate had decided, maybe on the night of the party that he wanted to take Hector down and grab everything. But with the new deal he made with Hector's contact, we all went from small time to big time. Our whole lives were about to change forever, and I resented Nate for making that kind of decision without talking to me about it.

I felt like I had to throw up. I got up and walked out of the room, and slammed the door. I got into the car and drove and cried, and drove and cried some more. I had plans, dreams, and with one deal, Nate wiped all of that away. When you're just selling some reefer, you're able to stop and get out one day, but when you're selling cocaine, especially so much cocaine, you're in it for life. I was terrified, I didn't know anything about that life, and neither did the others. They were just following Nate's blind ambition. What in the world were we gonna do now?

I had made a promise to Momma Williams to protect Nate and look out for him, but how could I do that now, in this game? I pulled the car over and put my head on the steering wheel. Two years ago, just two years ago, we were in high school, jumping around at house parties. I was an unremarkable, bookworm with dreams, and my brother Nate was a tough kid with an uncertain future. Now I was a confused, frightened young man with a bleak future, and my brother Nate was starting to become what he had been lusting to become for one year out of those two…a Drug Lord.

Chapter 5

Mercury Rises....

On November 25, 1987, a hero died in Chicago. Mayor Harold Washington was found slumped over at his desk in his office at City Hall and so, slumped the hopes of many people weary of machine politics and cronyism. Mayor Washington was a fair man, who wanted to run a fair city, and his appeal crossed racial and ethnic lines, and seemed to bring a city together. Many people in City Hall and on the police force felt secretly threatened by his appeal. One of those persons was Detective Trent, a staunch supporter of Richard Daley, who himself was making a secret bid to be the next mayor of Chicago. In the black community, there was a spirit of depression, hopelessness and despair. We all looked up to Washington, he was our political prince, the first black mayor this city had ever seen, and we poured much of our hope in him for a brighter future, now it was all over. Well, momma Williams always used to say black people were too messiah-prone, and that we should look to ourselves for a brighter future.

However, Nate didn't have to look to anybody he was deciding his own future. It had been a little over a year since the death of Hector, and Nate's newfound independence, and we had already made near one million dollars. The only problem was Nate wouldn't let anyone spend anything. Nate wanted desperately to spend and save with the premise of "organizational costs," whatever that was. We were one year and almost a million into the game and we were still wearing the same clothes and shoes. No one was allowed to spend a dime! When someone went to him about spending money on anything, he became irate. When he wanted to "treat" us, he would take us to Red Lobster or something, and even then, he told us to watch what we ordered. One thing I will say, though; he led by example. Nate spent nothing on himself; all of the money that was made was put into this underground area that he had dug under the house about a week after Hector was killed. Everyone was upset and angry, but no one ever said anything to Nate about it. Then, out of the blue Nate called a meeting. "I know you all have been bitching and moaning about the money and shit. Don't think I haven't heard about it." Nate said sternly. "But you all have to understand this ain't gonna be no damn gang. Shit is gonna be organized to a T."

With all of us assembled, he began to pass out two books to all of us, The Art of War by Sun Tzu and Cosa Nostra: A History of the Sicilian Mafia by John Dickie. He told us he wanted us to be the first crime family black folks had ever seen. He said we had to be organized, and that organization costs money. Nate always had a problem with gangs for that very reason. He always felt that gangs were a bunch of unorganized guys running around trying to get the same nickel. Nate said he believed gangs were more organized in prisons than they were on the street. Nate was up for days planning and strategizing. He wanted to come up with something unique, something that was not done before. He expressed a desire to imitate the organized crime families of the mafia. Nate wanted to originate a group of men not just scrambling around to get the same nickel, but a group that was organized and consolidated. During the mid-eighties, most of the reefer sellers on the south side were a few young gang bangers, and some older guys just freelancing to make ends meet. Nate told me that he wanted to give these people an option; either join our group or die, but the gang bangers were not to be given an option; they were to be exterminated. The freelancers and gang bangers were already starting to lose business. Word got around that our stuff was the best out, which caused the freelancers to virtually close shop and come to us anyway. The gangbanging street dealers had other ideas. Many of them reported to their people that they were losing street business to our group, and that we started dealing cocaine. The Gangster Disciples knew that it would not be long before they would lose the entire south side to us. At that time, I had a few eyes and ears on the street, and it was reported back to me that the Gangster Disciples were planning to make a move on our house and kill us all. My sources told me that they were gonna wait until winter, catch us off-guard one night, raid us and kill us. I was also told that Titus was at the helm of the plan. He was in control of the west side, and didn't want to lose the south side entirely. A few years before, Hector had street peace with the GD's because he never made a move on the black community. As it turned out, Hector had a few sit-downs with the GD's but the two groups could never agree to terms that would benefit both parties. Hector was using us to get a toehold on the black community right under the Gangster Disciples' noses, a direct violation to street peace that we would have paid the price for! When I gave this information to Nate, he didn't seem to be surprised. "You know G, I always knew we were gonna eventually have to fight for the south side call a meeting. It's time to get our hands dirty." Nate resigned.

"G has informed me of a plot to overthrow us and kill us, a plot directly from the Gangster Disciples," Nate

128

said.   "Now, from what I hear, it's not supposed to go down for a few months, so we have time. What we're going to do with that time is organize. Like I told you guys last meeting, organization is the key. I hope you all read the books I gave you; they'll help give each of you insight on how this group will be organized. As a matter of fact, from this point on we'll refer to this group as a family, because that's what we are, a family. First, this family will be structured in the old ways of the Sicilian Mafia, hence the necessity for the first book I gave you. The Sicilian Mafia system is the best blueprint given to us on how to organize our activities. During the late 1800's the Mafia was organized when the European Feudal system collapsed, and certain landowners and other powerful men built reputations as local leaders to protect their land. They called themselves "Capos," and they were structured into "regimes," Nate taught.

Nate went on all night practically, and he captivated everyone.   I don't remember anyone even taking a bathroom break! After going on about the old Sicilian Mafia, the Roman Empire, and how they were structured, he began to delegate authority.   He turned to Big Mike and said, "Mike, I want you to run the muscle in this family; I want you to be strategic, and vicious. I want members to understand that loyalty to the death is the only loyalty that will be tolerated. I want outsiders to be more afraid of us than the police, understand?" he asked.

"Understood," was Mikes reply.   He turned to Jon and instructed him. "Jon, you'll run the family's assets and money. Not a fucking dime will be spent unless I okay it. Everyone will receive a salary, and won't be given a quarter over or under get it?" "Got it." was Jon's reply.

"G, you'll head up intelligence. I want the eyes and ears of this family everywhere, even on the police force. I want you to work on getting people from all walks of life on spy and informant payroll. I want everyone from homeless people to council members giving us information and alerting us of any shakedowns or busts. Do you understand?"

"Yes." I said. "G will also be second in command, so don't be bringing me all of your complaints and problems. Follow the chain of command that I've set up. All bullshit will be filtered first by G, before it gets to me." As I looked around the room, I could see people smiling and nodding in agreement with Nate. The ass kissing had already started, I thought.

After Nate delegated responsibilities to everyone and told them what would be expected of them, we adjourned. He told us he'd work with each of us individually within our prospective regimes for a week, so we'd know exactly how he wanted it run. He gave us an organizational chart, and told us to write a report on the books and give it to him by the next meeting. I had already read the books before, but I had to revisit them to try to understand how they applied to what Nate wanted from us. Soon it all became clear; Nate wanted to rule the city's drug world with extreme violence, fear and intimidation. He wanted to control his enemies and keep them off balance, and incorporate the authorities and make them pseudo-partners. I thought secretly that Nate was a tough streetwise person, but he could never pull something like this off. I soon realized that Nate was not going to pull it off; we were going to help him do it!

Within the month, we all got back to Nate and gave him our "reports." Nate read them all and scheduled a follow-up meeting. We were all reacquainted with our duties once again.   He told us we must listen to him and carry out duties exactly as we were told. The only twist was that I would have to be right there during these "sessions," because I was the number two man; therefore, I would have to know everything Nate knew. Many men would have loved to be the number two man in a crime organization, but I loathed it. Some of the information that I gathered was downright revolting. One in particular was the formation of Mike's enforcement and security regime, the sadistic and brutal "South Side Mafia." Nate had done extensive research into the customs, culture and practices of the Sicilian Mafia, and came to admire them. He felt that one of the only things that prevented Blacks from truly imitating it was our inability to keep our mouths shut.

"Hey, G, the Sicilian's got this thing in their group called Omerta, which in essence means keep your motherfucking mouth shut. And if they don't, they get whacked. They have survived for a thousand years with that shit!" he exclaimed.   "That's what we're gonna have,G, that Omerta shit. If a motherfucker talks, he gets his ass whacked, no questions asked, no exceptions!"

The South Side Mafia started out with about fifteen people and Mike as their "Capo" or lieutenant.   Nate developed some old rituals and pricking of the fingers and all of that nonsense, but it definitely was not nonsense to them. These people ate it all up! It never ceases to amaze me how badly people, particularly black people, want to be a part of something, anything regardless of how crazy it is. The fifteen or so men who comprised the group were all young guys usually between the ages of seventeen and twenty-five, because as Nate said, they were the most impressionable. Most of these guys had been in and out of boys homes, and had done county time for petty theft or burglary, so they were well acquainted with the criminal culture. Nate taught Mike how to use intimidation and fear to control them. The fear of death was basically the only thing that kept these guys in line. But it wasn't just getting killed that frightened them, but the way it might have been done.

Nate and Mike talked of setting guys on fire, cutting off their heads and castration that frightened them into instant submission. However, with some guys, talk is cheap. They had been in the county jail and seen a lot. Seeing was definitely believing for them. Guys like Larry C, who was in the county jail for possession. Larry C didn't care for Nate. He figured Nate was some wannabe gangster, but didn't have the juice to be a real one. We were all playing basketball after one of Nate's teaching sessions at the park when he decided to test him. Nate was great at baseball, but was marginal at basketball, and Larry C had been elbowing him and trash talking Nate all night. "Where's your jumper boss, man? You ain't got no game!" Larry said.

"Just play the game man and shut your fucking mouth!" Nate said, obviously agitated.

This went on for the whole game. Whenever Nate had the ball on offense, Larry would take him on defense, steal the ball, and drive for a lay-up, or pass to a teammate for an easy two points. "Whoever heard of a nigga who can't play basketball? Shit man you can't be no crime boss. You ain't got no heart; you aint shit," Larry said as he drove for the winning points.

"You want me to handle his ass?" Mike asked.

"Nah baby, I got it. It's cool," Nate said as he walked to his gym bag. As I bent over dabbing sweat from my head with a towel, I wondered how Nate was going to handle it. Just then, I saw Nate draw a bat from his gym bag, walked up behind Larry as he was celebrating with the others and gave him a powerful blow to the small of his back that sent Larry to his knees.

"You couldn't just play the game, motherfucker. You had to run your fucking mouth," Nate said, smiling and throwing the bat down. Everyone looked on in nervous anticipation and disbelief. Mike tossed Nate a hunting knife, and Nate drew it from its sheath. Nate straddled Larry as he lay face down on the ground, grabbed him under the chin and drew his head back, completely exposing his neck and Adam's apple. Nate quickly reached across Larry's face and poked the blade into his neck just under the earlobe. "You had to come out here talking all of that shit!"

Just as Nate completed his sentence, he quickly sliced across Larry's throat with one quick powerful motion. I remember the cut being so deep and forceful; I thought Larry's head would come right off in Nate's hand! I had never seen a person get killed before like that except in the movies, so I threw up right there! Everyone looked on in utter horror as Nate wiped the blood from his hand and lower arm with a towel provided by Mike. One guy even pissed his pants! I remember Larry's body convulsing as he gurgled for life. There were some guys playing with us from the neighborhood standing there frozen in fear and disbelief at witnessing a man murdered over a pickup game of basketball! "Get your shit out!" Nate told them, referring to their identification. I could feel a tear rolling down my cheek as I wiped my mouth. My brother, a black man had just murdered another black man, in broad daylight over a game, I thought. Nate took all of their drivers' licenses and   state identification cards and gave them to Mike. "You didn't see shit, did you?" Nate asked them. They all replied no, those that could still muster the ability to speak. "I didn't think so," Nate said sarcastically.

Yep, seeing definitely is believing, and all of the young guys and perspective members of the S.S.M saw it and couldn't believe it. Neither did I. After we got back to the house, I confronted Nate about the murder. "What the hell did you just do? Why did you kill Larry over a fucking game, Nate?"

"Look, G, there's going to be a lot more of that. I'm not playing here, and it's time everybody sees that shit. Now, that motherfucker asked for that. I ain't nobody to be fucked with, G. I can't be showing no weaknesses to these guys. If that's what I have do to get their attention, then that's what I'll do. Besides, I never liked that asshole anyway." He said plainly.

"Was that your first kill, Nate?" I asked.

"Yeah, so what," he said as he walked out of the room. There was an animalistic rage in him when he was angry, a ruthless rage that knows no forgiveness, no sympathy, no reconciliation, no grace, no understanding or mercy. That frightened me; Nate was becoming something I didn't understand right before my eyes. He spent weeks breeding that same type of rage into the heart of Mike and the other members of the South Side Mafia. Nate was by far the worst of all because he had killed for no reason. The other guys could never have killed Larry over something so trivial. His rage was pretty much unrivaled in the group until Dana Oswald joined. Dana Oswald was a sexy but solidly built woman from Philadelphia who had been in and out of about ten group homes by the time she was fifteen. Her mother abandoned her and her younger sister and their father raised them, and frequently sexually abused Dana. She never gave any details, but she did admit to killing her father one night when she came home from a date and found him on top of her ten-year-old sister. The event traumatized her sister and she suffered a nervous

134

breakdown and was never the same mentally.   Dana's case was ruled justifiable homicide, due to the "cruel and unusual abuse" inflicted upon Dana and her sister by her father.   Dana's sister was placed in a state facility, and Dana went on to finish high school and became a bounty hunter.

Mike and I met her at a club up north one night. Some guy had gotten full of alcohol and got pretty fresh with her.   He obviously placed his hands where they didn't belong and she gave him a hard slap. Embarrassed, he gave her a fist to the face and knocked her down.   Mike and I stood up to move to her defense and one of the regulars held his hand out.   "No need, guys. She can handle it."

She stood, wiped her mouth and grinned, "That's the best you can do?"   As the men stood around laughing, the guy swung wildly at her, she ducked and gave him a hard right to the stomach and an elbow shot to the head that knocked him out cold. She rolled him over and straddled him.   "Since you have a problem touching what you see, I think I'll help you out." She gently opened the guy's right eyelid and jammed her thumb about two inches into his socket, more than likely blinding him from that eye permanently. As she stood, wiping her thumb off on her jeans, she looked around as people started moving away and whispering to each other. "Damn it, Dana, I told you not to pull that shit in here again!" the bartender shouted as he reached for the phone.

"Fuck you, Billy. You saw what he did to me!" she
shouted back.

"That's it. I want your psycho ass out of here!" he
yelled, obviously dialing 911.

"Can you guys give me a ride?" she asked me.

"I don't know uh" I muffled out.

"Yeah, let's go," Mike said, obviously excited.

We took to her immediately; she seemed to like us also.

"Hey, what's your name?" I asked.

"Dana. What's yours?" she replied.

"Everybody calls me G, and this is my friend Mike. You really handled yourself pretty good back there, Dana," I said, smiling.

"That was nothing. That motherfucker had it coming," she said proudly.

"Aren't you afraid about him retaliating against you?" I asked.

"No, he knows who I am and what I do. He's lucky I didn't kill him," she said flatly.

"What do you do, anyway?" Mike asked.

"I'm the Governor of Illinois, what the fuck do you do?" she said sarcastically. "No, for real, I want to know, are you a cop or something?" Mike asked.

"Look, man, I don't know you. Why the fuck are you asking me so many questions?" she said slightly agitated. She passed the first test, I thought. She knows how to keep her mouth shut. It was then that I noticed the flashing lights of a police car in the side mirror.

"Oh, shit, Mike, pull over. It's the police! Hey, Dana, there's some blankets on the floor back there. Lie on the floor and completely cover yourself with them." I also reached back to throw some boxes and other trash Mike had back there on top of her. As the cop approached the car, I began organizing lies in my head, if needed. I knew Mike had a driver's license, and the car was insured so that wasn't a problem. We only needed to B.S our way through this traffic stop and be on our way.

"May I see your driver's license, registration and proof of insurance please," the officer asked.

"Sure, is there a problem, officer?" Mike asked.

"Well, yeah, first off, you were speeding. Sit tight I'll be back," the cop said, walking away. I noticed as he walked away he flashed his light in the back seat and gave a quick look. All he saw was blankets and food stuff, a baby car seat and a bible. Nate always taught us to buy a baby seat and a bible and put it in the back seat, and be polite. That would always sway the opinion of the officer to believe he was law abiding and harmless. Criminals and dope dealers usually don't drive around with baby seats and bibles in their cars. Something as simple as a sixty-dollar baby seat and a bible might make the difference between going to jail or home. As the cop walked back to the car, I looked at Mike and told him to remain calm and be polite. If he writes a ticket, agree with him and take it. If he lets you go, thank him and wish him well.

"Everything checked out. I'm not going to write you a ticket this time. I just want you to slow down, okay? Consider this a warning," the cop instructed.

"Yes sir, thank you and God bless," Mike said humbly. "I'm just going to say it, that Nate is a fucking genius!" Mike said exuberantly.

"Be cool, Mike. He ain't gone yet," I cautioned.

As the cop drove off, Dana stuck her head up slightly and asked if the cop was gone. "Yeah, it's cool. You can get up. Now you owe us one, cause we could have turned your ass in, you know!" I said sarcastically.

"Whatever! Why didn't you?" she asked.

"Well, I like your flavor, your style. I want to get to know you and maybe offer you a job. How about that?" I said.

"Doing what motherfucker? You keep asking so many questions. Why are you asking so many damn questions!" she said agitated.

"In time, I'll tell you. What are you doing tonight?"

I asked.

"Riding in the back of a car with some weird motherfuckers, trying to get home, why?"

"Let me take you to meet someone, and he'll tell you what the job entails. I promise there won't be any funny business, and it'll be worth your while. Agreed?" I proposed.

Mike looked at me strangely, because he knew Nate always said not to bring strangers to meet him. But I had a good feeling about this girl, and I knew Nate would, too. Mike made a quick stop at Harold's Chicken Shack from which he became notorious for picking up his favorite meal, "a half white with extra mild sauce," and we were on our way. When we arrived at the house, Nate was working out. He was still in sweats when I approached him. "What's up, bro, what did ya'll do tonight?" Nate asked smiling.

"Nothing. A little drinking and stuff...There was a fight, but everything turned out cool," I said.

"A fight, it wasn't Mike, was it?" he asked worried.

"Nah, it was this chick. She kicked this guy's ass. She's a real trooper, man, and I brought her here to meet you. I think she can be a valuable asset for us," I explained.

"You know I don't like to talk to strangers, G. What if she's Five-O?" Nate said, wiping the sweat from his brow.

"Nah, not this broad, if she's five-o, the department is in trouble, not us," I said sarcastically.

Nate looked at me for a second and chuckled.

"Okay, man, bring her in, but frisk her first," he cautioned. When I frisked her, I found a thirty-two-caliber pistol in the small of her back and confiscated it.

"Hey motherfucker, what's up? I thought this shit was cool. I thought your man was cool. What the fuck is up!" she yelled.

"What the fuck is up is I don't know you, and don't yell in this motherfucking house, or you'll get shot. Now, my boys brought you here cause they say you're cool and you might work out with us, but I don't trust you," Nate said, emerging from the workout room. "Now you want to calm down, have a seat and a drink and we can talk. What are you drinking?" Nate asked in a mild tone.

"Cutty and water, and I don't want no generic scotch. If you don't have Cutty or JB, fuck it."

Damn, I thought, a woman drinking scotch. She had to be a tough broad!

"Now, what's your name?" Nate asked as he gave her a drink. She went on to give him her name and her story pretty easy, much to my surprise. I guess power respects power, cause she didn't give Nate half the lip she gave us in the car. "So what do you do now?" Nate inquired.

"I'm a bounty hunter. I catch motherfuckers and lock them up for money," she said sharply.

"I know what a bounty hunter is. How much do you make?" Nate asked calmly.

"How much can you pay me?" she came back.

"More than you ever made in your life, I'm sure," Nate said with confidence.

"Don't be too sure. I've made quite a bit in my life," she retorted. Nate laughed in a tickled sort of way.

"You're right, G. I like her, but I still don't trust her," Nate said with reservation.

"You still haven't told me what ya'll do around here," she said.

Nate looked at her for what seemed to be about thirty seconds. "Have you ever killed a man, Dana?" Nate asked plainly.

"No, why?" she asked curiously.

"Because it's not of any importance what we do. I feel all you should know for now is what you'll be doing. Fair enough?" Nate asked. "Cool, come with me, all of you," Nate instructed.

As we went downstairs, there was the strangest of smells. I had never smelled it before but it was making me sick that's for sure. When we arrived downstairs, Nate had a local member of the GD's gagged and duct taped to a chair. Members of the S.S.M had been torturing him all night. They had been burning him with cigarettes, pulling his toenails out and depriving him of sleep. The guy looked and smelled awful. "You see this little motherfucker, Dana? This ass gave the Gangster Disciples some information about us and told them where we lived. Now all I need to know is who he specifically told it to, but he won't tell us. Can you help us out?" Nate asked sarcastically.

"That's all you need? Shit, that's easy," she said seemingly delighted. She asked if we had a bottle of alcohol, then took a knife and made slices all over the guy's penis and scrotum as he yelled. "Now look, nigga, my man wants to know who the fuck you talked to, and your going tell me. I haven't made any permanent damage yet, but I can and I will, so talk!" she demanded.

The guy mumbled something that none of us could understand. She looked at him and shook her head no, and poured about a half a cup of alcohol all over the guy's lap and open cuts. I never heard a man scream and yell in agony before; I just wanted to go upstairs. I looked over at Nate and even he was wincing, but pleased at her zealousness. "Wipe his face," she instructed. One of the guys looked at Nate before taking any orders from Dana. Nate nodded in approval to show Dana he was in charge of the fiasco. After wiping the saliva, snot, and tears from the guy's face, she started talking to him again, "I'm going to fuck you up all night with this alcohol until you tell me, and if you don't, I'll cut that little piece of shit off with a rusty butter knife. I got all night!" "I, I, told ya'll T,T.,Titus, I told you all, already," the guy said, probably going into shock.

Dana looked at Nate incredulously and he smiled. Nate already had the name he was looking for; he just wanted to see how brutal Dana could be. He pulled a German Lugar from the small of his back.

"Put him to sleep, Dana," Nate said coldly.

The guy had already passed out from the pain. Nate emptied all of the bullets out of the gun, except one. "One in his dome, that's how we do it here," Nate said.

Dana took the gun, shaking her head, put the barrel to the guy's left eye, and pulled the trigger, blowing out most of the back of his head. Everyone looking on jumped as the weapon discharged, and witnessing the horror of skull fragments and brain matter exploding out of the young guy's head. Dana did little more than flinch as she handed the gun back to Nate.

"Good. Now I trust you. G, she's hired. Dana, if you work with us, you must live with us. We're a family, and we do everything together, no outsiders. Come with me," Nate said.

"Okay, everyone, we know what to do let's do it," I said.

We had to prepare the body for dumping, but there was more to getting rid of a body than just dumping it; it was a process. Nate taught us that a dead body had more forensic evidence on it than the crime scene itself. Both hands and feet had to be scrubbed with an acidic solution to get rid of prints. All teeth had to be pulled out or broken with pliers, to hamper dental records, and finally the head had to be separated from the body. The body would be dumped in one place usually the cornfields of southern Illinois, and the head was to be dumped in a body of water usually the Calumet River, Nate taught that most gang members were caught after committing murders because of shoddy work. He said that gang bangers would shoot a guy then let the body drop and leave it wherever it falls, along with all of the evidence on it. "In the family, we do shit the Mafiosi way. We take our time," Nate always said. The process usually took about an hour and a half, and then two people were designated to drive the "package" to the prospective destinations. Sometimes guys would complain about it, but Nate always gave his favorite saying, "If guys don't take the time, they end up doing time." As I sat there supervising the guys, my mind wandered back to those hot summer days when Nate and I would play strikeout, and Momma Williams would make us lunch and talk about how dirty we had gotten in such a short time. She always hated when we got dirty. I long for those days. We were innocent kids then; now we're living like demons. As I began to drift off deeper into thought Jon tapped me on the shoulder.

"What the hell happened down here?" he asked.

"Oh, Nate killed another gang banger," I resigned.

"Damn he hunts these guys for sport huh?" Jon said smiling.

"It's not funny, Jon. This shit is gonna get us in real trouble. I mean, these are human lives we're talking about here. This is the fourth person this month. We are not in the Middle East somewhere. You can't just kill people and go eat steak and talk about it!" I explained.

"G, Nate is right. You worry too much. Relax he has it all covered," Jon said confidently.

"You don't understand, Jon. These are somebody's sons, somebody's fathers, somebody's brothers. I mean, this shit is going catch up to us someday," I reasoned.

Planting a firm pat on my back, Jon replied, "Stop worrying. It's all covered. By the way, Nate said to have two guys take care of this."

As Jon handed me a piece of paper, I noticed an address scribbled on it. "What is this?" I asked. "Nate says this new Dana chick is going join us. He wants two guys to go over to her house and get all of her personal belongings; you know, clothes and shit, and bring them back here, but leave all of the furniture," he instructed.

"She doesn't want her furniture?" I asked surprised.

"Nate says she won't be needing it, and he wants to see you after this is done," Jon said flatly.

During my conversation with Jon I was hoping they would've been finished. I supervised three of these "preparations" and it still made me physically sick. I made up my mind right there that this would be my last. "Hey, Jon, send Mike down here right away!" I shouted.

As I heard Mike lumbering down the stairs, I rose from my chair, preparing to give it to him. "Supervise the rest," I stated to him.

"Nate told you to do it," he retorted.

"You're a Capo, aren't you?" I asked.

He replied, "Yes." "This is your regime, isn't it?" He again replied, "Yes." "Then supervise your regime, Capo!"

As I walked upstairs, I began wondering what Nate could have wanted to talk to me about. I wanted all of this to end, all of the killing and drug selling. I just

Evil Side Of Money   Jeff Robertson

wanted to be a regular person again, but I knew Nate wouldn't have such talk from any of us.

"Hey, G, good looking out with that Dana girl. She's going work out just fine. Did you see her go to work down there? I'm telling you, G, she might end up with her own regime; she's that good," Nate said admiringly.

"Did you want to see me?" I asked.

"Yeah. Look, we're gonna have an important meeting next week, but I need to get you up to speed on a few things. Can we do lunch tomorrow morning?" he asked.

"We can talk about it now, Nate," I acknowledged.

"Nah, I got a couple of broads waiting for me in the room, if you know what I mean," he said smiling. "Besides, I thought you and I could take a drive up to the cemetery afterwards to see our mom, what do you think?"

"It's cool. Where do you want to eat at?"

"You know I only like Army & Lou's, G. I don't eat lunch anywhere else, plus, Jon is going join us for breakfast. So let's say about nine-thirty okay?" He asked.

"Fine with me. Don't you think this house is getting a little crowded? With Dana moving in, that makes six or seven of us," I stated.

"We'll discuss that, too, I got it all taken care of, G," he said. I always got nervous when he has things "all taken care of."

144

Chapter 6

The Family

Somehow, I beat Jon and Nate to the restaurant. I sat down and ordered my usual, pancakes, turkey sausage and a coffee, and waited. Everyone was buzzing over the death of Harold Washington. There were conspiracy theories everywhere, ranging from the mayor committing suicide to the Daley people poisoning him. I knew the city would never be the same. I could tell Chicago was about to take a turn for the worse. There was political infighting going on every night at the city counsel dubbed, "counsel wars," by the media. There was a genuine feeling of disgust and despair on the streets, particularly in the black community. It was not a good time. People in the restaurant were quiet and reserved. The only hot topics in the city were the death of Harold Washington and the rise of a new sports phenom named Michael Jordan. I saw three members of the S.S.M walk in the door and I knew Nate and Jon weren't far behind. Nate came in and kissed me on the cheek. Jon did the same as they sat down and ordered their meals.

"Did you see that bullshit on the news last night, G, that counsel war's bullshit? All of those motherfuckers jockeying for position and power like a bunch of pariahs!" Nate said in disgust.

"Yeah, the shit is pretty disgusting. Everybody's talking about it," I replied.

"I tell you, this city is about to go to the fucking toilet," Nate said.

145

"You think so?" Jon asked.

"Open your eyes, baby, look at everybody's faces. All of these motherfuckers looking defeated and shit, like Washington was Jesus or something. G, you remember what mamma always said. Black people are too messiah prone. You kill the head and everyone starts meandering around like some fucking sheep," he reflected. "I'm surprised they haven't started tearing up the community like they did when King got killed," Nate said. "I think they would have. The only thing stopping them is how Washington died. If black people knew for a fact he was killed, they'd be tearing shit up," I injected. Jon wisely said nothing; a white person's point of view was definitely not needed at the time.

"Well, enough of that shit. Let's talk shop. G, we're about to make some real drastic moves, and Jon and I wanted to talk to you about it to get your opinion on things before we did anything," Nate explained.

"Cool, what's up?" I replied. "First, we're going to war with the GD's next week. Now the Family has swollen to about one hundred and fifty total. We can use the weight of that to gain total control of the south side, but we have to make a move before they make one on us. Like that little plan they have to rush the house this winter, I don't want to wait around for that shit. I say let's hit their asses now and get it over with. Now, Jon says that we have about ninety thousand dollars in our war chest. How many eyes and ears you got on the street?" he asked.

"Hmmm, about twenty-five guys, why?" I asked.

"Well, G, the way we see it, we don't need to spend too much money on this front. If we can get some good intel, we can wage and win this war in one night. What I

146

need is to get most of these street dealers from the GD's in one place and murder all of them at once, but just the ones that deal on the south side. If we can conjure up some fake meeting somewhere, where we can get them to congregate and I can have the mafia guys do the number and send a definitive message to these gang banging motherfuckers that we own the south side. You think you can help us with that?" He asked. "Let me think about it, and I will get back to you tonight okay?" I replied. "Cool, just don't forget, I need this done as soon as possible. Jon, what can we spare for this?" "Well we shouldn't need to spend too much, I say about ten thousand. We have the guns and the guys, the intelligence will be the challenge," Jon explained. "How so?" Nate asked. "Well depending on how G wants to go with this, you know Nate intelligence costs, more than guns and men, especially if it's good intelligence," Jon reasoned. I nodded in agreement. Nate sometimes forgot how costly good intelligence can be. Good intelligence is a dirty cop on the take who will get you information straight from the department, or a politician of some kind who can get you information or help you with some political stuff, or some crooked preacher who will give you information on one of his members whom you might need. That's good intelligence, and it doesn't come cheap! Yet, that was the kind of intelligence we were going to need to pull this one off. I needed to remind Nate of that. It helped that Jon already understood and endorsed the idea.

"Whatever you have to do, just make it fast, okay?" Nate resigned. "Now right after this move, the family is going to move into another home. It's getting too dangerous living on the south side, especially after this move we're going to make, plus, we aren't dealing with Hector's contact anymore," he said.

"What happened?" I asked. "Nate feels we can make and grow the stuff on our own, the reefer I mean. In addition, it's more economical for the family to go it alone on the reefer. However, we'll be selling a new product not yet out on the market full force," Jon said.

"Will our reefer be as good as Hector's contact?" I asked.

"Oh, yeah, maybe better. I got a better recipe, if you will, for making it, and with this new product, we won't need to sell too much reefer. This product is going to put us in an ivory tower, G!" Nate said.

"What is it?" "Well, it's a synthetic form of cocaine in rock form. Its street name is crack rock or crack cocaine. Motherfuckers are dying to get this shit, G! With the powder, people would order and come back in maybe a day or so and order more, right? Well, with this shit, G, they buy the shit and smoke and come back in an hour! Now, Jon and I have played with the numbers and if we can get the entire south side, we can be worth about fifty million in a matter of two to three years!" Nate said excitedly.

"I don't know, Nate, anything that has people that hooked, can have the potential to destroy an entire community. The powder was bad enough, but if this stuff is as bad as the propaganda I'm hearing, it can be fatal to the black community or any other community, for that matter," I said.

"Why should we care about that? Do you think any of the other drug dealers care about that shit, G? Do you think these drug pharmaceutical companies care if people are hooked on valium or painkillers? Do you think the tobacco industry cares how many people die each year from lung cancer? Do you think Seagram or Anheuser

Busch cares about how many people die in drunken driving accidents or cirrhosis of the liver? None of them give a fuck, G. They're in it for the profit, and so will we!" Nate said emphatically.

Strangely, Nate had a point. In a land of Capitalism, it seems the driving force is to capitalize at whomever or whoever's expense. "Okay, you win, Nate, but how will we produce the stuff? Do we have another contact?" I asked.

"Well, yes and no. We have a guy who knows how to mass produce the crack cocaine and is willing to teach us how, for a price, which leads me to my next topic, G. Like I said, the family is going to move into a new home, somewhere away from Chicago, but not too far that we can't closely monitor our business," Nate explained.

"Just how far are you talking, Nate?" I asked curiously.

"New Lenox," he said flatly.

As the waitress brought our food, there was a period of silence as we all prepared our food for eating. Nate seasoned his favorite T-bone steak medium well over medium eggs and grits, Jon jellied his English muffin and prepared his coffee and hardboiled eggs.

"You ever been out there, G? It's beautiful and largely pristine," he said.

"Nah, this is my first time hearing about it. Where is it exactly?"

"Right next to Joliet, out Interstate 80 West, not that far of a drive. We can run our business from there and be inconspicuous; we'll even be in a different county. We'll do all of our business from there; however, not even a joint will be sold in New Lennox. Everything will go straight to Chicago," he said as he took a bite of his steak.

"Nate has been building a house out there for us that you won't believe. It's large enough for all of us to live, and then some," Jon added.

"When can I see it?" I asked.

"Today, right after we finish eating, then we can go to the cemetery like we planned," Nate said.

As we finished eating, we small talked about a few things. Jon mentioned that Nate spent somewhere in the neighborhood of 1.5 million for the house, much of what we had left, with only about one-hundred thousand left to operate on. I strongly disagreed with that, but it was a good idea to get out of Chicago. With the Gangster Disciples breathing down our neck, Nate could have been killed at any time. Word on the street was that Titus had placed a fifty thousand dollar bounty on Nate's head. Nate heard about it and laughed, "That motherfucker probably doesn't even have fifty thousand dollars!" he joked.

Soon we were finished, paid our bill, and started out of the door. We barely got out of the door before a familiar face we hadn't seen in a while approached us.

"Well, hello, fellas long time-no-see. How have you been?" It was Officer Diane Jackson. Someone we hadn't seen since the death of our friend Donnel some four years ago.

"Well, I can't say that it's good to see you, but I've been good. What about yourself?" Nate said sarcastically.

"Pretty good. I've been promoted to Detective, and life has been good, but I do have one small problem, though. Maybe you guys could help me out," she said.

"Well, we don't have time. We've gotta go," I said.

"Oh, you've got a minute, Derrick. I was just coming to get breakfast and I ran right into you guys. How ironic? You guys ever heard of a guy named Lawrence Caldwell?" she asked.

"Can't say that we have," Nate said.

"Well, maybe you know him by his street name Larry C. Does that ring a bell?"
Nate hesitated, because he didn't know how to respond, so I rang in.
"Oh, Larry. Yeah, we know him. He's a pretty cool guy, why?" I asked.
"Well, he's a real cool guy now. He's dead. Somebody gave him a Columbian Necktie in the park a couple of months ago. You know anything about that, Nathan?" she asked.
"Wow, that's terrible. Larry was a nice guy, too, but no, I don't know anything about that at all," Nate said.

"Now that's interesting because a couple of people said they saw you playing basketball with him not more than an hour before he was killed. You know anything about that, Nathan? You know about playing basketball with Larry about a couple of months ago?" she asked.

"Maybe, I play a lot of basketball with a lot of guys, so maybe, maybe not, but maybe it's all just neighborhood talk," Nate said.
"There's a lot of neighborhood talk about you, Nathan. Some people in the neighborhood are saying that you're one of the biggest drug distributors on the south side. There's talk on the street about your involvement in a territorial power struggle with the Gangster Disciples.

Word on the street is you're growing stronger and stronger with each passing month. Talk is that you and Derrick here live off drug money. Have you heard any of that talk, Nathan?" she asked.

"No, but then again, I don't have to hear it, cause it's ridiculous. Do I look like a big time drug distributor, Detective? I drive an '81 Chevy. My friends here don't drive at all; they ride with me. Do I dress like a major drug distributor? I certainly don't live like one. I live in a two flat off Indiana Street, but then I assume you already know that. But let me ask you this, have you come up with any leads or arrests for my friend Donnell's murder? No, you haven't. He's been dead four years and there have been no leads, charges filed or arrests. So while you're running around here listening to rumors, maybe you should finish the case you started four years ago," Nate said agitated.

"Nathan, I was taken off that case four years ago. Don't you think for a minute had I still been on the case there would be no leads or arrests by now!" she said equally agitated.

"You know what I think, Detective? I think you and the Chicago Police Department are full of shit. You pick your battles. No one's gonna find out who killed Donnell, just like no one is gonna find out who killed Larry C, because no one cares. They are just a couple of dead black boys here in the inner city. Oh, you'll ask some questions, maybe even harass a couple of people, but nothing will become of it. Hundreds of young black men are murdered right here in the community each year, and it's always the same story, no leads, no charges filed, no arrests," Nate said smugly.

"You smug son of a bitch, this isn't about me or the Chicago Police Department. It's about you. Now, you may or may not be a drug distributor, but I believe you had something to do with that kid's murder, and I'm gonna find out what," she said angrily.

"Okay, Detective, you do that, but come back to me when you have something real and substantial. Until then, you deal with my lawyer, and stay away from me! Let's go, fellas," Nate said.

As we were walking away, Nate told me that maybe we should go to the house later that night.

He thought that maybe the police would be tailing us. Detective Jackson was telling the truth. She had been taken off Donnell's murder case, but she never said why. First, she was a low ranking officer at the time, and she had proven to be a little over zealous and too passionate for the case. Donnell was one of the first kids murdered in Chicago at the time, and some of the interviews she gave and people she questioned turned out to be a little obtuse and abrasive. The Chicago Police Department could not afford the negative press and public relations, so they took her off the case. By the time they assigned someone else, hot leads started to turn cold. By then, Titus had already left town, and he was never subpoenaed to court anyway. Like Nate said, Donnell turned out to be just another black kid murdered, without anyone being charged for it. Soon, other kids started getting in trouble and were murdered, and people started to forget about Donnell. Besides, his family gave up on the case and relocated to another state and started over, so that was that. Detective Jackson was a bulldog, I knew she wouldn't give up until she had us on something. From that point on, all of us had to be careful.

Later that night, Jon suggested driving to New Lenox so I could see the house.

"How am I going to see a house at night, Jon? It's too dark! I hate night driving!" I said.

"It's cool man. I got the keys and the lights are on. We should make a go of it. I can't wait for you to see it," Jon said, almost giddy.

"I don't know, Jon. What if that broad Jackson is out there lurking around? It might be too risky," Mike suggested. "Fuck it, let's go. It ain't no law against driving to see a house," Nate interjected.

Jon nodded in agreement, lit a joint and went to start up the car.

"Should we take Dana with us?" I asked Nate.

"Yeah, probably. I just don't want to tell her anything yet," Nate said.

"How is she working out?" I asked.

"Cool, She's been running a few errands for me here and there, you know, taking care of things. She's been asking a lot of questions, though."

"Maybe you better let her in on what's going on, Nate. If she's gonna roll with us, you gotta let her know what's up," I suggested.

"Yeah, maybe we'll tell her tonight at the house. What do you think?" he asked.

"You're the boss," I said plainly.

"Hey, let's go. The car is warm enough. What the fuck are you guys waiting for?" Jon asked, obviously high already.

As soon as we all got into the car, he put in a War tape and we got rolling. I kept checking on Jon the whole drive. I knew he was high, and I didn't want him falling asleep at the wheel. "Maybe we should let Mike drive, Jon. You've been smoking," I suggested.

"Fuck you, G. I can handle my shit. Everything's gonna   be   cool.   Just   relax," Jon shot back.

Nate looked at me and smiled. He loved to see Jon high. He felt Jon was his coolest after a joint or two.

"Where the fuck are we going?" Dana asked.

"To our new home out in New Lenox. We thought you'd like to check it out with us," Nate said.

"You bought a house big enough for all of us to live in?" she asked curiously.

"Sure why not? We're getting a little tight where we're at now, don't you think?" Nate said.

"It ain't no section eight fix up shit, is it? Cause I ain't doing no hammering and nailing and shit!" she insisted.

Nate laughed and began to tell her about our "business." He told her all of the details and how things were handled. He also explained that if she divulged any of that information, it would get her killed. She didn't seem surprised or taken aback by any of it; she seemed to fit right into the fold. She told us that her father peddled a little reefer back in his day. Just nickel bags, nothing big time. The only thing that seemed strange about her was the fact that she seemed totally devoid of feelings. I mean, we knew she had them, but she rarely showed them. She led us to believe that she was totally hard-core, and that showing feelings and emotion was for suckers and lames. I think with her upbringing and the horrors she was exposed to made her shut down emotionally, completely. The only time I ever saw her express emotion without reservation was when she spoke of her younger sister. She would go and visit her religiously every Saturday at the mental hospital, and spend at least three hours there with her. That was something she got squared away with Nate when she joined us. She told him that wasn't negotiable. Anyway, Nate didn't mind, he actually admired her for her loyalty to her sister. But Dana was just like that. She could kill a person with no remorse. I think maybe it might've had something to do with her father and his sexual abuse of

155

her and her sister. I believe all of those years of abuse burned the one thing in all of us that makes us care and love our fellow man, that something is called a heart. We were the only thing in her life that even resembled family. Everyone else she came in contact with was either afraid of her or flat out hated her for one reason or another. She stayed to herself for years and loosely involved herself in fugitive hunting. She hated the idea of being a bounty hunter. She despised the restraint of it all. If Dana collard a criminal, she wanted to be able to beat him down, and be verbally abusive, but law enforcements strongly discouraged it. She would tell us that during her years as a bounty hunter she'd beat the hell out of some of the guys, so much that many departments wouldn't employ her. Her violent ways actually started to cost her clients! There was one particular guy she told us about who she chased all the way to Phoenix, Arizona. She walked into a pub there and he took off running from her. After shooting him in the back of the leg to impair him, she proceeded to break his jaw, break two of his ribs and punctured a lung. When the paramedics finally arrived, they had to resuscitate the guy to keep him from dying! When we asked her why did she do all of that, she simply replied, "The motherfucker shouldn't have made me chase him!"

Needless to say that most law enforcement agencies don't want criminals that they have to hospitalize for weeks before they can bring them to trial, so she lost clients. She was a third degree black belt in Judo and Karate, and she was one of the strongest broads I ever met. Factor that in with a woman who has it in for men, and ice in her veins, and you have a force to deal with! Still, we loved her just the same. Nate always joked that if he ever got into a scrap with her, she would be one broad he would have to shoot right out of the gate!

As we pulled into the driveway, seeing the house for the first time, to say we were all impressed was an understatement, we were floored! This house was magnificent. It was an estate-sized home somewhere in the neighborhood of nine thousand square feet. Complete with eight bedrooms, six bathrooms, twelve-foot ceilings, marble floors and walls, full terraces in some of the bedrooms, eight foot French doors overlooking a fountain and courtyard, a gated wine room, four gas fireplaces, a workout room, inside basketball court, indoor pool, game room, steam rooms, a gourmet kitchen, a butlers quarters and many other amenities. The house was breathtaking!

"How did you do it, Nate?" Mike asked.

"I've never seen a house this big before!" Dana said, running through several rooms.

"I told you G, isn't it something?" Jon asked.

I just stood in the middle of the dining room with my mouth open. Nate stood in the middle of the room grinning and beaming with pride. He seemed to be happy that we were happy.

"Is this house paid for?" I asked. "Everything except the taxes. Nate had the construction people building this house for about a year," Jon said.

There was hardwood flooring everywhere, and in every room there was a different shade of hardwood. All of the kitchen cabinets were solid oak, with marble countertops. There were balconies, a spiral staircase and cathedral ceilings.

"Nate, how did you do this?" I asked in amazement.

"Planning, G.   With good planning, you can do whatever you want if you plan for it. I knew we'd need a new location, so Jon and I started planning, making calls and investing time, and here it is," Nate said.

"Whose name is it under; I mean who's the registered owner?" Mike asked.

"The owners on the title are Mr. and Ms. Ira Epstein. They were real estate developers," Jon explained. "They were? Where are they now?" Dana asked.

"They're dead; they died in a fire about two or three years ago," Jon said.

"Well, isn't somebody gonna check that shit out? I mean, what if we get busted?" Mike asked.

"We worked all of that out with the real estate company and the developers. I mean, we paid 2.5 million dollars for this place in cash. Why would they want to keep us from getting it? Also, one of my relatives actually helped out with the sale and paperwork. It's all legit," Jon reasoned.

Jon was good at that sort of thing, coming from a family of bankers and all. Jon was always good with numbers. His father owned his own bank, and his uncle and aunt were successful real estate bankers. He had a cousin who was a bank president somewhere. His whole family was into the banking business. Jon knew how to make money appear and disappear. He knew how to make the right investments to triple the money in short period of time. Jon was the type of person, where if someone found five-hundred thousand dollars, he would know how to allow you to spend it and hide it from the IRS, at the same time. He used to always say, "This country was founded on washing money. You just have to know how to do it within the channels of the law." When we'd sit around talking politics and how we hated Republicans, Jon used to say, "Most poor people hate Republicans until they become rich." Jon was such a

financier that I don't ever remember him having a job.
He got his first bank account at five years old, and his
first mutual fund portfolio at nine, and the guy always
made money. He used to live off his investments. Jon
only had one problem, though. He hated school. His
parents sent him to DePaul University to study
Economics. Jon spent most of his time getting high and
partying; he just wasn't the school type. When he
flunked out of DePaul, his father pulled some strings and
got him into University of Illinois at Chicago. Soon Jon
flunked out there also, prompting his family to cut him
off and disown him. Jon was always the type I thought
should have his own business, maybe be an entrepreneur.
I mean, the guy knew money; he just was never going to
be the type to get a degree. I didn't know the full extent
of Jon's expertise with money until I cornered him about
the financing on the estate. "Tell the truth, Jon, how the
hell did you and Nate get the money for all of this? We
didn't have that kind of money a year ago," I asked.

"Well, between you and me, we had investors," he
said smiling.

"What do you mean investors? We don't have any
investors?" I replied.

Jon was pretty vague. Later he confessed that he and
Nate paid a banker to electronically cipher fifty thousand
dollars out of various accounts around the country and
deposit them into an account for us. As soon as the
check to the real estate company and the construction
company cleared, he closed the account. I mean, these
were accounts of wealthy people; they weren't going to
miss fifty thousand dollars. I mean, he was an expert
with money, so much so, even other drug czars used to
ask for Jon's assistance with money matters. Of course,
Nate never obliged, but they always asked. Jon was an
integral part of the family; he kept us all cohesive

financially, with Nate's strong guidance, of course. Jon never got involved with the other aspects of the family, not directly, anyway. Nate wanted Jon to concentrate his efforts on keeping us all rich, and he did that well. He had a girlfriend whom he would see from time to time, but he never introduced her to us. It was part of Nate's rule of no outsiders. We knew of her, but she knew nothing of us or what Jon did for a living. Jon didn't mind. He knew some of the stuff we were into, and frankly, he wanted to protect her from that, especially when she turned up pregnant. I never saw her except from afar but he would talk to me about her pretty often. He told me her name was Theresa, and that he knew her from grade school. He said he bought her a house in Orland Park, and would go there from time to time to make sure she was doing well. He also said she was a stockbroker, and she wanted them to be married. They would have little spats about it, but Jon always felt he shouldn't marry a woman because of his line of work. "What kind of example would I set for a kid, G?" He would often ask me.

I always knew of their little arguments. Nate had all of the phones in the housed bugged, and he had me bug Theresa's house, too. This was Nate's way of knowing a little bit about everyone in the family. Nate had everybody's boyfriends, fiancées, girlfriends and parents' phones bugged, for security reasons. No one knew about it besides Nate and me, but I suspect everyone knew our house phones were bugged. It was all part of intelligence, so Nate would know when or if someone flipped against the family. No one took it personally; that's just how things were. He strongly discouraged us from talking on the phone, anyway. He told us to always keep phone conversations brief and general. He told us that state and federal wiretaps had sunk many mob figures over the years, and that we should always be cognizant of what we say over the phone. To be extra certain, he had a message engraved over every phone in the house that read "Loose lips sink ships," but Nate never talked on the phone. If we had something to tell him, we had to tell him in his ear, especially if it was incriminating. I remember once stopping at a gas station so Mike could tell Nate about a change in plan for a "pickup." Mike used a random pay phone to call him, and when Nate answered the phone, Mike started going into the details of the arrangement and Nate hung up. So, Mike called back and Nate hung up again. Mike gave me a strange look, and tried again. This time Nate said, "Motherfucker you got the wrong number!" Mike, came back to the car seemingly bewildered and told me about Nate's strange actions.

"Mike, you know Nate ain't gonna talk to you about that shit over no payphone!" I said disgusted.

When we got to Nate, he was livid. "Hey, Mike, what the fuck are you thinking? Don't ever call me and talk to me about that kind of shit over no phone again!" he said sternly.

"It was a random pay phone. The feds can't tap a payphone---"

"Fuck that shit man. Don't give me that shit. You aint no lawyer, so don't quote the law to me. You don't know what the fuck the feds can and cannot do!" Nate shouted.

"My fault, my fault, man, I'm sorry. My bad," Mike resigned.

Mike didn't mean any harm; that's just how he was. It took a while for Mike to learn how to function criminally. Mike was always a tough guy, but he as well as all of us, had to learn the ways of the criminal life. Mike, like us, grew up around crime, but he and his brother Peter were never exactly involved in the life. Their parents died in car accidents, so their grandmother raised them. Mike was always so much bigger than the rest of us. He always had the other boys afraid of him. Nate used to tell me how he met Mike in the first grade, and how they've been friends ever since. According to Nate, Mike always sort of looked up to Nate, because Nate had a mom and nice clothes and money, even if it was only a couple of quarters. Mike's grandmother was on disability, and she used to get assistance from the state to help take care of Mike and Peter. I imagine it was an uphill battle raising two boys in the inner city at her age. Mike was six when he and Peter went to live with their grandmother, and Peter was just three. Their parents died unexpectedly, so there was no money set aside for them. In the old days, people used to make fun of Mike and Pete because they wore clothes from the Salvation Army, and hand me downs from other families, but that was all their grandmother could afford. Nate used to tell me how he would stick up for Mike and they would have to fight on the way home from school sometimes, but it made them best of friends. It also honed Mike's skills for fighting. By the time I met him, that guy had more battle scars than an Army veteran. Fighting was never a big thing for Mike. He was used to it; it was no big deal. If a guy got disrespectful or out of line, Mike beat him down. No matter how big or strong a guy was, Mike took him on. Of course, it would be hard to find a guy bigger or stronger than Mike, standing six feet- four and two-hundred seventy pounds, but it didn't matter. I remember one time a guy got out of line with Nate at a craps game and Mike broke the guy's jaw with one punch. Mike was a real tough guy, but Peter was the mouth of the two. Peter wasn't as big as Mike, but Pete was the kind of guy who could talk a person into anything. He genuinely had the gift of gab. When we were growing up, Peter would talk himself into jobs he knew he could not perform and then quit after he got the first check. It was hilarious. Once when we were kids, Pete was caught by the police with a box full of illegal explosive just before Independence Day. Pete got them from a guy in Indiana, and was going to sell them for a little pocket cash. The police nabbed him in the alley, cuffed him, and placed him in the squad car. We watched the whole thing from our bedroom window, Pete sat back there and talked and talked, after about twenty minutes not only did the police cut him loose, but they gave him money for fireworks! This guy was an incredible talker, who could bullshit his way out of or into anything. Pete and Mike were an interesting couple of guys. Pete would talk himself into a fight, and Mike would have to end up fighting for him. Because of Pete's ability to negotiate well, Nate told him to work with me in intelligence, but later that was changed because Nate needed someone to oversee the large production operation of the crack cocaine that had to be made. Pete didn't know the first thing about drugs, much less mass production, but Nate didn't trust anyone else. I flew the idea of Dana overseeing it, but Nate said she was too valuable to him in security and enforcement. "Nate man, I want to do this thing for you but I don't know anything about coke man, I don't know shit," Pete said. "You can learn, I have a guy who will teach you all you need to know, don't worry. Plus you will have a crew working with you that has experience with the drug. It will all work out, don't worry," Nate assured. Before long, Pete went to the library and researched books on cocaine, asked different people in the neighborhood, and even sent off for documentaries on the drug. He amazingly taught himself everything about cocaine, and soon he was an expert. Nate admired Pete's diligence, but never told him about it. Nate always said as soon as you give a guy a compliment, it seems he then starts to slack off. Nate hooked Pete up with a guy named Lollie, who had done a twelve-year bid downstate for possession with intent. This guy taught Pete everything, how to "cut" cocaine, and what to "cut" it with, how to "package" it, even how to negotiate with big time guys on purchasing. Between Pete's self-education, and this guy's acquired knowledge, Pete knew all he needed to know. Lollie spent hours and days with Pete, giving him street knowledge and "powder" knowledge. We all started to like Lollie. He hung out with us at the house, played cards with us and everything. We all used to sit up for hours at night while Lollie shared stories about prison, and the drug game, it was great. I particularly liked him because Lollie was older and had a wealth of knowledge and wisdom. He used to say, "G, you're gonna do great things before it's over, 'cause you got something these other guys don't have, insight. You have the gift to see things before they happen." I don't think he meant I was psychic, just smart enough to look ahead, that's all. One night, we sat up for hours talking about God, and intelligent design versus evolution. I could talk to him about stuff I wouldn't dare talk to the others about; he and I were compatible mentally. One day I asked him how he ended up in prison. "Just a stupid kid I guess G, I wish I would have applied my knowledge to something else, but I didn't. Now I am fifty-eight and nowhere to go. Sometimes I swear I am terrified, G. Don't you make that mistake, you get the hell out of this game, it's a dead end, G. I don't want to see what happened to me happen to you," he said. He made me promise him I would get out and I did. I really started to look up to him as a man, a man who admitted he made mistakes, but refused to make excuses.

He gave me a list of books to read, books he knew I would like. I waited about a week or so and purchased them. I had been dragging my feet with it and he told me procrastination was a demon, so I was excited about finally getting them to show him I had finally done it. "Hey Dana, where is Lollie, I can't find him around anywhere?" I asked. "Oh he's gone," she said flatly. "What do you mean gone?" I questioned. "You know, G, he's gone, you know...gone," she said. "What...what do you mean?" I said slightly confused. "G, he's gone...that's it he's gone, I thought you knew?" she asked. Then it hit me. "You motherfucker, you lousy motherfuckers!" I yelled throwing the books at her and storming out of the room. "Hey nigga, wait a minute, wait!" she screamed. I ran to Nate's room and flung the door open. "What the fuck did you guys do to Lollie, and don't fucking lie to me Nate!" I shouted. "G, wait a minute just relax and calm down...," Nate said. "I am calm. What did you guys do to him, Nate? I want to know now. Dana said he's gone, what the fuck does that mean gone, what is that?" I asked. Nate glared at Dana. "Everyone, get out! I want to talk to G a minute, give us a minute please," Nate said. I felt everyone looking at me as they walked out of the room, I kept my eyes glued to Nate, I wasn't going to accept any of his bullshit this time. Nate let out a deep exhale, and spoke. "Ok G, Lollie is dead," he said in an admitting fashion. I slumped down on the couch and put my head in my hands. "We had to G, he was a security risk, he knew too much," Nate tried to reason. "The old guy was just trying to help us Nate, just trying to fit in and change. You were playing him the whole time, weren't you? You knew the whole time you were gonna kill him, didn't you?" I asked sincerely. Nate looked around the room uncomfortably. "G, I liked Lollie too, but he was a drug dealer just like us, that's all he was ever gonna be, you know that," Nate said. "Maybe, but you didn't give him an option did, you Nate?" I asked him. "And as far as him being a drug dealer, did you ever talk to him, Nate? I mean really talk to him, did you ever ask him what his dreams were, or his plans for the future? Did you ever ask him if he had family, or children? Did you ever ask him about anything other than drugs? No you didn't, you didn't give a damn. You just used him and killed him," I said looking at him in disgust. "No, I didn't ask him about anything but drugs, because that's what I do, G. I'm a drug dealer, that's what the fuck I do, that's what the fuck you do! I don't know if he had any kids, or if he had a wife or a mistress, or a dog or a cat or any of that bullshit. If I were a fucking biographer or an interviewer I would have asked him, but I am a drug dealer so I have to do that thing! I know you liked Lollie, G, I know you had established a rapport with him, and I understand and respect that. But let me give you some advice, and you better heed it, this is the life we have chosen, don't get close to anyone, G. Motherfuckers are disposable in this life, they're here today, gone tomorrow. So, don't get attached, ok? We are drug dealers, two brothers in the game trying to live until tomorrow. Don't ever forget that. You actually thought I was gonna let him live, G, knowing all that he knew about us. You had to know that there was no way he was gonna live. Now, I'm sorry you had to find out the way you did, but it's done, G, let it go," Nate advised. I felt lousy the rest of the day, but there was a ring of truth to what Nate said. Once we chose this life, we lost certain things; we gave up a lot to have a lot, and to many of us that had not sunk in yet. Later that night, Nate called a meeting, "I want everyone to listen to me, G was pretty broken up about what happened to Lollie, and I understand that, he's still pretty broke up about it. I don't like to see my brother like that; I don't want to see any of you like that, so I am instituting a rule. You don't have to follow it, it's up to you. I strongly discourage any attachments to anyone outside of the people that are in this room. Don't get close to anyone, people, it's the price we pay for the life we have chosen. People in this game are disposable, they are here today, gone tomorrow, and attachments cause problems, problems I don't need. So I'm warning everyone, don't get close to anybody," Nate said. "We can't have boyfriends or girlfriends, how are we supposed to get our freak on?" Dana asked. "Sure you can have friends and screw Dana, but keep it light, don't get serious with anyone, cause they could be gone the next day," Nate explained. "But what kind of fucking life is that?" Jon asked. "It's the fucking life you chose, Jon, it's the fucking life we all chose, live with it," Nate said coldly. We all looked at each other in disbelief. "We are a family, and family sticks together, no outsiders, ever. You are to trust no one outside of the family, and your loyalty is to the family first, anyone that tries it another way will suffer hurt, pain, and dire consequences, that's the rule," Nate instructed. Nevertheless, it was a rule no human could possibly follow, it was a rule that would cause even Nate hurt and spell our demise someday. Later I heard they found Lollie's body in an alley in Englewood badly decomposed with rats and dogs around him and a needle hanging out of his arm. Nate had told Dana to give Lollie a "hot dose." In the end, the way I saw it, he died like an animal, no man should die that way, but Lollie would certainly not be the last victim of the "Family."

CHAPTER 7

Bloodbath

Nate loved baseball, he always said he wanted to play professional ball, before all of this drug stuff happened. As I walked into the room, he happened to be watching his favorite team, the White Sox. I remember him always watching the games on television, yelling and cursing the television during the game. This time was no different. "Damn it, stop watching the first fucking pitch asshole, it's always gonna be a strike!" he yelled. "Nate, you ready to talk?" I asked quietly, he never liked to be interrupted during a game. "Hold on, G, it's over in a minute, these guys just cannot play ball for nine innings to save their lives." As the California Angels recorded the final out defeating his beloved White Sox, Nate threw a shoe at the television and cursed. "Fuck, that's two in a row, two losses in a row, G, these motherfuckers, are gonna give me a heart attack!" he said sternly. As I stood there, Big Mike, Dana, Pete, and Jon walked in the room. I motioned for them to be quiet as they all took seats. Nate listened to the commentator giving remarks for a moment and made his final comment. "Bullshit, the Sox aren't World Series material, faggot. They'll never win the World Series because Chicago don't support them," he griped. He was in a bad mood as he always was when the Sox lost. He flipped the television off and took a seat. "Ok G, you got the floor, but before you start I'd like to make an announcement. I'm making Dana a Capo and giving her a regime. Everyone looked shocked and surprised, especially Mike. "I made my decision based on how well she has performed for me and I need one more regime, I want Mike's group to work specifically on security. Mike, that's no slight on your part, but I need someone like Dana to handle enforcement," Nate said. "What's up Nate, I thought you wanted me to handle that stuff, why am I out?" Mike asked. "No offense, Mike, but Dana is a killer and you are not. I need someone more aggressive to handle some of the things I need done over the next few months. When it comes to security you are the best no doubt about it, but you don't have the stomach for what we are about to get involved in, you understand, don't you?" Nate asked. "Yeah, whatever you say Nate, I don't agree but you're the boss," Mike said. "What about that don't you agree with?" Nate asked. "Well Nate, Dana is still fairly new, does she have a full understanding of what we do here yet?" Mike asked. "She understands enough to me," Nate replied. Then Dana ringed in. "With all due respect, boss, maybe Mike is right, not that I am not flattered by it all but maybe I need more time," Dana said respectfully. "The switch is made and it will stand," Nate said finally. "Are you sure you want to do that, Nate? I mean Dana doesn't sound comfortable with the move," I said to make Dana accept the position. I knew Dana was uncomfortable with it, but her aggressive nature would not allow her to be "punked" in a room full of men. It worked. "No, G, I can handle it, I just wanted to make sure you guys really wanted to give me the position," Dana said. This move I totally agreed with Nate on. We were about to make a huge move and needed someone to handle the aggressive moves that we needed done. Dana was the person to handle these moves because she could kill with no remorse, we weren't sure if Mike could handle it for the long haul. "Ok, G, it's your show let's have it," Nate said. "Well, we need as many G.D's as we can that sell on the south side to congregate in one place at one time, now I have set up the intelligence to make it to happen, but we're gonna need a little more money than I expected," I said. "How much are you talking?" Nate asked cautiously. "About fifteen thousand to be exact," I said. "I don't know, G, why do we need that much?" Nate asked. "Because I have a few cops that need to be greased, and an informant that has to be paid, they are part of the con. We have to be very careful with this, if we are found out this thing can blow up in our faces," I warned. "Well how is all of this shit gonna go down, G?" Nate asked slightly frustrated. "Well, my informant is a close confidant to the G.D's, and we're going to give him a few thousand to throw a party for the south side dealers at an apartment near Hyde Park. Two of the cops that I have on payroll are going to be allegedly providing security for the south side dealers. They are going to let the dealers know where the party is going to be and when everything will go down. I even hired a few strippers to "perform" there, to make it look authentic. The "party" will start near midnight. My informant will make sure that everything is festive and the atmosphere is authentic. When all of the marks are in place, a little fun and frolic will commence. At about two a.m., Dana and a select crewmember will come in, mingle with the partygoers and position themselves at strategic areas near the doors and windows so no one has a chance to escape. My informant has already placed five AK-47s, two AR-15s, and a couple of UZI's under couches, and in other areas of the apartment. The women and the alcohol will be used to get them all relaxed, once they are, Dana and the crew will kill them all," I said. "Good, can we trust the informant and the cops?" Nate asked. "Yeah, I got them on tape agreeing to help us with this and I also have them on videotape getting high with Dana and Jon, playing cards and other incriminating stuff, they'll play along," I explained. "What about your informant, G?" Nate asked. "The informant's name is Pookie, he's been aching to join us and we have a complete background on him, he did a little stint in the county jail for possession, plus we told him if he fucks up we'll kill his little girl, I think he's cool," I assured Nate. He stared at me and looked around the room thinking. "Ok, G, run with it, but if anything goes wrong, Dana, I want you to murder that Pookie motherfucker, and everyone else in the room; cops and all, understand?" Nate advised. "You got it," Dana replied. On the night of the party everything went as planned, and almost too well. The south side dealers bit so easily, it made me nervous, they completely trusted Pookie, and he didn't disappoint. On that night, Dana and a few desperados murdered about fifteen to twenty dealers of the Gangster Disciples in an effort to solidify our hold on the south side. The newspapers dubbed it "Mass Homicide in Hyde Park." The newspaper showed the gruesome pictures of the crime scene. There were bullet holes in all of the walls; blood spattered everywhere and dead bodies in abundance. I remember Nate telling Dana before going to the party to make sure there were no survivors, and that he wanted the people to look like hamburger meat. Dana didn't disappoint. Many of the guys were so badly shot that some of their body parts had to be "bagged" separately. The murder scene was a bloody mess, the Chicago police tried to brush for prints but weren't very successful. The place looked like a southern slaughterhouse. The Gangster Disciples were rumored to be livid, and vowed to get even with Nate and the family, but we were way ahead of them. The night after the massacre Nate moved us to New Lenox. "G, make sure Dana is out of visibility, while we are on this move, I don't want her "fingered" by anyone," Nate insisted. The street sales were through the roof, some of the older people wanted the powder cocaine, and many of the younger kids still loved the reefer, but everyone loved crack! We couldn't sell it fast enough. Just as Nate predicted, people bought, went and got high and came right back in a matter of minutes! The sale of crack totally financed our move and much of our operations, the powder and refer served as extra cash. Jon had a staff of about eight people whose job was just to count cash all day! I mean there were stacks of cash piled up to near six feet at one time. I approached Nate on why we were keeping that kind of money around the house. "What would you propose, G, maybe putting it in a bank?" Nate asked. "Well, maybe some of the other guys in the business have gotten pretty good deals with banks maybe we should try," I proposed. "Why, G, so some banker can charge me a quarter on a dollar to keep it, no thanks. I'll just keep my shit here in the house," he insisted. We lived in a massive home, an estate really, and Nate's theory was, why shouldn't we take advantage of it? So Nate had a room constructed just to house our cash, there was cash slotted into the walls and the floor! I don't know how he did it, but the walls and the floor looked like they were made of one-hundred dollar bills. There were walls on wheels that you could turn a handle and they would roll, he actually had tracks built into the floor, it was amazing. Jon would stay up all night with his staff counting and wrapping the money. Each stack comprised of about two-hundred thousand dollars. After they were compressed together, Jon and his staff wrapped the stack in heavy-duty wax paper. They had some type of instrument to suck all of the air out, to keep it airtight for storage. The stack was then slid into slots into the wall. Of course, no one was allowed into the room, only Jon, Nate and I knew where the room was, or that a cash room even existed. Jon even had the room humidified and the temperature regulated. We were getting about twenty-five thousand dollars a night in that house, more than enough to go around. Nate decided to pay Dana and Mike one million dollars a year, but pay them weekly which came to about twenty-thousand dollars. Jon wanted to be paid one percent of the total profits a year per week, which completely pissed Nate off. "You gotta be kidding me, that's sixty-eight thousand dollars a week, there ain't no way we are paying Jon that kind of fucking money, G. You go tell that motherfucker, to put the joint down and get real!" I didn't say anything to Nate; I knew he was pissed off. Instead, I tried to reason with Jon. "C'mon Jon, you know that's a lot of cash, way more than we are paying the Capos. It's just not fair," I reasoned. "G, fuck the Capos, you know I am invaluable to this family, my worth far exceeds the worth of the Capos. You and Nate could easily find someone to kill and beat up people, but those motherfuckers would be lost in the fucking count room and you know it!" Jon said angrily. I could see two things, first Jon was already high, which meant there was no reasoning in him, and two Jon had started to "smell himself" a little too much, so I put him on ice for a while. "Ok Jon, give me a day or so and I will talk to Nate and we will all have a sit down and work this thing out. Just give me a couple of days, ok?" I asked. "Whatever man," Jon responded. Now I had to soften Nate up. As arrogant as Jon was, he did have a point. He was invaluable to the family, but I don't know if it was sixty eight thousand dollars worth a week. This was going to be a tough negotiation process to say the least. "As far as I'm concerned, he's out of his mind, G. We can't afford to pay him that kind of fucking money and you know it,"

Nate said. "I know, I know but we have to meet him half way, Nate. We can't just tell him no," I reasoned. "Why the fuck not? I mean he ain't trying to reason with us. He's just being the typical white man, gouge the niggas and let the chips fall where they may!" Nate said frustrated. "You know Jon ain't like that, you know he loves us all Nate," I responded. "Yeah I know, I just don't like this shit at all, G. Set up a meeting with him tonight and maybe we can find a way to work all of this out somehow," Nate said. Well we did, we agreed to pay Jon forty-four thousand a week- a number that had to be haggled upon for more than six hours! After the "negotiation," Nate and I agreed to keep everyone's salary a secret that way there would be no discrepancies. Soon everyone was satisfied with their money and Nate could get on with his business of running things. And boy were things running well. Nate set up a room in the lower level of the house to mass-produce the marijuana. Pete was placed in charge of it. Nate had researched all of what was needed. He had the room specially constructed for special lighting, water for irrigation, and a special device to keep the humidity in the room just right. Pete and the guys could grow about one-hundred pounds of marijuana in about sixty days, which would take at least four and a half months to grow outside. The room was huge, about twenty feet high and could only be entered through secret entrances, it was amazing! As if that was not amazing enough, the room designated to mass produce crack cocaine was out of this world! It was actually a laboratory! With the South Side under the Family's control, everyone getting paid and the house fully moved into, we were all set up to make our mark. We all got together at the house to have our usual game of Bid Whiz and to party. These were wild parties full of trash talking and extravagant betting, plenty of marijuana and alcohol, women, the hole nine yards. "Hey Nate, there's a couple of guys downstairs that claim to know you, what do you want me to do?" Dana asked. "Give me some names, Dana, I need some names!" Nate said frustrated. "Some cat named Fingers, and another older guy claiming to be your father! Dana exclaimed. Nate's eye lit up upon hearing about fingers, our long lost friend and running buddy, but was predictably confused about the old guy and the father thing. "Bring them both up, but frisk them first," Nate instructed. "Did you hear that, G? It's Fingers! I wonder where the hell he's been. Call Mike and tell him and Pete to get their asses up hear. I can't believe this!" Nate said with excitement. I guess Nate figured the older guy to be some crackpot, which he would easily dismiss.   Also, it was two-thirty in the morning, and he was a bit high. "Wow, I wonder if it is really him, Nate?" I asked. Just then, the door opened and low and behold, it was Fingers. We jumped and hugged each other with boyhood excitement. "Where have you been, nigga? We've been looking all over for you, what's been up?" Nate asked. "Yeah, Fingers where have you been, we thought you was in jail or something," I said. "I've been from boys home to boys' home, since eighty-five, and then I stayed with my aunt in Broadview. I tried to get in touch, but no one in the hood' knew where to find you guys. I see you all have been into something real big, huh?" Fingers said coyly. "Just a little something, that's all, we'll talk to you all about that later, but look at you, gained weight and shit. I see your aunt been feedin' you're skinny ass, huh?" Nate teased.   "Fuck you nigga," Fingers said slightly embarrassed. "Ah, that's my nigga. Dana, please get this man a drink or whatever else he wants. Hook him up," Nate said proudly. We all looked at Nate and looked back at the older man, and quickly looked back at Nate.

As Nate looked at the man, his demeanor quickly changed from that of joy and excitement over Fingers, to disdain and mistrust to the stranger. "Alright Nigga, what's your story?" Nate asked smugly. "I....I have no story Nathan, I am your father, I just wanted to see you. Boy! You have grown to be a handsome man, and successful, too, I see. Uh, I have some identification and some pictures of me and your mother." As the man reached for his wallet Dana and a few of her guys pulled out their guns and pointed them about two inches from his face. "Nigga, you ain't my father, my father died years ago, somebody get this clown ass nigga out of here," Nate said dismissively. "No, Nate, I think he is real man, he has pictures and everything, he owns a barber shop in Broadview. I used to go there and get my haircut and we found out we both knew you. We would talk about you and the old days for hours, it's cool man," Fingers said convincingly. Nate snatched the pictures out of the man's hand, as the older man looked down hurtfully. "Let's see what the fuck you got here," Nate said agitated. As I peeked over Nate's shoulder, sure enough they were pictures of mamma Williams, and Nate as a young baby, and another picture of mamma Williams pregnant with Nate and the older man holding her with his hand on her stomach. "What the fuck is your name, man?" Nate asked curiously. "Nathan Williams...Sr.," the man said. Nate motioned for Dana and the crew to put their weapons down. Everyone stood around looking at Nate to see what his response would be. "Ok, I believe you, so you're my father, so what? My mamma is dead, I haven't seen you and don't know you. Now you show up talking about I'm your father, now what the fuck am I supposed to do? Hug you and cry, I don't think so. What do you want, man?" Nate asked. "I just wanted to see you; I haven't seen you

176

since you were a baby, that's all," the man said. This was a sticky situation; frankly the man looked just like Nate, or vice-versa. Nate had to handle the situation well enough. He obviously had no feelings for the man, but he was also very intrigued by him and wanted to ask the man many questions. "Well, have a plate, sit down and have a drink. Dana, give him a drink. What are you drinking?" Nate asked. "Tom Collins, I'll have a Tom Collins," he said proudly. "What the fuck is that? I don't know how to fix that shit," Dana said. The whole room burst into laughter. "What do you know about Bid Whist old man?" Nate asked him. "I'm pretty good, I think I will watch," he replied. I didn't trust Nate in this matter; I felt he had something up his sleeve concerning the man. When no one was looking, he whispered to me. "Check this motherfucker out, G. He could be five-o for all we know." "I got you, but he does seem to be your father, and he looks just like you!" I added. "Nevertheless, check him out," Nate retorted. After careful checking, he did turn out to be Nate's father all right, and he had a pretty clean background. He did own a barbershop in Broadview like Fingers said. However, after careful digging, I found out that the reason he and mamma Williams broke up was he turned her on to prostitution, and he beat her from time to time. This I found out from a longtime friend of his named "Gator." You would be surprised what you can find out about people if the right sources are asked, and bribed. I could never tell Nate this information, though. Nate would kill him for sure. So I told him Nathan Sr. checked out, I felt whatever was in the past should stay in the past. "Gator" told me that back in those days Nathan Sr. was hooked on coke. After losing jobs, he could no longer pay for it outright, so he made a deal with the pusher that he would turn mamma Williams over to him for some coke "credit." According to "Gator," mamma Williams refused the first time and the dealer sent some goons over to the apartment and beat Nathan Sr. to a pulp. Mamma Williams was so in love with him and afraid they would kill him, so she gave in. After about a year or so of this, mamma Williams packed up Nate and disappeared. Nathan Sr. tried to find them, but couldn't. To keep from being murdered by the dealer, he threw himself into rehab under an anonymous name. When he got out, the dealer had been killed in a drug raid, so Nathan Sr. moved to Broadview cleaned up his life and never searched for his family again until he ran into Fingers. "Did he check out or what?" Nate asked. "Oh, yeah he's clean and he is your father. Now what are you gonna do? Personally, I think it's cool to have your dad around, don't you think?" I asked. "We'll see," Nate said

Things were going real well, the Family had total control of the entire south side of Chicago, our drugs were selling real well, and Nate and his father were getting along. They went to see the White Sox together, they went to Bulls games together, and sometimes they would sit up all night talking. I didn't get in the way, although I considered myself Nate's brother and Nate introduced me to his father as such. He even told his father my story on how we met and how close I was to him and mamma Williams. He told his father that he loved me like a brother. That made me feel special. Nate never told his father what we were into, although I believe Nathan Sr. figured it out on his own. He and I would talk from time to time and he said he didn't care what we did, he was just glad to get a second chance with Nate and it was all good. As luck would have it, our cocaine contact got busted by the cops and convicted; he wasn't in the "pen" two weeks before somebody killed him. Nate had already made contact with another supplier, some guy in Bolivia. He told me the guy was cool and that he was hooked up with a cartel over there. "I think we are gonna have to go to Bolivia, G. This guy wants to meet with us over there to check us out. I need you to check him out and this whole Bolivian connection with Dana before we leave. I want to leave after NBA championship run, sometime in late May. Is that enough time?" Nate asked. "Yeah, but why am I doing it with Dana?" I replied. "I thought you would want to have her around for security, you know?" he said. "Personally Nate, I don't care for her, she may do a good job and all, but she is reckless and short tempered. I would rather work with Mike and his people," I said. "Suit yourself, man. I'll keep Dana around for my security then." "You know, Nate, Mike is our friend, and you have kind of kicked him to the curb for Dana, like he ain't good enough or something. What's up with that?" I asked. "Nothing, G, it's just that I respect Mike and Dana will do shit that I just don't want Mike to do that's all. Shit that I don't want on his conscience, it's nothing personal at all," Nate assured. "Maybe you should tell him that, because he is certainly not under that impression," I said. "Why, did he say something to you?" "No, I just think that communication is always a great thing to have with people, that's all," I said. "Tell you what, let's you, me, my father, and Mike go to breakfast tomorrow and I will iron it all out," Nate said. I thought it was a good idea, except I thought Jon should join us. We had to find a good restaurant in Joliet, it was way too hot for any of us to be seen anywhere near the South Side streets. Nate was able to get tickets for me, his dad and him to go to a Bulls playoff game at the Stadium later that week and I was really looking forward to it. I wanted to see first hand how Nate would interact with his father during some down time. This time Nate set up security for us

179

with Dana and Mike with members of their respective regimes. Nate got us a skybox. It was great. There were beers in the portable refrigerator couches and everything. Nate's father seemed to really like it. Nate wanted all of us to dress up; he wanted us to look nice when we went down to the west side. I was a little nervous, though, the west side was Gangster Disciple territory, and Titus' drug territory, anything could happen. Nate had to be fitted for his suit; he had gotten pretty big from all of that working out with Mike. Nate was also getting pretty well known as a stylish dresser. Some of the pimps on the west side labeled him the "best dressed Gangster." We all looked great. Nate even took his father to get fitted for a suit. We all went to the Stadium in a chauffeured limousine. As we approached the stadium, people were looking at us as if we were movie stars. Nate's father showed pride all across his face. It was the first time we all attended anything public together. It was the 1989 playoffs, and the Bulls were playing the Detroit Pistons, led by Isaiah Thomas and his band of thugs known affectionately in Detroit as "the bad boys." We made our move directly to the skyboxes as Mike made a trip to the concession stand. "We already got shit up in the box, Mike. You don't need to stop," Nate said. "It's cool man, I want one of those concession stands, it's been a while since I had one," Mike answered. Things were going so well, and wouldn't you know it, of all nights and all people we run into Titus and a couple of his men. "Well, well look at this, motherfuckers all dressed up and doin' the town!" Titus chided. "Step back, nigga, give us some room!" Dana insisted. "Bitch, fuck you, you ain't running shit!" Titus screamed. "Bitch, nigga I'll…," Dana said forcefully. "Some other time, Dana. It's cool. This ain't nothing but a common gang bangin' punk ass nigga, he ain't no real threat!"

Nate said smiling. "I know about that shit you pulled on the south side a month ago. It's cool, we weren't making no money out there any way, but if you even think about coming out here you gone end up in a world of shit boy! Cause you see, I run shit out here, and I'll bury your little young ass and the rest of these clowns you with, believe that!" Titus said loudly. "Titus, listen to me and listen good, I'm not out here cause I ain't interested in being out here.....yet, but when I am interested, you will be the first motherfucker to be put to sleep believe that!" Nate said mockingly. Then a cop came by, just in the nick of time. The exchanges were getting a little tense. "Alright, let's go keep the line moving guys, c'mon let's go!" the cop grunted. As the respective parties dispersed, Nate and Titus glared at each other signifying a near fifteen-year rivalry that would definitely leave one of them dead. "Fucking gangbanger. I really believe I hate that nigga, G. As soon as we get all of this shit straight, I am definitely going for the west side, if nothing else, but to kill that motherfucker!" Nate growled. The rest of the night went pretty well. Nate's father never asked about the exchange between Nate and Titus, which to me was strange, most parents would have. I guess he was so afraid of offending Nate and destroying their newfound relationship, he just wisely kept his mouth shut.

      Over the next couple of weeks, Nate spent much of his time getting ready for our trip to Bolivia. Everyone in the family received their first payments Dana and Mike got their twenty thousand, and Jon got his forty-four thousand and they were responsible for their respective regimes and workers. The rule was the same as it had always been; don't buy nothing big, nothing gaudy. However, trying to get black people to be discrete making that kind of money was a battle in and of itself. "Hey c'mere G, I want you to see something,"

Mike said. "What, man? I am busy, does it have to be now?" I asked slightly irritated. "Yeah nigga, it ain't gonna take but a second, shit!" Mike said. As I came out to the huge driveway, I saw one of the most repulsive vehicles I have ever seen. Mike took his money and purchased a brand new 1989 Chevy Blazer painted in a complete wood grain color, tinted headlights, huge chrome wheels, limousine tint on the windows, a personalized plate that read "Enfcer 1" and a host of Frankenstein gadgets in the interior. "I had the Mexicans hook me up. Man this truck is beautiful, you know, G, the first word that came to mind when I saw it was "Gorgeous." What's the first word that came to your mind when you first saw it, G? Tell the truth," Mike said gleefully. "The first word, truthfully?" I asked. "Yeah man," Mike said in anticipation. "Nigger," I said plainly. Mike's whole demeanor changed. "Nigger.....man, fuck you. This truck is bad and you know it!" Mike said, obviously offended. "Just playing man, but you know Nate ain't gonna let you keep this truck, man. He said nothing big and extravagant. You know that," I said reminding him. "Yeah, he'll let me keep it, you'll see," he said with hope in his eyes. Dana was just as bad, she went out and purchased a brand knew candy apple red Chevy Corvette, also with big chrome wheels and "Enfcer 2" on the license plate. She and Mike had gotten together on that one. But as predicted Nate told them to take it back. "You know ya'll need to take all of that Nigga shit back, ya'll may as well wear a sign on your heads saying, "drug dealers." I told you nothing gaudy, one goes and buys a new Blazer, and the other gets a Corvette!" Nate said agitated. But Nate was consistent with his beliefs. He purchased a 1985 Volvo, and I purchased an 85' Maxima. Jon purchased a Volvo also. Mike and Dana secretly kept their cars and hid them in one of the far garages of the estate far away from Nate's eyesight. Nate was too busy furnishing the house and getting ready for our trip to Bolivia. I think everyone did some crazy things with their money, just depends on how you look at it. Take Nate for instance, he did keep it simple in the area of a car, but he did purchase two solid black female Rottwielers and placed diamond crusted dog collars on both of them. That was stranger than the cars in my opinion, especially since I have never been very fond of dogs. The furniture that Nate purchased for the house was nothing less than breathtaking. He had an interior decorator come in and furnish the entire place. Every room was exquisitely furnished to taste and very lavish to say the least. Nate also hired some domestic help to cook and clean for us. I never really knew any of them but we all knew the cooks; a Spanish woman named Lolita, and a black woman named Glodine both in their mid fifties. They were very good cooks, and great personalities to have around the house. Having taken care of all of that, Nate could concentrate fully on Bolivia. Nate's father was really starting to grow on us all, and I even think Nate was getting used to him being around. "Is your father going with us to Bolivia?" I asked. "Nah, I'm not ready to disclose all of that to him right now. I think he will just stay here," Nate answered. "You know you will have to tell him eventually, right?" "Yeah, in time but not right now," he said. "Have you seen Dana, I need some info from her concerning Chicago?" I asked. "Oh, yeah I got her on a mission for me. She should be back tonight. Is everything cool?" Nate asked. "Yeah, just some info on some safe houses I am looking into," I replied. Over the next couple of days everything flowed nice, Nate and his father went to check out a movie on the eve of our trip. He told Jon and me that he wanted to have a card game that night and to have everything set up. Jon loved to play Bid Whist with us, he was always better at it than we were. He and Dana's right hand "Pookie" beat Nate and me most of the time. We didn't care; it was always a good time for us. Nate thought a nice card game might help us unwind before the long trip.   That night we had the music playing and some drinks and the mood was real light. "If you don't mind, G, I think I want to play with my father tonight, he says he is a good player, I want to see. Plus, Jon and that damn Pookie have beaten us four straight, I want to give them a different look," Nate explained. "Cool, its ok, play with your dad. Are you feeling a little better about him now?" I asked. "Make sure members of the mafia are there tonight, from both regimes ok?" Nate asked.   "Uh…yeah Nate, but I asked you a question. How do you feel about your dad?" I asked. "It's cool, G, I got it all taken care of, ok?" he said dismissively.

From the onset, all was good. Nate and his dad actually beat Jon and Pookie. Nate's dad turned out to be good at the game after all. "I can't believe you made that bid Mr. Williams, that was a good call and make," Pookie said. "Yeah, I think Nate will actually win some money tonight for a change," Jon joked. Jon leaned over and whispered to me, "Why are all of these people here tonight?" "I don't know. Nate said have members of the mafia from both regimes here tonight. I am just as confused as you are," I said.   After playing another couple of hands, Nate rose to fix himself another drink. "Good game, my man, you really are a good player. I didn't think we were gonna make that six downtown bid," Nate said to his father. "Well son, I been playing a lot longer, and after so many years you just know," his father said proudly. "Yeah, you just know. I'm getting another drink, what are you having?" Nate asked cordially. "I think I will just have a little Cognac tonight," he replied. "Cognac it is, anyone else?" Nate asked graciously. Everyone else was drinking beers for the most part. As he squeezed himself behind his father who was sitting across from him, but in front of the bar he asked him a strange question. "So pops, you know a guy named "Gator", my friend here met him yesterday, he says he knows you?" Nate asked. "Oh…uh yeah Gator I've known him since your mamma and I were young. Your mother and I used to double date with he and his wife all the time, good person. How's he doing these days?" his father asked. "Oh, I guess ok, he talked my friend Dana here to death about you and mamma and the old days. He says if there is anything to know about you he would know it. Says you and him go back a long ways, huh?" Nate asked with his back still to his father. "Yeah, yeah, he didn't tell you too much did he young lady, I don't want him telling everyone my secrets!" he replied with a chuckle. "Too late….he already did!" Nate said. Just then, he whipped around in one motion and wrapped a cable wire around his father's neck, and tightened it so tight, it cut off his windpipe! "Secrets, huh motherfucker? So you put mamma on whore's row for your fucking drug habit, huh….answer me bitch!" Nate yelled. Everyone jumped in shock and horror and stood frozen in fear and bewilderment. "Nate, no….don't!" I screamed. "Yeah, nigga come around me talking all that daddy son shit, didn't think I would find out, did you?" Nate said still yelling. The elder Nathan managed to slightly breathe out some words. "Nate, I...can…explain…Just let me explain-" he said barely above a whisper. "Nigga, fuck you! This ain't for me, this is for my mamma. This is for every time she had to lay down for your junkie ass!" Nate continued to yell. Nate yanked the older man out of the chair with the strength of an ox, and dragged him by the neck to the middle of the floor. The cable wire was starting to cut through the elder man's skin and bleed. The man tried to wiggle himself free, but Nate only tightened his grip with his muscular arms. Mr. Williams tried to bring his arms around to grab Nate, scratch him or anything, as he felt life slipping away. "Nate, you're killing him, stop!" I yelled from across the room. Seeing enough I jumped up and started toward Nate and Dana whipped a gun to my face faster than I could think, stopping me cold in my tracks. The scene was complete horror and pandemonium. "You all gonna sit here and watch him kill his father?" I asked in desperation. As the life slipped from the old man and he fell unconscious, Nate slipped the wire from around his neck and with one hand, he grabbed his father by the chin and top of his head and twisted repeatedly until he heard the snap of his neck. I fell to the floor as terror engulfed me in waves. Dana gave a sly smile as she placed her gun back in her side holster. Everyone else stood frozen not believing what just transpired. Nate looked at everyone with an evil about his face I cannot explain, he looked like a mad dog as sweat ran down his face. I have never professed to be a religious man, but I can honestly say I saw evil personified on his face. He looked possessed! "Anybody got a problem with what the fuck I just did?" Nate snarled. Everyone shook their heads in unison no. Then he looked at me with that beastly look in his eyes. "You fucked up, G, whenever I tell you to get some info on a motherfucker I want you to get all of the info!" he growled pointing the bloody wire cord at me. "I.....thought.....you...." I said as I felt a tear roll down my cheek. "I know what the fuck you thought. You thought if you told me I would kill him, well G, I found out anyway. And there he is.....dead. So what did you

accomplish?" he said. "Next time get me the information
I ask you to get me, understood?" he asked in authority.
I just sat there weeping, weeping for him more than his
father. Nate was losing his soul, and I wept for him.
"UNDERSTOOD?" he yelled. "Yeah..." I whispered.
"Good....Good," Nate said smiling and nodding in
agreement. "Clean this shit up. Take his ass to the city
and give him to the undertaker for cremation, and then
find a manhole and dump his fucking ashes down in it,
you got it Dana?" he instructed. "Got it boss," she
replied.   I sat there as waves of emotion overtook my
body. Streams of tears rolled down my cheeks. In any
normal situation, I would have been concerned about
how I looked in front of all of the men in the room. I
didn't care anymore; I sat there staring into nothingness,
thinking, reflecting, on all of the death and mayhem I had
been a part of. One thing was for sure I made a decision
sitting right there on the floor. I wanted out immediately,
just as I promised Lollie. I just couldn't take anymore. I
decided to go to Bolivia with the Family, but when I got
back stateside, I was leaving. I wanted to leave this
whole scene....my heart couldn't take anymore.

CHAPTER 8

Bolivia

As it turned out Dana got all of the info on Mr. Williams from "Gator" herself and gave it all to Nate. He was suspicious of what I told him and knew I was the type to avoid confrontation, so he checked behind me. It was ok; I didn't care because he was right. I knew how Nate was and I wanted to minimize the amount of murder and chaos in the Family. It was a long ride to O'Hare Airport the next day. Everyone got packed and ready as the limousines arrived to pick us all up. I didn't say anything to anyone, not even Nate. I didn't want to convey that I approved of the slaughter of Mr. Williams. But the rest of these "yes men," it seemed that whatever Nate did they were ok with it. It didn't take Fingers long to fit into the mold either. "That Nate is a true gangster, huh?" Fingers said trying to start conversation. "Whatever," I replied. I guess he could see I wasn't up for conversation. Nate instructed Dana to stay home and take care of things, and the rest of the Family to accompany him on the trip. Dana was given strict guidelines on what to do and what not to do, and how to contact him if anything went wrong. He confided to Mike how nervous he was about leaving Dana here considering how reckless she was and all. In my opinion, leaving Dana anywhere on the planet was a risk. "It's all good, Nate, I got everything under control, and I know how and when to get in touch with you," she assured. "Alright, don't fuck up now," Nate said. "It's all good, baby I got it. Just get us a good deal. Ya'll better go before you miss your flight," she said trying to reassure him. Dana was a woman but she was definitely an imposing figure. She constantly walked around with two huge guns in a double side arm holster ready to use at any time. Most of the servants Nate hired assisted us with the baggage to the cars. "G, you got a minute?" Jon asked. "Yeah, what's up?" I answered. "I know you're still pissed off about last night. Frankly, the shit didn't set well with me either. I hate violence. But you gotta let it go, G, like Nate said it's the life we chose, things will get better and easier you'll see," Jon said. Jon was a little different from the rest. He handled the money issues, and never got involved directly with the violent or drug ends of the Family. "Not me, Jon, I didn't sign up for any of this shit. I appreciate what you're trying to do, but I have had enough of all of this, really I have. I want a life man, a real life, and I am going to get one," I exclaimed. As we loaded the limos for the airport, there was a strange hush among everyone. I believe people were still reeling from the previous night's events. Nate instructed everyone that he wanted a meeting on the plane. Bolivia, I thought would be a nice way for all of us to get a break, and change environments. Surely, none of us had ever been there, and that was exciting in and of itself. Weeks prior to this trip, Nate asked me to check out the contact, which I did through my sources. The contact; Hugo Zamora had ties to a Columbian drug cartel, and had heard about how lucrative it would be to start getting drugs into the states. A few of the local rivals had already done it and they were amassing fortunes, and Hugo wanted in. The problem for him was he had no contacts. He desperately needed distributors in the States to get the ball rolling, and to share the risk. He had heard of some guys but there was always a trust issue involved. I heard about this through some of our friends from the Latin Kings. They still held Nate in high regard from the Hector hit, and told him about Hugo, as long as they were cut into the deal. The county and local authorities were watching the Latin Kings because they figured if anyone was filtering drugs in from Latin America, or South America, it would come from them. But few would suspect a bunch of black guys to have ties to drug cartels in Bolivia. Police intelligence knew that relations with Latinos and Blacks as far as the drug world was concerned were strained, and one side didn't trust the other. To an extent they were right, what they underestimated though was that the power and love for money and profit could sometimes make strange bedfellows!

Still, there were risks, big risks! Despite the fact that I was the one who chiefly set up this meeting with help from the Latin Kings, I didn't trust it. I had never met Hugo before and really didn't know much about his character and business savvy. I didn't know if state or federal officials were setting us up, or if the Latin Kings had betrayed us, I didn't know if we were going to be killed in a strange country or if we would end up in some Bolivian jail. If we did, we were just fucked because the State Department or the Ambassador certainly was not going to raise a fuss over a bunch of drug dealing niggers!

The only thing we were riding on was that Hugo's people guaranteed our safety to the Latin Kings, a guarantee that didn't make me feel safe at all. Nate and I were the only ones concerned about the whole thing, and we really weren't talking! Everyone else acted as if no one had a care in the world. Mike and Pete were playing cards, Fingers was busy trying to get phone numbers from the stewardesses, and the rest of Mike's regime

were either sleeping or in their own little worlds. They
thought we were high rollers and big time, like we were
"Scarface" or "Don Corleone" or some shit! They were
totally oblivious to the danger of this trip! I guess the
cliché is right…ignorance truly is bliss. I was happy that
Nate booked us in first class, there was no way I wanted
to sit for a long ass flight to Bolivia in coach! After we
boarded the plane and checked our bags, I took a seat
near the window. As one of Mike's bodyguards sat next
to me, which was customary security protocol in the
Family, I turned and stared out of the window. The next
thing I knew the bodyguard was gone and Nate had taken
his spot next to me, it scared the shit out of me! "G, we
need to talk, you got a minute?" he asked. "I guess so,
Nate, I'm on the plane now, where am I gonna go?" I
said condescendingly. "G, I am sorry about last night, I
really didn't want to expose you to all of that, but I
thought you kind of undermined me a little with the
whole intelligence breach," he said. "Undermined you?
Nate, there was no intelligence breach, I knew all about
the guy, I just wanted all of the violence and killing to
cease a little. But I see you all are hell bent on it, so it's
cool, I just have to distance myself from it, that's all," I
said flatly. "What do you mean, G?" Nate asked
confused. "What I am trying to tell you Nate is I am out,
I can't take all of this shit anymore. I didn't sign on for
this. I want a life, Nate, a real life. I am twenty-one
years old and I have never had a real girlfriend, I mean I
get a woman here and there, but never a real relationship.
One day I want to get married, argue with my wife and
work a nine to five like normal people do, have a bunch
of kids and wonder how I am gonna pay bills, you
know…normal shit!" I reasoned. "You think I don't
want that too, G? I get tired of fucking different women
too, I want a baby and a wife too, it just ain't in the cards

right now. It'll come, you'll see," Nate assured. "How can you guarantee me something, Nate? You can't even guarantee that we will come back from this trip alive. You know I was at a motel with this broad last week and while she was gone for food I started flipping through one of those Bible's that's always in the top drawer you know, and it was saying that God is real, and tomorrow is not promised, and moral sin is terrible and it talked about hell and stuff. What if all of that is true, Nate, what if we are writing a moral bill that we are not prepared to cover, what if all of this killing and drug sales and stuff is damning our souls, have you ever thought about that? If we do get our lives together how do we pay that kind of debt to a God?" I asked. "I don't know, G, I am not a religious man. All of that stuff is too heavy for me to think about right now. All I know is if our shit is not together when we meet Hugo, you might get a chance to ask God yourself this week!" I let out a deep sigh, turned and looked back out of the window shaking my head. Nate was neck deep in this drug world and the existence of anything else was totally oblivious to him. "Now look, G, I need you to have a clear head, the rest of these guys are ok, but they're clowns and this trip is life and death, understand? No matter what, we are still brothers," Nate said. "Why didn't you tell them about the importance of this trip?" I asked. "Why, so they can be all shaken and nervous? So they can go there and fuck up and get us all killed? No thanks, G, I would rather keep them happy and ignorant. Besides, I'm calling a meeting when we change birds to fill them in on some protocol while we are there, I'll tell them a little then," he assured. Although I was angry, I felt sorry for Nate, he just didn't get it and maybe he never will. I have always been a believer of consequences, consequences for actions and decisions that we make.

The deeper we got into this world, the more remote our chances were of all of us coming out of it alive.

CHICAGO, IL POLICE HEADQUARTERS:

"So, you going on the golfing trip Harry or what? Because if you are, I'm gonna need to carpool with you," a young detective said. "I don't know. I haven't made a decision yet. Are you on your way downstairs?" Inspector Trent asked. "Yeah, what do you need?" The detective replied. "Bring me a coffee, will ya? And send up Detective Jackson, it's an emergency," Inspector Trent yelled. "You got it," the detective responded. "You needed to see me chief?" Jackson asked. "Yeah Diane, come in and have a seat please. I have been going over your file on the young kid Nathan Williams and it looks as though you are close to an arrest....according to your file," Trent stated. "Yeah, I have compiled enough evidence to tie him to the Lawrence Caldwell murder in the park near St Colubanus Church," she said. "I am familiar with it detective, remember I told you I've been in the file," he asserted. "Yes Sir," she replied apologetically. "You know, it's good but the evidence is a little light, too light for a conviction to stick, therefore too light for an arrest and indictment," Trent said. "I know it's not the best, sir, but I think I can push it through, make it stick," Jackson said. "Detective, you have hearsay, testimonies from drunks, and convicted felons here. Look, this guy just got out of Marion State eight months ago, none of this will stick," Trent instructed. "Sir, I want this guy off the streets. Inspector, there is a good chance that Nathan Williams is one of, if not the biggest, drug distributors on the south side, now if we move now we can also get a large amount of drugs off the street, and collar a murderer to boot," Jackson urged. "Detective, I have been on the force for a little over thirty years now, I know how to get criminals off the street. And with over thirty years of experience I know you don't do it with circumstantial evidence and hearsay from horrible character witnesses. Now I want you to stall your arrest of this man until you come back to me with something that will stick, and not some bullshit that won't even make it to trial, understand?" Trent said agitated. "But Inspector with all due respect....." Jackson said trying to plead her case. "You have a good day Detective!" Trent said cutting her off. "You too, sir," Jackson said giving up the argument. "Close the door behind you detective," Trent said. "What was that all about?" Jackson's partner asked. "He said our file on the Caldwell murder is too thin to arrest Williams. I don't know what he wants," Jackson said frustrated. "Probably a confession, huh?" her partner joked.

BACK ON THE PLANE:

"Ok guys listen up we will be in Bolivia in about an hour I want to go over some things with you. First, the only ones who will do the talking will be myself, G, and Pete, everyone else keep quiet and watch my back. Next, watch these Bolivians; watch what you say and who you say it to. G's intelligence report says that these motherfuckers are short tempered and easy to offend so be cool, demand respect but don't offend," Nate instructed. "How do we do that, Nate?" Mike asked. "These assholes think all niggas are fools, we have to beat through that stereotype, we have to let them know that we know how to conduct business too, we have to let them know we aren't down here on some Moe, Larry, and Curly shit! Negotiators, if we get to the negotiation part, Hugo and his people are going to want us to buy high and take all of the risks. Fuck that! We are going there to buy, but not high, and our aim is to share the risk. They grow this shit over here by the tons, so they can afford to cut us some slack. Remember, they need us as much as we want the coke and the price, so haggle a little with them; we're not going there to buy the farm. We want them to guarantee us at least to the Baltimore Port, and we will take it from there. G and his people have some Coast Guard guys and some guys that work at the Port on payroll, but they don't have to know that, understand?" Nate said. "Jon, we are going there to set a deal for two-hundred pounds a quarter, we already discussed the price last night, don't let these motherfuckers talk you too far up from that. You got that purchase money, right?" Nate asked. "Yeah, I got it all," Jon replied. "Good, don't let these motherfuckers know what we are worth, but let them know we aren't amateurs either. I don't want to see anyone high on this trip, there will be enough time for that when we get back home. If Hugo or any of these yokels offer you food or a drink, or invite you to a party, don't refuse, they take that shit as an insult. Is everybody up to speed?" Nate asked. "Oh, and I almost forgot....don't drink the water!" Nate said jokingly. As Nate wrapped up his instructional pep talk, I started to feel myself getting a headache, probably from nervous anticipation. As I looked out of my window, all I could see was what looked to me like jungles or rain forests, we were definitely not in Chicago anymore. "Excuse me, Miss, do you have any aspirin?" I asked the stewardess. "Sure sir, I will bring you two, would you like water or milk to take that with?" she asked. "Water will be fine," I replied. "What's wrong, G, you got a headache?" Jon asked. "Yeah, I think it's this long ass plane ride, I hope we never have to do this again. You know this was my first flight," I revealed. "No shit, why would you make your first flight one this damn long, G?" Jon asked. "It's not like any of us had a choice?" I replied. "Yeah, you think we will get a good deal?" Jon asked concerned. "Jon, our first objective should be to avoid getting into a world of shit, I just want to make the deal and get out!" I confessed. "You and me both, we are way out of our element," Jon said. As the pilot announced the temperature and our arrival in Bolivia, I felt waves of tense nervousness all over my body. Something about this whole thing did not feel right. Screw it, I said. We were there and there was no turning back. As we arrived in Bolivia, I looked out of the window and the view was breathtaking. Bolivia was a beautiful country from about ten-thousand feet in the air, but then again so was Chicago. When the plane touched down at El Alto International Airport, we all gathered our luggage, with an air of uncertainty. Jon kept the purchase money close of course, but some of the members of the South Side Mafia helped us by carrying our stuff. The first thing I noticed was the heat, for me it was unbearable. "Damn, it's hot out here, ain't it, G?" Nate asked. "Yeah, we've only been off the plane a minute and I am burning up," I replied. Jon was turning red and looked slightly irritated, the rest of our entourage seemed overtaken also. As soon as we stepped off the plane, I also noticed about five limos approaching while walking toward the airport. "What the fuck is this shit?" Jon asked as they approached. As the limos screeched to a halt, a salt and pepper haired man approached us. "Which one of you is Nate Williams?" the man asked with a thick Hispanic accent. "We are the Nate Williams entourage, who are you?" one of our bodyguards responded. "Hugo Zamora desires your presence at his compound; we need you to follow us," the man instructed. We all looked at Nate and he started toward the limos, so we all followed. We got into the cars that were cool, and smelled of garlic, at least the one I was in did. The limos led us out of La Paz, and we drove for a long time until we reached what I later found out was a small wooded compound in the middle of nowhere just outside the town of Coroico. Hugo's compound was massive, the house was huge, but what made it so imposing was the land, there were acres and acres of land. Most of it looked like forest land, but it was all his. There were armed guards everywhere, on the roof of the mansion, all through the forest land, and even some up in the trees. While we were traveling up the winding road toward the home, we approached some huge gates; all of the limos stood in line and waited for what seemed like an hour. Then four guards pulled the gates open and we drove through, I have to admit it was a beautiful country. We were all in awe of the area, and couldn't believe that some snot-nosed guys from Chicago had come this far. I must say there was a sense of accomplishment.

New Lenox:

"One-forty eight….One-forty nine….One-fifty. Good Dana, but you know you got one more set," the trainer said. "Yeah, thanks Terry. Whew! I am tired, but I will do that last set," Dana said slightly winded. "Excuse me, Dana, can I see you a minute?" a young man asked. "What motherfucker? You know I don't like my workouts interrupted, what do you want?" Dana asked agitated. "I'm sorry, but a couple of the guys and Pookie got into a fight at the club. Some of them got shot up and they are at the hospital," the young man explained. "What the hell happened and what hospital are they at?" Dana asked in a panic. "They're at some hospital on the east side….uh I think its Saint Bernard's," the young man said nervously. "You think, nigga, go find out what the fuck is going on and get right back to me you hear!"

Dana said angrily. "Yes....ma'am, I will," the young man said. "You're still here, boy? Get going!" Dana screamed. The young man ran from the room.

Two Hours Later...

"Yeah.....Dana, it's Tony.   Here's the lowdown; Pookie and a couple of the guys from the mafia were at the club last night, he had a few drinks and got into a little heated discussion about the streets and shit, turns out these were some of Titus' guys. Well you know how Pookie is, especially after a few drinks, he told the guys to go fuck themselves and their mothers too. Well, that's when the shit hit the fan. Dana the whole place went up. There were shots fired from everywhere, that's when a couple of our guys went down. Pookie pulled out an Uzi and sprayed the place. When the smoke cleared, me and a couple of the guys got the truck and pulled around back and put Pookie and Anthony in the truck and took off before the cops got there. Pookie's arm is broken and Anthony got shot in the leg, but he's ok. Five members of Titus' gang are dead. I got the rest of the mafia guys, Mack 10's, Uzi's and shit what you wanna do boss?" Tony said over the phone. "Good job Tony, call me back in about an hour. Give me a minute to think," Dana said. Dana walked over to the massive bay window in the kitchen and looked out. She could feel the anger swelling inside. She wanted revenge for what they did to her people. However, she dared not to make a move without Nate or G's approval, so she thought.

BOLIVIA:

As we approached the massive home, about eight Spanish men rushed to the car and opened the door. "Welcome, please allow me to introduce myself, I am Alonzo Rodriguez, I will be your translator while you are here, Mr. Zamora does not speak English well, as with many of his handlers. I also hope to show you the country of Bolivia; you know the nightlife so to speak. However, I must ask you if you have the money?" he asked. "Yeah…sure, of course," I replied. "Do you have it now?" Alonzo asked. "Yes, man but we aren't showing anything until we meet Hugo, that's the deal," Nate replied. Alonzo just stared at us for a moment then smiled. "Of course my friend, follow me," he replied. As we approached the home, I noticed all of the windows were tinted black. I knew folks on the inside could see us, but we couldn't see them. We were once again frisked inside, which was cool, we knew all about security, we just made sure that the purchase money never left our sight. Actually, there were two bags, one with the real purchase money, and another bag with about twenty thousand dollars in hundred dollar bills with paper underneath in case we were robbed. We walked into a huge elegant dining room. In fact, the whole place was elegantly decorated, we were all impressed, to say the least. "Here is where you will meet with Mr. Zamora in approximately an hour. He wants you and your entourage to get cleaned up and ready for dinner where we will get better acquainted," Alonzo instructed. "Cool, I think we will need about…" Nate said as Alonzo interrupted. "We have you well accommodated my friend," Alonzo replied. As well they did, Alonzo took us to a whole floor full of rooms to ourselves, along with our own personal butlers and wait staff. All of the rooms were Victorian styled with huge beds and many pillows. All of the rooms had fresh cut flowers and smelled great. There were huge screen televisions, gold plated telephones, sterling silver water pitchers, Persian rugs, balconies, and the works! Nate was very impressed. "Man, you see how these

199

mother..." Nate said before I interrupted. I placed my index finger over my perched lips giving the universal sign to be quiet. I then grabbed him by the coat, led him to the bathroom and turned the water up high. "Be cool, it's probably more bugs in this room than on sixty-third street in Chicago, so don't say anything aloud that you don't want taped," I whispered in his ear. "Right, right...you think we are being videotaped too?" Nate whispered. "Don't know for sure, I noticed all of the hallways have cameras, though, the rooms probably have hidden cameras, I think," I replied. "Good looking out, G! I think they respect us though, they're treating us like dope dealer royalty, don't you think?" Nate asked excitedly. "Hold your horses Tonto, this could all be part of the setup, you know fatten the turkey before Thanksgiving! The real test will be after they get the purchase money, but personally, I won't feel safe until I get back to O'Hare airport," I revealed. "Be cool, G, I got a feeling it's gonna be all good. I got a good feeling about this trip. You'll see what I mean later," Nate assured. I didn't care what he said we were in unfamiliar territory, and it's two things I really don't like; unfamiliar territory and night driving! I instructed the rest of the group about the probable bugs in the rooms so they wouldn't say anything incriminating. Nate and I decided to take a shower. I let Nate go first and figured while he was in I would unpack. I grabbed the bag of real purchase money and it felt heavier than I thought it should, so I opened it. I knew we were supposed to bring one-million, but this felt like at least double that! "You know, G, that has to be the hardest water I have ever..." Nate said coming out of the bathroom. "What is this, Nate, why do we have so much money?" I whispered. "What, that's more than a million?" Nate whispered. "At least double that, look," I said. When Nate looked in the bag, he grimaced. He and I threw on some jeans and t-shirts, walked down the hall and knocked on Jon and Pete's room door. When Jon cracked the door, we barged in. We grabbed Jon by the shirt collar, pulled him into the bathroom and again turned the faucet on high. "What the fuck is all of that money doing in the purchase bag, Jon?" Nate asked loudly. "Oh shit, you scared the hell out of me, man. You should always have more money than you need on a venture like this, so I grabbed some extra cash," Jon whispered relieved. "So when were you gonna tell us about it?" Nate asked. "In about twenty minutes after we got cleaned up, honest," Jon said convincingly. Nate looked at him and looked at me. "Don't be late for the dinner," Nate said as he walked out of the bathroom. "What's going on?" Pete asked as we walked out of the room and closed the door.

We had an impromptu meeting in our room shortly before we were to meet with Hugo. "Ok listen up, if he asks for the money before negotiating we are screwed and it's a setup, but if he negotiates first then we are cool, understood?" Nate got up and took the purchase money in the bathroom, turned the lights out and hid the money in the ceiling, in case someone wanted to take it while we were negotiating. He told Pete where it was and instructed Big Mike to escort Pete to it, if the time came. It wasn't much of a plan, but it's all we had, we were in their domain what the hell else could we do? When we got to dinner, Hugo was not there, but Alonzo and Hugo's handlers were in attendance. "Ah, welcome…has a seat. Now which one of you is Nate?" Alonzo asked. "Which one of you is Hugo?" Nate asked. Alonzo laughed loudly, "I like you, you must be Nate huh, tell me about Chicago and the States. How are the women there, huh?" Alonzo asked. "Same as the women here, can we cut the crap? We flew out here to see Hugo. We have been here for two hours and have not met him yet. No disrespect Alonzo, but we didn't fly all the way out here to talk to an underling, we want to meet Hugo himself," Nate said slightly irritated. I almost shit in my pants I knew Nate had a temper, but he told us not to piss these guys off, now we were about to die. "I Hugo," a man sitting adjacent to Nate said in broken English. The man waived everyone to relax as men started to get fidgety after Nate's comment. Hugo Zamora stood about six feet tall and what the ladies would call a handsome Latin man. He was a bit older than expected and had salt and pepper hair slicked back and neatly cropped. He wore a linen Italian suit with sandals and a cigar poking from his mouth. As he spoke, Alonzo translated. "Hugo apologizes for the inconvenience, but we wanted to make sure you guys were not the CIA." "The CIA, do we look like agents to you guys?" I asked incredulously. "No my friend, but he does," Alonzo said pointing to Jon. "No, he's cool he's just white. You're not going to hold that against him or us, are you?" Nate said smiling. Hugo looked at Nate and responded in Spanish, Alonzo translated. "No, as long as you don't hold being Columbian against us!" Nate laughed and extended his hand for a handshake toward Hugo. Hugo looked at Nate's hand and shook it. Then spoke in Spanish, as Alonzo translated. "He says he knew you guys were not agents he could smell the street on you." Nate smiled condescendingly and responded. "Yeah, and we could smell the Coke and tacos on you guys," Alonzo looked angrily at Nate. "Tell him," Nate said confidently. Alonzo translated to Hugo. Hugo looked at Nate sternly and replied in Spanish, as Alonzo interpreted. "He said he is not Mexican!" Alonzo said as if to imply Hugo was offended. "Good, cause we're not street niggers!" Nate said proudly.

Alonzo translated back to Hugo Nate's response. Hugo looked at Nate hard for ten seconds, as Nate looked at him equally as hard. Just then, Hugo burst into hearty laughter from Nate's response, and spoke in Spanish between chuckles, as Alonzo translated. "He said he likes you, you have balls, and speak from the heart," Alonzo said smiling. "Tell him likewise," Nate responded. Everyone stood laughing and relaxed. The ice was broken.

NEW LENOX:

As Dana stood looking out of the window, the phone rang. "Yeah, who is it?" she asked agitated. "It's me Pookie, we got the mark, what you want us to do now?" he asked. "Take him to the safe house on the southwest side, you know where, right?" she asked "Yeah, how long you gonna be?" Pookie asked. "Just get your ass over there and wait. I'll be there when I get there, and don't touch him until I get there!" she said. As Dana hung up the phone, she wondered if she was about to do the right thing or not. She summoned a member of her regime and ordered him to get the car for her. Four more members of the regime came to her near the front door. "You need us, boss?" one of the men asked. "Yeah, get the cars and meet me in the foyer, we have to make a run. Use the black trucks, and get my corvette," she instructed. As she started toward the front door, the butler and caretaker approached her, "Will you be taking your jacket, it is a bit nippy out this evening Ms. Oswald?" "Yes, my red jacket please," Dana responded. Dana stood dressed completely in black, black t-shirt, jeans and gym shoes. As she put on her side holsters and placed two huge shiny nickel-plated guns in each, she took in a deep breath, took the jacket from the butler and walked out into the night air. "You think you will need the jacket?" a young man also dressed in black asked. "Yeah, I'm taking my corvette and dropping the top. We better ride in formation on the Ryan, just make sure everyone knows that we are getting off on 95th, and going west, before we go see Pookie," she instructed. Another member of her regime approached her and gave her two additional guns; one black 9mm Glock, and another shiny nickel-plated cannon of a gun. She placed the 9mm in an ankle holster, and the nickel-plated gun in the small of her back. She breathed in the night air and looked around wishing Nate or G was around to give her assurance that what she was about to do was right and just. She cupped her right hand around her mouth and yelled out, "Listen up we are riding in formation on the highway, and getting off on 95th to go west. At that time I want three in front and three in back." All six cars tapped their horns to acknowledge that they heard her. Dana put on her jacket and hopped into the red vehicle and let the top down, inserted a rap tape into the cassette player and blasted it. She raced the engine and lit a joint up for the ride, she threw the car into drive and they all sped off into the night headed for Chicago like desperados.

BOLIVIA

After eating a great dinner, we all sat around and talked about the drug game, how it is in the states as opposed to overseas. Hugo proved to be a real cool guy. He clearly had lots of money, but he was down to earth. He explained how he was hooked up with a cartel near the Andes, and his group needed an attaché, so to speak in the states. He said we fit the bill because no one would suspect a bunch of black guys directly linked to a drug cartel. Most of the time, the black men were street dealers, hundreds of men removed from the cartel, it would work out perfectly. We thought it would work out because the Hispanics and the Blacks could finally get together, cut out the government and the white man and keep all of the profits for ourselves. Of course, we had to cut the Latin Kings in on the deal, but we didn't care, it was the least we could do. Besides, they only wanted a small piece, and the right to deal in their community exclusively, no problem. Everything was going smooth until we started to iron out just how to get the stuff to the states. "You know, Nate, Hugo thinks we should be responsible for our port here, and you guys take it from there," Alonzo said as Hugo nodded his head in agreement. "We can't do that, we have no contacts here, besides where is the risk for you guys? Outside of you all, we know no one here," Pete said. Hugo spoke in Spanish as Alonzo translated. "What do you propose?" "If you could get us to Maryland, the Baltimore port, we can take it from there. We have guys that will get it to Chicago," Pete replied. "Right, I think everyone should be responsible for their own native land, I think that's fair," Nate added. Hugo spoke in Spanish as Alonzo translated. "How much are we talking here exactly?" "Well, we agreed on ninety-one kilos a quarter, now that's a bit over three million dollars, two of which we have here with us, the other million you get when we get the powder," Jon said. "Now Hugo, we are taking a tremendous risk here, we are giving you two million dollars for coke that we won't see for a month! You have got to understand our position here," Nate added. Alonzo translated what was said to Hugo and Hugo took a long pull from his cigar, leaned back in his chair and tilted his head toward the Bolivian landscape. We all looked around, and Jon whispered something to Pete as Hugo snapped back up to attention. He leaned toward Alonzo and spoke into his ear in Spanish. Alonzo stood and walked over to Nate and whispered into his ear, "You have a deal my friend, we will get you to Baltimore, but Hugo wants an additional two-hundred for his trouble." "No problem, we have a deal," Nate whispered back, and nodded to Jon. Jon was right; there should always be more money on hand than needed. As Nate leaned back in his chair, he was fixated on a young woman watering the flowers in the house. She had on a staff uniform. She was part of the help on the compound. I caught him staring hard at her. I didn't even think he blinked! As she turned around, she caught him looking at her, and threw him a smile and walked away. Nate got flushed in the face and his hands started to get sweaty. "What the fuck is wrong with you man, you know her?" I asked. "How would I know her, G? But I would like to get to know her," Nate replied. Hugo arose from his chair and spoke in Spanish as Alonzo translated, "Hugo would like to have a get together tonight in celebration of this new business venture before you leave for the states tomorrow." "Absolutely," Nate responded. I was starting to feel a little better about this trip.

CHICAGO, SOUTH SIDE:

As Dana walked up the steps to the apartment, she took her black gloves off and rubbed her already slick hair back, while the other members of her regime walking with her formed a circle around her. As they approached the apartment, she pulled out her gun and cocked it and one of the members of the regime gave a signaled knock to the door. "What took you so long? I was starting to get nervous," Pookie said. "Be cool Pook, where is he at?" Dana asked. "In the kitchen," Pookie replied. Dana peeked around the corner to look and saw Titus, bound, gagged, blindfolded, slightly bruised and duck taped to a chair. "What did he tell you?" Dana asked. "Shit, he keeps saying he didn't know about it, I think he lying, though!" Pookie said angrily. Dana smiled and looked over at him with his arm still in a sling and his bruised face from the skirmish the night before. "How are you, you doing, ok?" Dana asked. "Yeah, I'm cool I just want that motherfucker dead, that's all," Pookie said angrily. "Me too, but you know we can't do that, but what I did is just as good," Dana said confidently. She got a duffle bag from a member of her regime and walked into the kitchen. "What the fuck is going on!" Titus yelled. Dana snatched the duck tape from his eye's pulling away some of his eyebrows as Titus flinched. "What's up dude, remember me?" Dana asked. "Hell no, I don't know you bitch, who the fuck are you?" Titus asked. "Remember you saw me at the Stadium a month ago with my boss?" Titus started looking at her through squinting eyes. "Oh yeah bitch, I know you, you and that faggot ass Nate!" Titus said grinning. Dana pulled a gun from her holster and slapped him across his face drawing blood from his mouth. "Watch your mouth gang banger," Dana said forcefully. "Now, some of your *homies* shot up some of my guys a couple of nights ago, you know anything about that?" Dana asked. "Yeah, I remember them niggas, they was drunk and talking shit so they got blasted. So what?" Titus said arrogantly. "So, I would kill your ass, but I can't, so I did the next best thing," Dana said laughing. "What the fuck you're talking about, crazy bitch?" Titus said irritated. Dana gave him a fist to the face. "I can't kill you, but I can beat the fuck out of you, I'm not going to be too many more bitches, faggot!" She stood looking at him as she took a cup of coffee from one of her crewmember. "You read the Bible at all Titus?" she asked. "What the fuck you asking me that for?" she pulled a gun from her holster and cocked it and pointed it to his right temple.

"I said, have you read the Bible at all, nigga?" she asked through gritted teeth. "Uh, yeah a little, why?" Titus replied after a deep swallow. "Good...what was Kane's punishment for killing his brother Abel?" Dana asked looking at him. "Uh I don't know what?" he asked. "God made him a vagabond in the land, he had to run for the rest of his life, remember?" she explained. "That's you Titus, you're gonna be on the run," Dana revealed. "From you, I don't think so," Titus said confidently. "Not me fool, you'll be running from the police." "For what, I didn't do shit," Titus said. "Yeah you did, you did this!" She pulled about five pictures from her duffle bag. There were gruesome photos of about four people gunned to death in a convenience store with the letters BGDN spray painted one the wall. There was even a little girl shot in the neck and dragged to the back of the store. When Titus saw the pictures, he threw up right in his own lap. "Look at this shit, Pookie, Big Bad ass Titus got a weak stomach," Dana said laughing. Titus looked up at Dana with residue around his mouth. "I didn't do that shit. You can't put that shit on me!" Titus yelled. "Yeah you did, here's the gun you used with your prints all over it and the spray paint can!" Everyone in the room began to laugh. "You framed me. I'll call the police and tell them, they will believe me!" Titus said desperately. "With your record, nigga, I doubt it. Looks like an open and shut case to me. How it look to you, Pook?" Dana said smiling. "Looks open and shut from here, too," he said glaring at Titus. "I'll get your ass for this, believe that!" Titus promised. "How you gonna track me down running from the police, dumb motherfucker? I got four white people and a little blond haired white girl here, shot in the face dead," Dana said. "Why you doing this shit to me, you think this is a fucking game or something?" Titus asked. "Yeah, it is a game called the running man," Dana said laughing. "What kind of consolation prize does this fool get?" Pookie asked Dana. "Well, you get an all expenses paid trip to the electric chair! That's right, you will get to lounge in a nice comfortable wooden chair complete with restraints and a nice cap for your head, but before then you will get to relax for at least ten years or so in the friendly confines of Stateville prison! That's right; you and a few friends will get to reminisce about the good old days while receiving three meals and a nice cot. All of this and maybe a little ass raping is yours for playing every gang banger's favorite game show THE RUNNING MAN!" Dana said mimicking a game show host. "You're sick…you're really sick," Titus said looking at her in amazement. "Yeah, and don't you ever forget it, motherfucker, don't EVER forget it! Pookie take this nigga and dump his stupid ass under a viaduct somewhere and get him out of my sight!" Dana said angrily. As all of Dana's henchmen bound Titus, she and Pookie walked to the front door. "You know what to do, right?" Dana asked. "Yeah I know," Pookie answered. "What do you think the backlash on this shit will be, Dana?" he asked. "I don't know, we'll have to see, don't worry, though, if there is any hell to be caught, I'll catch it," she said reflecting.

BOLIVIA:

"You know, G, I think I want to stay here one more day. You know to see the sights," Nate said. "What sights, Nate? Let's just seal the deal, hop on the plane and get the fuck out of here!" I said anxiously. "Wait a minute; this ain't about no damn sights. This is about that broad you saw earlier tonight, ain't it?" I said, guessing right. Nate just looked at me and gave me a sly grin. "G, she is breathtaking, I just can't get her out of my head. I've been sneaking all around this damn place trying to find her. I can't seem to find her ass anywhere," Nate said desperately. "Well, why don't you ask Hugo, or one of the other staff members?" I asked. "Nah, I ain't trying to look desperate or nothing," Nate said trying to maintain cool. "Yeah, but you are desperate," I said laughing. Then there was a knock at the door. After I opened it, there she was with freshly folded sheets and pillowcases in her arms. To Nate's credit, she was beautiful and very exotic looking. She stood about five feet four inches, with long black hair that seemed to reach her mid back. She had olive colored skin, deep dimples, and the brightest eyes. She was what the brothers would call "thick" with nice hips and a beauty mark right over her top lip. She was exquisite. "I am here to make the beds," she said with a sexy accent. "Uh, cool, come on in," I said, looking at Nate and raising my eyebrows in approval. As she turned her back to walk toward the bed, Nate waved me into the other room. She neatly placed the fresh sheets on a chair and walked toward the huge windows and opened them, letting in the warm Bolivian air. As she walked by Nate, she gave him a nice smile and gently placed her hands on the small of his back to ever so gently, move him. "Excuse me," she said coyly, obviously flirting. I excused myself and walked into the next room, but stood near the door to listen. "Hey uh, I didn't get your name," Nate said. "I didn't give it," she replied. "Ok, what is your name...please?" Nate asked boyishly. "Gabriella," she answered while stripping the bed of its crumpled sheets. "That is a beautiful name, and you are a beautiful woman, I might add," Nate said advancing. She stopped for a second, gave Nate a stoned face look and continued with her work. "Uh, are you married or single?" Nate asked. "I no married," she replied. Her English was not so good. "I see...what time do you get off today?" Nate asked. "Why, why you asking me this?" she said half smiling. "Because you are one of the most beautiful women I have ever laid eyes on, and I would like to take you out to dinner tonight before I leave town, if it's ok with you Gabriella," Nate asked "Thank you no," she said flatly. "Why not, please?" Nate asked again boyishly. "Cause I no attracted to you," she said maneuvering around him to finish making the bed. "Ok, then let me take you for a walk, please just give me a chance?" Nate said almost begging. He sounded pitiful. She slapped the bed tight, put her hands on her hips, walked toward him and stood very close to him, enough for her body to just barely touch the front of his. She put her mouth close to his right ear and spoke to him in a sensual accent, "You like what you see, Chico?" Nate took a deep swallow and shook his head yes. "Good, then be aggressive, me like aggressive man," she whispered sexily in his ear. Then she gently, but firmly grabbed Nate's crouch. "Me like a man with balls, a man sure himself. Now ask me again with balls this time," she lightly demanded. Nate's eyes were as wide as a golf ball, she was truly in charge, and Nate was clay in her hands. He cleared his throat and spoke, "Let's go out this evening, about seven o'clock, I'll pick you up in front of the estate, baby," Nate said with more confidence. "Good, now I interested. Don't be late," she whispered. She released his crouch and walked toward the door. "You can stop listening now, compadre," she said referring to me. "Wow, she's something else," I said after she left. "Yeah, G, I need two more days here. Tell the rest of the crew we're staying here until Monday morning, and then we will catch the early morning flight. Ask Hugo to help you get a secure line to Chicago. Also, call Dana and tell her we will be home Monday and find

211

out what's been going on," Nate instructed. "Nate, let's just get the fuck out of here, can't you chase that broad another time, we are here on business," I said. "G, I just need a couple of days to score with her, that's all," Nate said. "A couple of days? As aggressive as that broad is, you should be able to score tonight," I remarked. "G, I need this solid please, do it for your brother. Give me until Monday and we will be on the first bird out of here, I promise," Nate pleaded. "Whatever, man, but you tell the guys I don't want to have to hear all of their bullshit when they find out," I said disgusted. As I walked around the estate to look for one of Hugo's men, I noticed there was a beautiful grove of trees just down the road. The whole scene was very peaceful. Nate was right, Bolivia was a nice country, but to me it just wasn't home. I finally located Alonzo and managed to get a secure line back to the States. I had to collect myself before dialing the number to remember the code language we had set up for when speaking on the phone with Dana to check on things.

NEW LENOX:

"Hello?" Dana answered. "Oh, how's the trip?" Dana asked. "Everything is cool, how's the baby?" I asked. We always referred to the drug as "the baby." "The baby's fine he's asleep now, but he was getting into shit earlier but I quieted him down and put him to sleep," Dana replied. In coded terms, she mentioned there was problem, but she took care of it. "Oh he didn't hurt himself, did he?" I asked. I wanted to know if she had killed anyone. "Yeah he did, but he's fine now. I gave him some medicine to settle him down. I've got it all taken care of," she replied. She basically confirmed that some people had to be shot, but it was done in a clean way. "Well, as long as he is asleep, but don't give him anymore medicine if you can keep from it. The president wants us to stay here until Monday morning. He's having us attend some more seminars," I said. I simply told her to try not to kill anybody else, as Nate wanted to stay in Bolivia until Monday for more negotiations. "Everything is ok, right?" Dana asked. "Yeah, just him being himself making sure things are sealed tight," I said. "Oh, are you bringing some souvenirs back with you?" Dana asked. She wanted to know if we were bringing drugs back with us. "Nah, we've got enough with the luggage and everything. We purchased all of the souvenirs and we are gonna have them flown back in a month or so," I said. "Look, I gotta go, but don't forget what I said about the medicine, no more until we get home if you can help it," I said. I reiterated to her that she should avoid killing anybody until we got back. "I remember when you told me the first time," Dana said, trying to be a smart ass. "Ok, kiss the baby for me, and tell him we miss him," I said jokingly. "Hello....Hello?" I said realizing that Dana hung up on me.

"Who was that?" Pookie asked. "That was G, they're gonna get here on Monday instead of tomorrow. They're trying to haggle Hugo some more for a better price," Dana said. "Did you tell him about what went on here?" Pookie asked. "Nah, I told him a little bit. I'll fill them in on everything when they get back. I am tired as hell; I think I am going to bed," Dana said. "Let's share a joint first. Weed always makes me sleep better," Pookie admitted. "Good idea, but first go run a check on everything, so I can turn the alarm on," Dana instructed. When Pookie left, Dana reflected quickly on her life, wondering what would become of it all. Reflecting on her sister, she decided to take advantage of Nate and the crew's extended stay and went to visit her sister a little longer the next morning. Her sister brought her peace amid the chaos. She really enjoyed her visiting her sister. "Everything is cool, turn the alarm on while I fire this shit up," Pookie said as he walked into the television room with a joint about five inches long. It was three in the morning and the chaos that would be discovered the next day would last in the memories of people for years to come.

CHAPTER 9

The Uncertain Future

Nate and the crew had no idea whether we were going to make it out of Bolivia in one piece. Chasing after beautiful women was part of the drug world and that weakness has always been the reason for the fall of so many drug dealers. Nate's selfish ways placed us all in harm's way. I knew I did not feel comfortable staying in Bolivia for one more hour, but Nate stopped thinking with his brain as his dick took over.

Stay tuned to find out if we ever made it back to Chicago...

A sample chapter from Evil Side of Money II

Chapter 1

LOVE AND MURDER

Saturday Morning, Chicago Ridge

As Detective Jackson parked her vehicle along the road she noticed what she would describe as a circus. There were police squad cars from every agency within a ten-mile radius present. There were also community activists, a throng of news reporters from all of the local stations, members of the local religious community, politicians, and general onlookers – the scene was a bit chaotic.

"Who's in charge here?" Detective Jackson asked flashing her badge.

"That would be Detective Sergeant Faulkner over there," a policeman replied.

"Detective Faulkner, I am Lieutenant Detective Diane Jackson from area one in Chicago. I was sent over to help out and get some information about the situation here," Diane said.

"Humph…now you guys come. Well here's the information Detective. I got a husband, his wife, their seven-year-old daughter, and a member of their staff…all shot gunned to death on a robbery. Is that enough information?" Detective Faulkner said angrily.

"Ok…may I see the scene please?" Jackson asked.

"Sure, go right ahead," Faulkner said sarcastically.

As Jackson walked past the various policemen and other law enforcement, she could feel the tension and contempt they had for her. Some even pointed and whispered. Jackson took off her jacket and placed on some latex gloves. Then she walked into the convenience store. The scene was a bloody mess, as people from ballistics and the coroner's office were brushing for

216

prints and taking pictures. Behind the counter were Thomas Kennebrew and his wife, Becky, both shot in the chest and lying on their backs wearing looks of terror on their faces as death masks. Upon first noticing them Jackson flinched and closed her eyes briefly in sorrow. Slumped over the counter was nineteen-year-old Eric Simpson shot in the head, with his pockets turned inside out signifying that someone had taken his money. In the corner was the most horrific sight. It appeared to be a little girl shot in the face and neck area, but because of all the blood, Detective Jackson wasn't sure. She had been lying on top of a teddy bear. The sight made Detective Jackson walk away in tears.

"Yeah, that was my first reaction, too. That's their daughter, Elizabeth. She was a sweet little girl who always hung out here with her parents. It's a damn shame. I am Sergeant Sanders with Chicago Ridge and you are?" the man said.

"I'm sorry…..I am Detective Jackson from area one in Chicago," Jackson said between sobs.

"Good to meet you…uh do you have anything? Any leads at all for us?" Sanders asked.

"I was hoping *you* all had something that *I* could use," Jackson replied.

"Just the kid over there…he's the one that discovered the bodies this morning. He says he was coming in for work and the lights were on and the door was opened," Sanders said.

"Can I talk to him?" Jackson asked.

"Be my guest," Sanders said.

Jackson felt sorry for the kid. As she walked toward him he seemed grief stricken and extremely nervous.

"Hello, my name is Detective Jackson and you are?" Jackson said.

"Perry…David Perry and I didn't do nothing…..I," the young man said nervously.

"No one said you did anything David. We just want to ask you some questions, that's all. Are you ok with that? May I ask you some questions?" Jackson asked.

"Uh-huh," he replied just as nervously.

"How long have you worked here?" Jackson asked.

"Just a month...I was on the night shift, but Mr. Kennebrew said I could switch over to days because he was thinking about just closing the place after midnight," he said.

"Did you like Mr. Kennebrew?" Jackson asked.

"Yeah, he gave me a job. You see I just got out of the county jail and nobody would let me work. My parole officer pulled some strings and got me work with Mr. Kennebrew. He and I got along well. He was always nice to me and I was nice to him. I didn't have nothin' against him," Perry said.

"David what were you in jail for, may I ask?" Jackson said.

"Well, it was armed robbery, but I didn't do nothing this time, honest. I really liked Mr. Kennebrew and his wife. I would never do anything to hurt them or their little girl!" Perry said standing up excitedly.

Detective Jackson looked long and hard into David Perry's eyes and drew her conclusion.

"Ok David, have a seat I believe you," Jackson said sincerely.

"It don't matter Miss...they done already drew their conclusions," Perry said pointing to the onlookers and police.

"If you are innocent David, what are you worried about?" Jackson asked.

"They gonna stick it on me and when something like this is stuck on a black man, it stays stuck!" Perry said shaking.

"Look, that's not gonna happen David. You stay with the truth and nobody's gonna stick anything on you at all. Look, I want you to take this and call this man. He is a lawyer. Tell him I referred you to him. Call him today David. Here's my card if anything happens or if you remember anything give me a call," Jackson said earnestly.

Jackson walked away thinking. While heading toward the crime seen again, Detective Faulkner approached her.

"What are you doing? Is that all you have to say to him? This guy could very well be the killer or know who the killers are and you just give him a damn card and walk away?" Faulkner said bewildered.

"He's innocent…he doesn't have anything to do with this," Jackson said confidently.

"How do you know that? He just told you that?" Faulkner asked.

"I just know…it's in the eyes. I have been doing this a long time Detective. I know when a criminal is lying or withholding something. That kid over there is scared shitless and he's shaking like a leaf. No he's innocent," Jackson restated confidently. As Detective Faulkner went on and on, Jackson noticed something of importance across the room and excused herself from Faulkner. "What's this?" Jackson asked a policeman who was dusting for prints.

"Shoe print. We found it not long after we got here…it belongs to the wife," the policeman said.

Jackson walked over to the dead wife's body and lifted her foot up. The tracks from the dead woman did not match the bloody print by the dead man. Also the bottom of the woman's shoes had no blood.

"Can you get me a mold of that bloody print please?" Jackson asked.

"I guess, what's wrong?" the young cop asked.

"There may have been a grave mistake made here today and I have to make sure that's all." Jackson said thinking.

Bolivia

As Nate got ready for his "date" with Gabriella, he went on and on about her and how fabulous she was. She was an exotic looking woman and very sexy, but I think Nate was taking it a little too far.

"Man, G, I tell you…this woman is invigorating. I mean she wakes up shit in me I thought never existed. She's definitely the best I have ever been with," Nate said.

"Yeah man, she's cool," I said casually.

"Cool? She's the bomb man. I just hope she digs *me*," Nate said excitedly.

"Oh I think she will. As a matter of fact Nate do you know anything about her? She might be up to anything you know?" I said.

"Yeah I'm gonna ask her some questions tonight…try and see where her head is," Nate explained.

"Good luck and be careful," I cautioned.

"G, the first chance you get, try and snoop around and find out a little more about her if you can. I know we are out of our element, but just try to get what you can," Nate asked.

What the hell was I going to find out? I mean I knew absolutely no one here! It didn't matter to Nate what I found out; he was sold on this woman. And to be honest I was concerned about that. I guess Nate was right; I am basically a suspicious person. On my way to meet Jon, I ran into Alonzo near the courtyard.

"Ah G, I have been looking for you. Tell Nate that we will be looking for him to make the drop tonight before you guys leave," Alonzo said.

"No need, we will be staying for a couple more days after all," I explained.

"Oh, want to see more of our country, huh?" he asked. on

"Not exactly. Nate wants us to stay because he is some personal interest," I said coyly.

"Ah a beautiful lady has his interest, huh? Great! Just tell him to be careful. The ladies here love American men. They are all looking to get to the States any way they can!" he said.

The last part of that comment worried me: *any way they can. Was this chick looking to use Nate to get to the States?*

"Hey Gabriella, I'm over here!" Nate said.

"Hey baby, I see you," she replied.

"What do you want to do tonight?" Nate asked.

"Take me dancing!" Gabriella said enthusiastically.

"Well I'm not much of a dancer. Back in the States, I am considered a good stepper," Nate confided.

"Follow me. I will show you how. Over here, we Salsa. Baby, me like to Salsa!" Gabriella said with her Bolivian accent.

"I'll do my best. Look these are a couple of my bodyguards, they are gonna drive us ok?" Nate said.

"We don't need them baby…I want to be with you alone ok?" she asked.

"I don't know. I always travel with my guards back home," Nate said.

"You are not home. Baby, you are with me here in Bolivia. C'mon please?" Gabriella asked.

Nate released his bodyguards and they hopped into the jeep and sped off into the street.

Chicago Police Headquarters:

"Chief, I need to talk to you. I think I have something on the convenience store murders. You got a minute?" Detective Jackson asked.

"Yeah! Come into my office," Trent resigned.

"I just got back from ballistics and I think we might have something. The bloody footprint near the bodies seems to be that of a woman. The print is small and the tracks on the bottom fit that of a popular women's shoe…I have found out," Detective Jackson exclaimed.

"Is that so? What have you concluded?" Trent asked sarcastically.

"Well Inspector, I think a woman was involved with the killings," Jackson said cautiously.

"A woman? You've got to be kidding me Jackson, because you have a footprint? What makes you think a woman could have committed such a heinous crime like this?" Trent asked.

"Well because of the print and there were small handprints on the counter top. I think that stands for something," Jackson said slightly offended.

"Look Diane you aren't going to get anyone to believe that a woman stormed into a convenience store shotgunned three adults *and* a small child no less. I just don't think it is possible," Trent said.

"Ok. How do you explain the footprint and the small handprints on the counter?" Jackson asked defensively.

"I don't explain them! Maybe the mother struggled and touched the counter before she was shot. Maybe she had on a pair of shoes and changed them later. Maybe someone came in took some stuff and left out. Shit I don't know Jackson, but I don't believe a woman killed these people!" Trent said loudly.

"Why...because of the fact that it is a woman? Maybe that is exactly what the killer wants you to think. You don't have a murder weapon or anything that says it isn't. I think that it's sexist and naïve to think that a woman cannot commit crimes, boss," Jackson said challenging her boss.

"Now look Jack-..." As Trent started his harangue the phone rang. He answered it, had a brief conversation with someone and hung up abruptly. "Well Jackson, you can put that ludicrous theory of yours away. We have the murder weapon now. It was found in an alley not one mile away from the murder scene, along with the spray paint can. Prints were run and they fit exactly to a member of the Gangster Disciples. A petty drug dealer from the west side named Titus Thompson. Looks like we have our man!" Trent said proudly.

Detective Jackson hung her head slightly in defeat.

Bolivia

"I have had a wonderful time with you tonight. I didn't know you were such a good dancer," Nate admitted.

"There's a lot you don't know about me chico," Gabriella said.

"Oh yeah? Tell me. Tell me more about you," Nate said inquisitively.

"In time my man…in time," she said coyly.

"No, I want to get to know you. Look I'll tell you about me if you tell me about yourself," Nate said bargaining.

As they sat in the jeep, Gabriella moved closer to Nate and put her head in his lap looking up at the sky.

"I have had a hard life amigo…harder than you can imagine. We grew up very poor and my mamma had to work very hard to feed us – mostly labor jobs," Gabriella admitted.

"What about your father…where is he?" Nate asked.

"He died when I was a baby. Some of the local gangsters kill him because he did not pay tribute. He owned a fruit and flower stand in town, and they kill him," Gabriella said sorrowfully.

"I'm sorry to hear that, you must wish you knew him more, huh?" Nate asked.

"Not really…then I miss him even more," Gabriella said wiping a tear from her eye. "I hate it here baby. It's like if you poor, you no matter. You know?" Gabriella said with her native accent.

"Yeah, but it's beautiful here. Back home it's like a concrete jungle. But here, there are trees, groves of trees, and beautiful flowers and the smell of fruit…it's wonderful," Nate said admiringly. "And the sky, look at the sky. Shit, Gabriella, I can't tell you the last time I looked up at the sky and actually saw stars like that. The sky seems so much clearer here."

Gabriella looked deep into Nate's eyes and rubbed his chest while deep in thought.

"I'm going to miss you so much chico," Gabriella admitted.   "

"You just met me. You probably have a ton of guys, Nate said.

"You are different chico. You handsome, smart, daring, and a lot of fun," Gabriella said.

"Look Gabriella, do you know what I do for a living? I mean do you really know?" Nate asked.

"I no care...I really like you baby and I know when you leave, I never see you again," Gabriella said.

"Well I'll come back to visit. I got a lot of business with Hugo you know. I'm doing really well and Hugo and I are gonna do even better. I'll come back to see you, you'll see. You think I'm gonna know a fine ass woman like you and never come to see you?" Nate reasoned.

"Baby there are fine women everywhere. You will forget me and soon I will forget you. How you say....out of sight, out of mind?" Gabriella replied.

"I doubt that. I think we have real chemistry. We went dancing, eating, and more dancing, and I loved it. I even......,"

Before Nate could get another word out Gabriella kissed him passionately. Nate grabbed her gently by the hair and began to caress her body. The kiss seemed to last forever in the moonlit night.

"Take me home baby...I want to be with you tonight. I know I never see you again. I want something to remember you," Gabriella said with her passionate accent. Nate couldn't resist. Once they arrived at Hugo's estate Nate carried her to his and G's quarters. Once in the room Nate tossed her on the bed lustfully and began to undress. "You ready for me baby, can you handle me?" Gabriella asked with passion and lust in her eyes. Nate gave a devious smile and ripped his silk shirt off exposing his bare chest and large necklace. Gabriella looked at him with animalistic lust. "Come to me baby. I want you now," she purred. They made love with the perfect mix of lust and passion as the moonlight gave them a romantic setting.

~ . ~ . ~ . ~ . ~

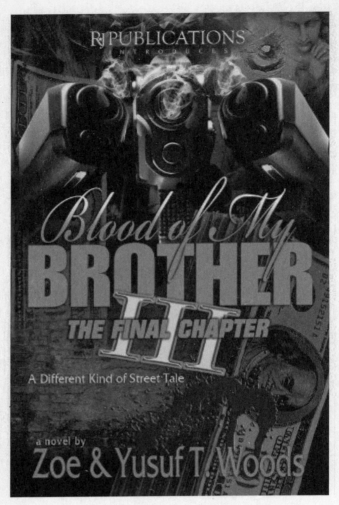

RJ PUBLICATIONS
INTRODUCES

Blood of My
BROTHER
III
THE FINAL CHAPTER

A Different Kind of Street Tale

a novel by
Zoe & Yusuf T. Woods

Retiring is no longer an option for Roc, who is now forced to restudy Philly's vicious streets through blood filled eyes. He realizes that his brother's killer is none other than his mentor, Mr. Holmes. With this knowledge, the strategic game of chess that began with the pushing of a pawn in the Blood of My Brother series, symbolizes one of love, loyalty, blood, mayhem, and death. In the end, the streets of Philadelphia will never be the same...

In Stores!!!

RICHARD JEANTY

Author of Neglected Souls and Neglected No More

WARNING
HIGHLY
ADDICTIVE
READING MATERIAL

The women always
ensure the "Bandit"
has a way in to give
them the ultimate
pleasure!

The Bedroom BANDIT

It may not be Histeria Lane, but these desperate housewives are fed up with their neglecting husbands. Their sexual needs take precedence over the millions of dollars their husbands bring home every year to keep them happy in their affluent neighborhood. While their husbands claim to be hard at work, these wives are doing a little work of their own with the bedroom bandit. Is the bandit swift enough to evade these angry husbands?

In Stores!!

Neglected SOULS

"Dark alleys, cold and lonely nights just trying to survive... Who can you run to? Neglected Souls made me gasp and grip my heart."
—Rashamba Williams, Best Selling Author of *Driven* and *At The Court's Mercy*.

RICHARD JEANTY

NEGLECTED SOULS

Motherhood and the trials of loving too hard and not enough frame this story...The realism of these characters will bring tears to your spirit as you discover the hero in the villain you never saw coming...

In Stores!!!

Jimmy and Nina continue to feel a void in their lives
because they haven't a clue about their genealogical
make-up. Jimmy falls victims to a life threatening illness
and only the right organ donor can save his life. Will the
donor be the bridge to reconnect Jimmy and Nina to their
biological family? Will Nina be the strength for her
brother in his time of need? Will they ever find out what
really happened to their mother?

In Stores!!!

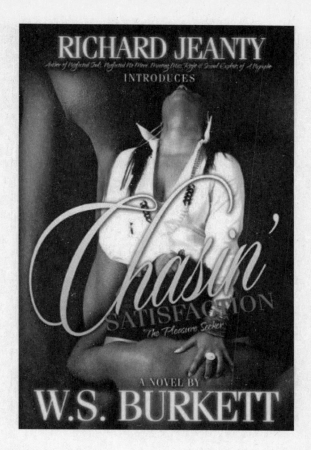

RICHARD JEANTY

Author of Neglected Soul, Neglected No More, Praying Man's Wish & Sexual Exploits of A Nympho

INTRODUCES

Chasin'

SATISFACTION

The Pleasure Seeker

A NOVEL BY

W.S. BURKETT

Betrayal, lust, lies, murder, deception, sex and tainted love frame this story... Julian Stevens lacks the ambition and freak ability that Miko looks for in a man, but she married him despite his flaws to spite an ex-boyfriend. When Miko least expects it, the old boyfriend shows up and ready to sweep her off her feet again. She wants to have her cake and eat it too. While Miko's doing her own thing, Julian is determined to become everything Miko ever wanted in a man and more, but will he go to extreme lengths to prove he's worthy of Miko's love? Julian Stevens soon finds out that he's capable of being more than he could ever imagine as he embarks on a journey that will change his life forever.

In Stores!!!

The police in New York and other major cities around the country are increasingly victimizing black men. The violence has escalated to deadly force, most of the time without justification. In this controversial book, noted author Richard Jeanty, tackles the problem of police brutality and the unfair treatment of Black men at the hands of police in New York City and the rest of the country.

In Stores!!!

RICHARD JEANTY

Author of Neglected Souls, Minding Your Night & Sexual Exploits of A Nympho

WARNING
HIGHLY
ADDICTIVE
READING MATERIAL

SEXUAL
exploits of a
NYMPHO

PART 2
"The Relapse"

Just when Darren thinks his relationship with Tina is flourishing, there is yet another hurdle on the road hindering their bliss. Tina saw a therapist for months to deal with her sexual addiction, but now Darren is wondering if she was ever treated completely. Darren has not been taking care of home and Tina's frustrated and agrees to a break-up with Darren. Will Darren lose Tina for good? Will Tina ever realize that Darren is the best man for her?

In Stores!!

SEXUAL Jeopardy

RICHARD JEANTY

Author of Neglected Souls, Meeting Mrs. Right & Sexual Cyphen of A Nympho

Ronald Murphy was a player all his life until he and his best friend, Myles, met the women of their dreams during a brief vacation in South Beach, Florida. Sexual Jeopardy is story of trust, betrayal, forgiveness, friendship and hope.

In Stores!!!

A NEW NOVEL FROM THE AUTHOR OF "NEGLECTED SOULS" AND "MEETING MS. RIGHT"

RICHARD JEANTY

SEXUAL
exploits of a
NYMPHO

" The book is hotter, steamier and sexier
than the title suggests. Jeanty has done it again."
—Treasure E. Blue Essence best selling author of
Harlem Girl Lost

Tina develops an insatiable sexual appetite very early in
life. She
only loves her boyfriend, Darren, but he's too far away in
college to satisfy her sexual needs.
Tina decides to get buck wild away in college
Will her sexual trysts jeopardize the lives of the men in
her life?

In Stores!!!

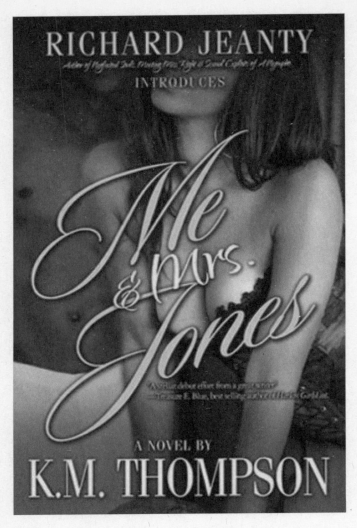

RICHARD JEANTY

Author of Neglected Souls, Honey Wiz Enigh & Sexual Exploits of A Nympho

INTRODUCES

Me & Mrs. & Jones

"A stellar debut effort from a great author"
author Carmen D. Blue, best selling author of Harlem Confidential

A NOVEL BY

K.M. THOMPSON

Faith Jones, a woman in her mid-thirties, has given up on ever finding love again until she met her son's best friend, Darius. Faith Jones is walking a thin line of betrayal against her son for the love of Darius. Will Faith allow her emotions to outweigh her common sense?

In Stores!!!

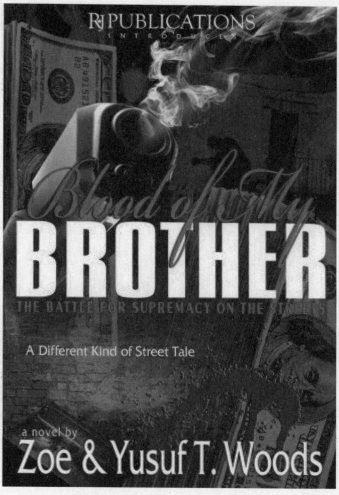

RJ PUBLICATIONS
INTRODUCES

Blood of My
BROTHER
THE BATTLE FOR SUPREMACY ON THE STREETS

A Different Kind of Street Tale

a novel by
Zoe & Yusuf T. Woods

Roc was the man on the streets of Philadelphia, until his younger brother decided it was time to become his own man by wreaking havoc on Roc's crew without any regards for the blood relation they share. Drug, murder, mayhem and the pursuit of happiness can lead to deadly consequences. This story can only be told by a person who has lived it.

In Stores!!!

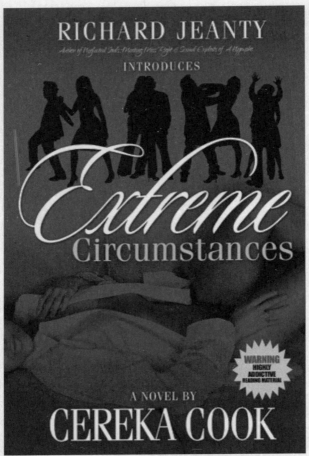

RICHARD JEANTY

Author of Neglected Souls, Meeting Miss Right & Sexual Exploits of A Nympho

INTRODUCES

Extreme
Circumstances

WARNING HIGHLY ADDICTIVE READING MATERIAL

A NOVEL BY

CEREKA COOK

What happens when a devoted woman is betrayed?
Come take a ride with Chanel as she takes her boyfriend,
Donnell, to circumstances beyond belief after he betrays
her trust with his endless infidelities. How long can
Chanel's friend, Janai, use her looks to get what she
wants from men before it catches up to her? Find out as
Janai's gold-digging ways catch up with and she has to
face the consequences of her extreme actions.

In Stores!!!

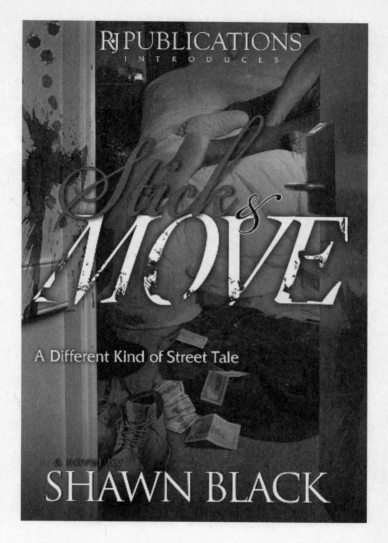

RJ PUBLICATIONS
INTRODUCES

Stack & MOVE

A Different Kind of Street Tale

a novel by

SHAWN BLACK

Yasmina witnessed the brutal murder of her parents at a young age at the hand of a drug dealer. This event stained her mind and upbringing as a result. Will Yamina's life come full circle with her past? Find out as Yasmina's crew, The Platinum Chicks, set out to make a name for themselves on the street.

Ashland's mother, Bianca, fights hard to suppress the truth from her daughter because she doesn't want her to marry Jordan, the grandson of an ex-lover she loathes. Ashland soon finds out how cruel and vengeful her mother can be, but what price will Bianca pay for redemption?

Malcolm is a wealthy virgin who decides to conceal his wealth From the world until he meets the right woman. His wealthy best friend, Dexter, hides his wealth from no one. Malcolm struggles to find love in an environment where vanity and materialism are rampant, while Dexter is getting more than enough of his share of women. Malcolm needs develop self-esteem and confidence to meet the right woman and Dexter's confidence is borderline arrogance.
Will bad boys like Dexter continue to take women for a ride?

Or will nice guys like Malcolm continue to finish last?

In Stores!!!

RICHARD JEANTY

INTRODUCES

Cater to Her

A NOVEL BY
SEAN MITCHELL

What happens when a woman's devotion to her fiancee is tested weeks before she gets married? What if her fiancee is just hiding behind the veil of ministry to deceive her? Find out as Sean Mitchell takes you on a journey you'll never forget into the lives of Angelica, Titus and Aurelius.

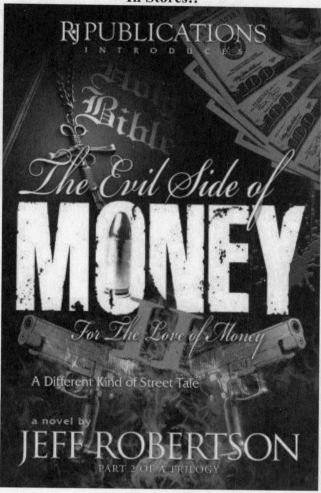

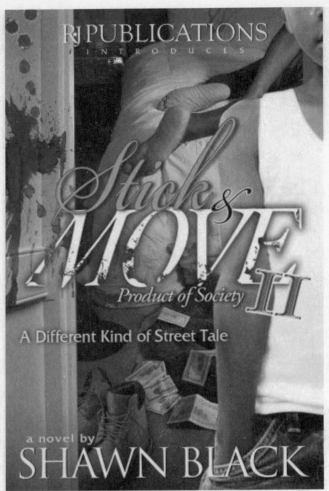

RJ PUBLICATIONS
INTRODUCES

Stick &
MOVE II
Product of Society

A Different Kind of Street Tale

a novel by
SHAWN BLACK

Scorcher and Yasmina's low key lifestyle was interrupted when they were taken down by the Feds, but their daughter, Serosa, was left to be raised by the foster care system. Will Serosa become a product of her environment or will she rise above it all? Her bloodline is undeniable, but will she be able to control it?

In Stores!!

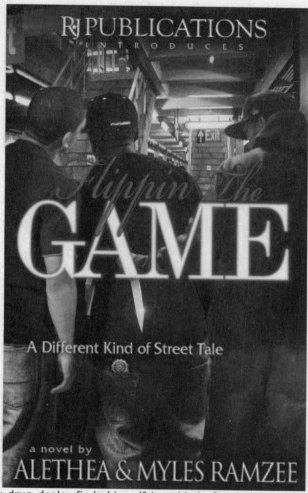

RJ PUBLICATIONS
I N T R O D U C E S

Flippin' The
GAME

A Different Kind of Street Tale

a novel by
ALETHEA & MYLES RAMZEE

An ex-drug dealer finds himself in a bind after he's caught by the
Feds. He has to decide which is more important, his family or his
loyalty to the game. As he fights hard to make a decision, those
who helped him to the top fear the worse from him. Will he get the
chance to tell the govt. whole story, or will someone get to him
before he becomes a snitch?

In Stores!!!

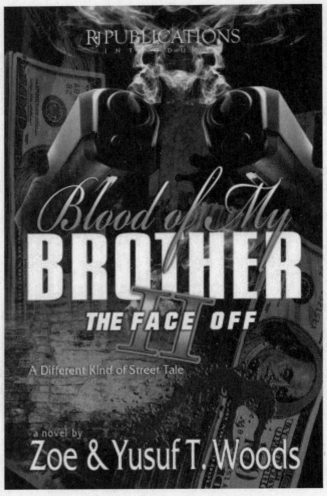

What will Roc do when he finds out the true identity of Solo? Will the blood shed come from his own brother Lil Mac? Will Roc and Solo take their beef to an explosive height on the street? Find out as Zoe and Yusuf bring the second installment to their hot street joint, Blood of My Brother.

In Stores!!!

RICHARD JEANTY

Author of Neglected Souls and Neglected No More

mr. Erotica

Jealousy can be a dangerous game for anyone...

WARNING HIGHLY ADDICTIVE READING MATERIAL

Dave Richardson is enjoying success as his second book became a New York Times best-seller. He left the life of The Bedroom behind to settle with his family, but an obsessed fan has not had enough of Dave and she will go to great length to get a piece of him. How far will a woman go to get a man that doesn't belong to her?

Coming September 2010

RJ PUBLICATIONS

INTRODUCES

Flippin' The
GAME II

A Different Kind of Street Tale

a novel by
ALETHEA & MYLES RAMZEE

Nafys Muhammad managed to beat the charges in court,
but will he beat them on the street? There will be many
revelations in this story as betrayal, greed, sex scandal
corruption and murder unravels throughout every page.
Get ready for a rough ride.

Coming December 2009

RJPUBLICATIONS
INTRODUCES

HOODFELLAS II
American Gangster

A Different Kind of Street Tale

a novel by
RICHARD JEANTY

Deon is at the mercy of a ruthless gang that kidnapped
him. In a foreign land where he knows nothing about the
culture, he has to use his survival instincts and his wit to
outsmart his captors. Will the Hoodfellas show up in
time to rescue Deon, or will Crazy D take over once
again and fight an all out war by himself?
Coming March 2010

RJ PUBLICATIONS

Stick &
MOVE
No Way Out... III

A Different Kind of Street Tale

a novel by
SHAWN BLACK

While Yasmina sits on death row awaiting her fate, her
daughter, Serosa, is fighting the fight of her life on the
outside. Her genetic structure that indirectly bins her to
her parents could also be her downfall and force her to
see that there's no way out!

Coming January 2010

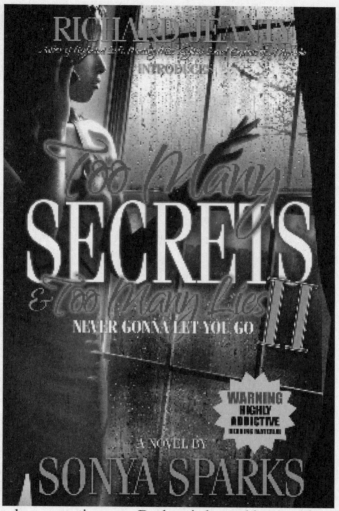

RICHARD JEANTY
INTRODUCES

Too Many
SECRETS
& Too Many Lies
NEVER GONNA LET YOU GO

WARNING
HIGHLY
ADDICTIVE
READING MATERIAL

A NOVEL BY
SONYA SPARKS

The drama continues as Deshun is hunted by Angela who
still feels that ex-girlfriend Kayla is still trying to win his
heart, though he brutally raped her. Angela will kill
anyone who gets in her way, but is DeShun worth all the
aggravation?

In Stores!!!

RICHARD JEANTY

Author of Neglected Souls and Neglected No More

Ignorant SOULS

THE FINAL EPISODE TO THE NEGLECTED SOULS SERIES

Buck Johnson was forced to make the best out of worst situation. He has witnessed the most cruel events in his life and it is those events who the man that he has become. Was the Johnson family ignorant souls through no fault of their own?

In Stores!!!

RJ PUBLICATIONS
PRESENTS

HOODFELLAS

A Different Kind of Street Tale

a novel by
RICHARD JEANTY

When an Ex-con finds himself destitute and in dire need of the basic
necessities after he's released from prison, he turns to what he knows
best, crime, but at what cost? Extortion, murder and mayhem drives
him back to the top, but will he stay there?

In Stores !!!

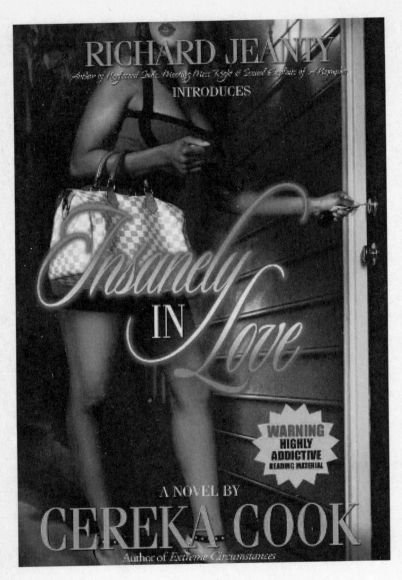

RICHARD JEANTY

Author of Neglected Souls, Meeting Miss Right & Sexual Exploits of A Nympho

INTRODUCES

Insanely

IN

Love

WARNING
HIGHLY
ADDICTIVE
READING MATERIAL

A NOVEL BY

CEREKA COOK

Author of Extreme Circumstances

What happens when someone falls insanely in love?
Stalking is just the beginning.
In Stores!!!

PUBLICATIONS
BRINGING EXCITEMENT, FUN AND JOY TO READING

Use this coupon to order by mail

1. Neglected Souls, Richard Jeanty $14.95 Available
2. Neglected No More, Richard Jeanty $14.95 Avail
3. Ignorant Souls, Richard Jeanty $15.00, Available
4. Sexual Exploits of Nympho I, Richard Jeanty $14.95 Available
5. Sexual Exploits of A Nympho II $15.00 available
6. Sexual Exploits of a Nympho III $15.00 Available
7. Meeting Ms. Right's Whip Appeal, Richard Jeanty $14.95
8. Me and Mrs. Jones, K.M Thompson $14.95 Available
9. Chasin' Satisfaction, W.S Burkett $14.95 out of stock til 6/15/13
10. Extreme Circumstances, Cereka Cook $14.95 Available
11. The Most Dangerous Gang In America, R. Jeanty $15.00 Avail.
12. Sexual Jeopardy, Richard Jeanty $14.95 Available
13. Too Many Secrets, Too Many Lies, Sonya Sparks $15.00 Avail
14. Too Many Secrets, Too Many Lies II, S. Sparks, $15.00 Available
15. Evil Side Of Money, Jeff Robertson $15.00 out of stock til 5/15/13
16. Evil Side Of Money II, Jeff Robertson $15.00 out of stock til 5/15/13
17. Evil Side Of Money III, Jeff Robertson $15.00 Available
18. Flippin' The Game, Alethea and M. Ramzee, $15.00 Available
19. Flippin' The Game II, Alethea and M. Ramzee, $15.00 Available
20. Cater To Her, W.S Burkett $15.00 Available
21. Blood of My Brother I, Zoe & Yusuf Woods $15.00 Avail.
22. Blood of my Brother II, Zoe & Yusuf Woods $15.00 Avail.
23. Blood of My Brother III, Zoe & Yusuf Woods $15.00 Avail.
24. Hoodfella s I, Richard Jeanty $15.00 available
25. Hoodfellas II, Richard Jeanty, $15.00 Available
26. Hoodfellas III, Richard Jeanty, $15.00 Avail
27. Bedroom Bandit, Richard Jeanty $15.00 Out of Stock til 6/15/13
28. Mr. Erotica, Richard Jeanty, $15.00, Available
29. Stick N Move I, Shawn Black, $15.00 Available
30. Stick N Move II, Shawn Black $15.00 Available
31. Stick N Move III, Shawn Black $15.00 Available
32. Miami Noire, W.S. Burkett $15.00 Available
33. Insanely In Love, Cereka Cook $15.00 Available
34. My partner's wife available
35. Deceived I, The Phantom $15.00 Available
36. Deceived II, The Phantom, $15.00 Available
37. Deceived III, The Phantom, $15.00 Available
38. Going All Out I, Dorian Sykes, $15.00 Available

39. Going All Out II, Dorian Sykes, $15.00 Available
40. Going All Out III, Dorian Sykes, $15.00 Available
41. King of Detroit, Dorian Sykes, $15.00, Available
42. Kwame, $15.00 Richard Jeanty Available
43.

Name_____

Address_____

City_____State_____Zip Code_____

Please send novels circled above; Shipping and Handling: Free

Total Number of Books_____

Tax $1.50 per book_____

Total Amount Due_____

Buy 3 books and get 1 free. Allow 2-3 weeks for delivery

Send institution check or money order only (no cash, personal check, or CODs) to:

RJ Publications

PO Box 300310

Jamaica, NY 11434